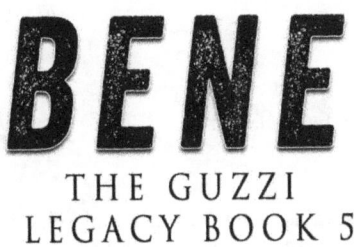

THE GUZZI
LEGACY BOOK 5

BETHANY-KRIS

www.bethanykris.com

Editor: Elizabeth Peters

Proofreaders: Tracy A., Mia B., Tori W. and Felicia F.

Cover Design © Under Cover Designs

Interior Design: Under Cover Designs

ISBN: 978-1-989658-03-1

CONTENTS

PROLOGUE

"What do you mean, you're *not sure*?"

Vanna Falco had rules. She followed them no matter what. Her number one rule? When her father became loud, she stayed quiet and got out of his way. Not that Adam ever yelled at her because he certainly didn't. He also never imposed his very large presence on her in such a way that would intimidate her like he did with nearly everyone else around them.

Still, she stayed true to that rule.

One of many, honestly.

Through the Bluetooth speakers in the car, the man her father had been conversing with during the drive tried to reply to Adam with, "This plan of yours, that's all I am saying. It won't work the way you think it will. You're going to get us all kill—"

"Or you're afraid."

"I'm not afraid! It won't *work*."

"It will. Just do what you were told."

"You're delusional, Adam, and if you didn't force my hand here, I would have handed your ass over to the boss for this ... *scheme*."

"Except you can't," Adam replied coldly, "not without outing the fact I knew you were stealing to fund your wife's gambling habit. So, either way, whether you help or hurt me here, you're still *fucked*. Remember that the next time you want to back out."

A beep sounded through the car speakers, saying the call cut off. The silence crawled on, a lot like their vehicle in downtown Toronto traffic.

The passing city streets, and the phone in her hands where she scrolled through her social media feed, held her attention up until the moment Adam spoke again from the front seat. Although, this time he talked to her, and not someone through the Bluetooth. He navigated the inner-city traffic with ease, and patience—*driving relaxes me,* he would say.

"Do you know what we Italians respect the most, Vanna?"

When her father spoke, Vanna *always* listened. Her friends, the few she did make at her private high school, never understood why she preferred spending time with her father instead of doing something with them.

"Do you?" he asked again, dark eyes darting to the Mercedes rearview mirror to meet her stare in the back seat.

"God."

He smiled. "And?"

"Family."

Adam tilted his head to the side. "That depends on—"

"Their loyalty to the clan."

If her father thought he would trip her up with that question, she had a surprise for him. Fifteen years of her life spent under his feet taught her a great many things—the most prominent, and *constant*, lessons had been about their ways; their *rules.*

The Camorra way.

The mafia life.

"Good, good. But no, those aren't the things I mean."

Vanna frowned, chewing over her thoughts as she tried to

pinpoint the lesson her father hinted at with his question. He smiled briefly, the strong line of his jaw softening when she glanced at his profile; it told her that he did, in fact, know he managed to make her hesitate with an answer.

"Maybe I posed the question wrong," her father mused.

"Maybe?"

He chuckled. "If we hold God and family closest to our hearts, then what would we hold even closer, hmm?"

Ah.

Now she understood.

Their life in a nutshell.

Her father talked.

She *listened*.

Adam was all she had, after all. Her blood relatives were long gone. Her grandfather, Gabriel Canali, murdered, and her aunt—Elena, her father's half-sister—had committed suicide shortly after, leaving Adam alone as the bastard son of a dead Camorra boss, with a criminal organization in ruins, and the clan in shambles. Shunned by his father before his murder, as his now-dead mother did her best to keep him away from the life, Adam was lower than dirt and treated the same for years after.

All because of one family.

One man.

Gian Guzzi.

He'd married her aunt, killed their grandfather, which caused Elena's suicide, or so she had always been told, and ruined the Canali name forever. It might have happened decades ago, but to them ... to Vanna and her father, who lived with the knowledge of what transpired way back then, and suffered the consequences of it long after, well, they simply couldn't forget.

They couldn't afford to.

It didn't matter they were Falcos—using the last name

given to Adam by his mother—because they were still Camorra. And this was their *way*.

"Well?" her father asked, bringing her back to the present with a bang. "Do you have an answer for me?"

She did.

"Vendettas," Vanna replied, parroting the only appropriate answer. "Our vendettas are *most* important."

That smile graced Adam's lips again.

Faint as it was.

He grew quiet, and so she turned her attention back to the phone in her hands. Traffic crawled on, but soon they would arrive at the restaurant where her father intended to make his next move to take over the Camorra clan. A goal of his, he made clear, that he had worked on since it was ripped from his hands after his father's murder.

That was two decades ago.

Finally, he had the chance to take his rightful place again heading the clan. *Rome didn't get built in a day*, Adam said, *and I won't take over in one, either.* He talked a lot, and she thought he said these things to her because she was all he had, too.

"Vanna?"

"Hmm?"

"I need you to remember that … about our vendettas —*always*."

She glanced up from the screen of her phone, meeting her father's stare in the rearview once more. It also allowed her the chance to see where they currently were in the city. A couple of blocks away from her school where he dropped her off every morning before going about his day and business, only to be right there at three PM sharp to pick her up. No excuses.

He listened to her day.

She listened to his.

People didn't understand why she never disobeyed her father—always his *good* girl, following every rule set out for her. She never wondered why. He nursed her when she was sick, read her bedtime story after bedtime story, and he was all she knew.

Her mother, a transient, neglectful *thing,* hadn't been in her life since before she could remember. She resented Rose for that the most, and while anyone who had known her mother often said Vanna took after the woman in appearance, she had no memories of her. Her dainty features made up of a button nose, delicate cheekbones, dark brown eyes the same shade as her wild hair, and heart-shaped lips didn't match her father at all, so she knew it had to come from her mother.

And yet, she still found a better sense of familiarity looking at her father than she did staring into a mirror at herself. She blamed her mother for that, but at least she had her dad.

She loved him.

He loved her.

"And someday," Adam said, bringing their vehicle to a crawl behind the car in front of theirs that slowed for a yellow light up ahead, "we will finally be able to fulfill our vendetta, won't we?"

"Of course, Papa."

"Why is that?"

The words that he repeated to her for years slipped out of her mouth without her even needing to think about it, really. "Because they took from us."

"Yes."

"They *almost* ruined us."

"But not quite."

Vanna nodded. "And so, they have to answer for it."

"Exactly, my girl. *Exactly*. We're the only ones who care

what the Guzzi family did to us all those years ago, but we also won't ever forget. It's our way—our *life*. An eye for an eye. They took from us, and we will take from them, no matter what."

Familiar buildings passed them by.

Silence stretched on.

"You can't forget the vendetta, Vanna," he said quietly.

"I won't."

"Promise me."

She didn't understand why he demanded that promise at all. She would do anything for her father—her one constant; a hero in her mind's eye. Out of love, and little else, her loyalties would forever be with him.

"I promise," Vanna said.

Adam let out a heavy stream of air, his fingers tightening rhythmically around the leather-wrapped steering wheel. "That's what I want to hear."

"Papa?"

"Yes?"

"Everything is okay, right?"

He took a second to answer.

She didn't like that.

Today would be *huge* for him, if the move he planned against the current Camorra boss of their clan went off the way he said it would. All the shame of being the son of a man who had nearly allowed their clan to be run into the ground because of his dealings with Gian Guzzi would go away.

They would be *great* again.

It just had to go right.

"It's fine," Adam murmured, "I promise, but you still have to remember what I told you. All of it, Vanna."

She would.

And her father lied.

It was not fine.

In a week, he would be dead. She buried him on her sixteenth birthday. Vanna never forgot about the vendetta, though.

She couldn't.

He made her promise.

Didn't she owe him that?

CHAPTER
1

There's a moment where a person meets their reflection, and they smile. No one really knows why, and it doesn't have to be a huge smile, either. Sometimes, it's done with the lips lifting at the corners, and other times, it's all in the eyes. A glow that just says *happiness*.

Benedetto Guzzi always thought one smiled at their reflection because they felt fondness in familiarity. Seeing something he recognized every single inch of, like his face, was comforting. More so than something strange and unknown.

It used to be that way with his twin, too. Identical in every sense of the very word, Bene never failed to smile when he looked at Beni's face. Except lately, that wasn't the case at all, and it was getting harder to hide it.

Not that it was Beni's fault.

Or anyone else's.

This was all on Bene.

Speaking of which …

"You good?"

"Yeah, of course," Bene replied.

"You sure?" his brother prodded. "Because you spent two minutes staring at the wall instead of knotting your tie."

God.

Why did Beni have to know him so well?

"A lot on my mind, that's all."

In the mirror, Beni arched a brow. He wished he could say his identical features did the same, but since Bene had fallen into this pit of hell within his own mind these last few months, all the strange similarities and quirks he shared with his brother slowed to a stop. Beni's continued, sure, like he hadn't changed at all, but Bene?

A different story.

One he didn't know how to tell.

That was part of the problem—for so long, it had been just the two of them. Bene and Beni. *The twins.* Stuck together, if you asked anyone who knew them. The same soul, if you asked people who were *really* close to the twins.

Except they weren't those things. Oh, sure. They looked alike and acted the same. They spent their entire childhood, teenage years, and even the first bit of their adulthood together, being extensions of one another, but it just … changed.

All at once.

Bene blinked, and that was over.

In the end, they still came out being two entirely different men. Beni was ready to be the man he knew he could be without his twin to hold him up on his own two feet, and Bene didn't know what in the fuck he was doing anymore. He still needed to figure that out somehow, and he used to do shit like that with his brother. Now, he would have to do it alone, and he wasn't sure how he felt about that.

Not at all.

"I'm worried about you, huh?"

Bene cleared his throat and shook his head. Forcing a smile on his face so his brother would see it, and not think something was up. Today wasn't the day for the dark shit in his mind, and surely he could suck up his emotions for a few hours so that his brother could have his moment.

Right?

Right, he told himself.

He'd probably need to say it a few more times before the day was out. So was his goddamn life lately. A whole fucking joke, it seemed.

"I'm good," Bene said, clapping his brother on the shoulder and keeping that same smile firmly in place. He could tell by the way his brother's lips drew down at the corners that Beni didn't believe him, but he probably wouldn't call him out on his shit. "Besides," he added, checking the watch on his wrist, "we've got twenty more minutes before I need to have you downstairs, and ready to get married. Are we wasting time talking about our feelings, or are we getting you *married*?"

Beni laughed. "*Prick.*"

"What?"

"Say married with a little less … disgust, yeah?"

Bene shrugged. "I just don't see the appeal, that's all."

It wasn't *who* his brother chose to marry, either. August Rivera was a great chick—smart as fuck, looked good on his twin's arm, and could hold her own against the rest of them. She never took any of Bene's nonsense when she first started hanging around with Beni, and even now, she was usually the first one to call him out on something when he had one of his days. Their mother adored her. Their father thought August was everything good for Beni.

And she was.

Bene wouldn't deny that.

He liked August.

It was just … *marriage*. In general. He wasn't scared to get married—didn't fear falling in love. He couldn't when his mother and father gave their five sons the best example of love and marriage for their entire lives. He simply didn't understand how a person could get married at their age, twenty-two, like they didn't have their best years ahead of them. That was all.

Then again, Beni found *her*, right?

That's what his father said.

His brothers, too.

And when a Guzzi found *that* woman, he didn't care about his best years yet to come, or whatever else. He only cared about her.

Beni found August.

Bene was still alone.

Great.

Now he was back to that shit.

Perfect.

"Seriously," Bene said, doing his best to hide the gruffness in his voice, "are we getting you married, or talking about me? Because if Ma comes in here and sees that you're still not dressed, she's going to blame *me*."

"But you *are* good, aren't you?"

"I'm fine."

And that was the last time he would say it, too.

Bene glanced away at the sight of his brother meeting his gaze in the reflection of the tall mirror the two of them used to get ready. *For the wedding.* Beni's wedding. After today, his twin would no longer be just one room over in their shared penthouse. Although, to be fair, Beni hadn't been living with Bene for a while now.

Still, this felt permanent.

More, in a way, because of the whole marriage thing. His twin would head back to Chicago—a place Bene *hated*—to live with his new wife. For good. Whatever hope Bene held that his brother would come back to Toronto to live again was basically gone now. Beni found something he wanted in Chicago, and he didn't mind staying there to keep it.

And where did that leave Bene?

He'd learned a lot of things in the past few months, but the most prominent thing was that he didn't know anything. Not about himself, anyway. Bene didn't know who he was without Beni. He had no clue who he wanted to be, either, and he didn't think he was going to figure it out anytime soon. So far, all he managed to do without his brother was drown his troubles in a bottle of liquor or a few hours of high and fun.

What is wrong with you?

Great.

Now, even his own mind was asking that question. Usually, it was one of his other brothers—more often Marcus, than Chris or Corrado—or even his parents daring to ask the question. It seemed like his mind was ready to get in on the fucking party, too.

Bene could do without that.

All of it.

At least, for today.

Just fucking let me get through today, please.

"Hey."

Bene found his brother still stared at him in the mirror. Shocker. Beni knew when shit was up; hiding it was pointless, but he would still *try*. What else could he do at this point?

"Yeah?"

"Since you're the best man and all—"

"What, thinking of changing that last minute?"

"Never."

That did make Bene smile.

A genuine one, too.

"What, then?"

Beni shrugged, and pulled a small white box with a satin bow on the top from his pocket. "It's a gift for August—I wanted her to have something before she walks down the aisle, and yeah."

"You want me to take it to her?"

"I'm not supposed to go to the other side of the church today. I was warned."

Bene chuckled. "It's bad luck."

"Superstitious bullshit, is what it is."

"And yet, you're still on this side of the church."

Beni scowled, though it still looked playful. "Are you going to take it to her, or what?"

"Of course, man."

He took the box and slapped his brother on the back as Beni turned to face the mirror once more. Leaving the room without another word, Bene did stop just long enough in the doorway to glance over his shoulder and take in his brother silently without Beni knowing he did so.

Like this, someone might not be able to tell them apart. The same high fade hairstyle, matching features they took from their mother and father—cut from steel jawlines, lips that always seemed to be smirking from the shape alone, dark brown eyes with flecks of gold near the irises, and olive-toned skin tanned from the bright June sun they had been getting.

Identical.

And right now, they were two identical men in two entirely different places.

Funny how that worked.

They could be so alike.

Yet, so different.

Bene would figure out his path eventually. He wished his brother luck walking on his own. It was all he could do now.

Besides, he had a job to do.

A best man to be.

The gift in his hand felt heavy.

A gift to deliver.

He'd deal with everything else later.

Later always came.

~

"I'm pleased to say those dancing lessons with me when you were younger paid off," Bene's mother said as they moved gracefully across the main floor. All around them, others waltzed and spun circles with their own partners, showing off for the guests at the reception. The wedding went off without a hitch, as long as the traditional Catholic ceremony could be, but the rest of the night? That would be a party. One long, *fun* party. "You always did like those lessons of ours."

He smiled. "Because I was spending time with you."

Cara laughed. "You know, I always wondered about that."

"About what?"

Pulling back slightly so that she could stare into his eyes, Cara shrugged. "I worried we never gave enough one on one attention to each of you. That with so many siblings, someone would feel left out of the rest."

"Never," he assured.

Both his parents made a great effort to ensure all their sons were loved and had exactly what they needed. Time, attention, and affection included. For him and his mother, that meant dance lessons twice a week, never failed. He caught on quickly, enjoyed it too, and never complained when his mother said it was time to practice.

"You certainly put on a happy face today," Cara said, her palm coming up to pat him on the cheek with a gentle touch. *Motherly.* Always the mother, no matter the situation. She simply knew when one of her boys were feeling off, or whatever the case may be. "But how are you really feeling tonight, hmm?"

Bene's gaze drifted over his mother's shoulder to peer

across the large ballroom floor. The hotel had really transformed for the dinner and reception after Beni and August's wedding. Gone were the tables, now pushed along the side of the walls for the guests who preferred to sit instead of getting up to dance. A popular DJ kept everyone moving and having fun. Servers walked around with free liquor for anyone who wanted to drink, and the large canopy of silk and chiffon lining the ceilings hung among twinkle lights.

All in all, it was a good night.

A *Guzzi* party.

At the other end of the room, he found his twin dancing with his new wife. The song was a little fast, but still slow enough for a fast waltz. Except Beni and August weren't dancing fast, and in fact, stayed close together.

Sweet, really.

As it should be.

"He's so happy," Bene murmured.

Cara sighed. "He is."

"And I'm not sure what I am, Ma."

Her hand on his cheek stroked again, softer that time. Her silent acknowledgement of a problem that he had been dealing with for a long time now, but alone. Mostly because he didn't know how to tell them—his family; his *twin*—that things were just confusing for him right now. He *was* happy for Beni, but he was also unhappy for himself.

But wasn't that selfish?

Petty?

Bene didn't want to be those things.

He didn't know how to stop it, either.

"Except today isn't about me," Bene continued, wishing he could settle himself on that fact instead of just *saying* it, "it's about them, so that's what I want everyone to focus on, Ma, even you, okay?"

Cara shook her head, letting him lead them further

toward the middle of the floor when the song sped up in tempo. "That isn't how a mother's mind works. I worry about all of you individually, and together. It's what I do."

"I'm fine."

He kept saying that.

Bene couldn't mean it.

Not yet.

Fake it until you make it.

That was going to be his new mantra. Until he could say it, and fucking *mean* it, Bene would simply do what he had to do.

"Also," his mother said, stopping their dance suddenly with one of her sly smiles and then patting his shoulder when they let go of one another, "you have yet to ask your brother's new wife for a dance, and all of your other brothers already did. I think it's your turn."

"I wasn't avoiding it."

"I never said that."

Bene glanced across the room again.

Beni and August were still dancing, as close as ever, and seemingly oblivious to the rest of the room. He wasn't sure it was very fair of him to go and break that up only because his mother thought it was his turn to dance with August. Not that it mattered. Cara got her way—it never failed. What she said went, as simple as that.

"When Beni asks me why I interrupted his time with her tonight," he said, "I am blaming you, Ma."

"*And?*"

Ha.

And they wondered where the Guzzi brothers got their attitudes from, really. They got it honestly—straight from the mouth of their mother.

"Love you, Ma."

Cara beamed. "I love you. Now, go dance so I can get pictures."

Bene pulled his mother in for a kiss to her cheek, which she then decided to use to hug him once more. He needed that, even if it didn't linger, and he wouldn't say it out loud. Not that he needed to because his mother likely already knew.

So was his life.

His mother hadn't been wrong—Beni didn't seem to mind when Bene stepped in, tapped his brother on the shoulder, and asked if he could cut in to finish the dance with August.

It did earn him a clap to the cheek as Beni asked, "How much longer do you think I have to entertain these people before I can get her out of here?"

"Beni," August admonished.

His brother only shrugged, walking away while tossing over his shoulder, "Not a lie."

Bene had already taken his brother's spot, only he kept his hand a lot higher on August's lower back, the silk fabric of her wedding dress soft against his palm while he led her back into the waltz. "Welcome to the family."

August laughed. "Thank you."

"I saw the floor plans for the house."

"Did you?"

"Quite a home he's building you."

"There's even a studio office."

Bene nodded. "To write … create, whatever."

"You helped him design it, didn't you?"

He had.

Beni asked, so.

"Needed something to remind me of home when I come to visit," he joked, "seeing as how Chicago always makes me want to dig out my eyeballs."

"It does not."

"A little."

"Just not home, huh?"

"Not my home," he admitted. "How are your parents liking Toronto?"

"Love it."

He figured.

Her parents came for the wedding, but three weeks early to help with any final preparations. It certainly gave the Guzzis lots of time to get to know the Riveras. It wasn't lost on Bene how August's small family seemed to fall right into step with theirs like it had always been that way.

Meant to be, his father would say.

"Bene?"

"Hmm?"

He smiled down at August.

She grinned back.

"I hope you don't think I took him away from you."

It took him a second.

And then two.

She was genuine.

He just hurt.

In his chest, the ache spread like a wild fire. Fast, and intent on devastating the peaceful balance he had somehow managed to find today. It wasn't August's fault, and he understood why she said what she did, but that changed nothing about how he felt.

Nothing changed that.

Across the room, over August's silk covered shoulder, he found his brother talking to their oldest sibling, Marcus. As though Beni could feel the sudden stab of pain that had taken over Bene in his chest, Beni rubbed at the same spot on his own body. Yet, he didn't stop his conversation, and he continued like nothing was wrong.

Subconscious.

It had always been that way.

Still was, even like this.

"Bene?"

He went back to August, never faltering in his happy expression. "I know you didn't take him away from me."

That was the truth.

He felt it in his bones.

"Sometimes, I wonder," she whispered.

"Don't."

He loved this woman. Certainly *not* in the same way his brother did, but he loved her nonetheless. He loved August simply because Beni fell in love with her, and she was the perfect fit for him, no question about it. His guilt was a killer, if only because he had said and done things early on in August and Beni's relationship that he thought left his brother with bad feelings, and despite it seeming good between them now … Bene couldn't say that it was. Not that his brother ever gave him any indication otherwise, and he made every effort he could to fix what he'd done wrong.

Still, the guilt raged on.

Killing him slowly.

It was the icing on his fucked up cake.

No, August hadn't taken his brother away. Things would just be different now. Bene had to figure it out, and he had to do that by himself.

Soon, the song changed and someone else interrupted Bene's dance with August to take over. A friend of her father, apparently. He stepped back, and let the man take over, but only after he gave August a kiss to her cheek, and one more congratulations. She deserved it, after all, the same way his brother did.

Plus, Bene was back in that space again.

The dark one.

His chest hurt.

It wouldn't stop.

Bad things always seemed to happen whenever he got in this place—bad in his heart, and bleak in his mind. He acted out, not that it made any sense, or like he intended to do it at all. He didn't want to do that here, not at his brother's wedding reception.

That wasn't fair.

Opposite to him in the room, he watched Beni rub his chest again.

Bene rubbed his, too.

Fuck that pain.

It told the truth when he didn't.

Not tonight, though.

No one would notice him gone.

Surely.

The party was almost over. Beni said it himself. With over three-hundred guests, no one would even notice he wasn't there to send his brother off on his week-long honeymoon in Italy.

Bene headed out of the hall before someone might notice he intended to leave, the background noise and pain in his chest fading with every step he took. It wasn't long before he was in his car, driving down the highway, and heading for the heart of the city.

His phone didn't ring.

No one called him back to the party.

A distraction, his mind repeated.

That's what he needed right now.

A fucking distraction.

Bene planned on finding it.

CHAPTER 2

The dates on the headstone mocked Vanna the longer she stared at the engraved numbers. Something about the reminder that her sixteenth birthday had been spent standing right here in this very spot, dry-eyed because she cried so much at that point, her body just *stopped* producing tears.

Instead, she'd dry-sobbed, an ugly cry that ached deep in her chest, left her throat raw, and kept her gasping for air when she just couldn't take in enough. Her sobs had carried over the graveyard long after all the mourners left, although none of those people felt the same way she did about the man she was forced to bury that day.

None of them understood her pain.

Or they did but didn't care.

That's how she remembered her father's funeral.

Painfully.

That was five years ago.

To the fucking day.

She stopped visiting her father's grave as much as she used to that first couple of years after his murder. Instead of twice a week, it was only on Sundays after church. And then she slowed to a couple of times a month, and now it was just once.

Did that mean the grief was settling?

That it hurt less?

That she didn't feel alone?

No.

It simply meant that standing here didn't give her the same tangible connection to her father that she used to have when she came to the grave. Sometimes, she felt it more when she was walking down a street and passed one of Adam's favorite places—things had changed in five years, sure, but some things remained the same. Other times, she felt him better when she stood at this spot, and looked down at his grave.

It did hurt more here, though.

She had to remember the funeral.

And what came before.

"Hey."

Vanna's head popped up at the familiar voice, finding Mario standing just outside her classroom. The Detti principe, people called him. Or the clan—the grandson of the Camorra boss, he was fucking royalty in their circles. Maybe it was his bloodline and the last name, but Mario got whatever he wanted, whenever he wanted it. All he had to do was snap his fingers, and someone would jump to fill his demands.

He was just another boy *to her, though.*

A boy who seemed to like her, sure, but Vanna wasn't interested.

She liked Mario well enough, but just not like that. And usually, when he was waiting for her at their private school, it was because something bad happened. Especially after a class. It meant someone would be waiting outside to take them home. So was the Camorra way. When shit went bad, they protected the clan first.

"What's wrong?" she asked.

Mario tried to smile.

It didn't come.

"Mario?"

He glanced to the side, and Vanna followed his stare. Down the hallway, she found a familiar man—no, that was wrong. Two men stood there, waiting. One stood a little ahead of the other, his arms crossed at his front, and his three-piece, black suit tailored to perfectly fit his form. He was an imposing sight, Mario's father.

Senior, they called him.

The right-hand man to the current Camorra boss, Senior's father. Senior would likely follow his father's footsteps, and someday head the clan as the boss. Like Mario, too. Or that's what people liked to say. Vanna didn't know if she believed it, or if she even cared. After all, her father promised it would be him as the boss soon enough.

Very soon, if his plans went off as he said they would.

Behind Mario's father, the other man stood as stoic and silent as he did. Waiting, she thought. It seemed like they were waiting for them. But why?

"I asked him to let me tell you," Mario said, his tone low.

"Tell me what?"

"Vanna—"

Her head snapped back and forth, glancing between the people down the hallway of her private school, and Mario. It was only then that she realized how empty the place was. The last class of the day, so it made sense that most of the kids had run the hell out of there because freedom was now at their fingertips.

Something in her heart said that freedom was nowhere for her. It was too heavy—too harsh, even. A weight had come to sit in her stomach, just like the ones sitting on her shoulders now, too. It almost made her feel sick, really.

One always knew when bad news was coming.

They only had to pay attention.

"What's happened?" Vanna asked, her voice rising and coming out sharper. Desperate. "Where's my dad? He's supposed to be the one who picks me up from school? Is he outside?"

"Vanna—"

"Where's my father?"

Mario wasn't even trying to smile now. Vanna wished her heart didn't hurt as much as it did in those moments.

"I'm sorry," Mario said, "but your dad was killed—"

"Hey."

Vanna blinked out of the memory at the voice echoing behind her. Just like that day as she was coming out of her final class of the day, how he greeted her ... it was exactly the same, and given how she felt in those moments, not very much had fucking changed.

If only Mario understood how much she hated him for that. Because *he* asked to be the one to deliver the news—he caused her more pain than he knew, and she would never be able to forgive him for it, either. He hadn't killed her father —his grandfather did that when he learned Adam was plotting against him to take over—but it didn't matter to Vanna.

That memory seared into her brain.

In her very soul.

And so did Mario's voice as he told her.

Glancing over her shoulder, she found Mario waiting at the end of the walkway, near the statue of the angel that appeared to be protecting the plots of graves beneath her. To his benefit, he didn't step off the walkway to come closer to Vanna. Mario never cared, really. Not that her dad died, or that she was left alone as an orphan, taken in by his mother and father, and she understood why, too. Because her father was the traitor. He proved his bloodline *true*.

The clan always said he would go against them. That, like his father before him, he would prove to be the bastard son of Gabriel Canali, and he did exactly that. But her? Well, she was just a girl, and that didn't mean very much to them. She certainly couldn't do anything to hurt them, or their organization. Well, that's what they thought. God knew, during those first couple of months, revenge on the people who took her father from her was the only thing on her mind. She might be *just* a girl, but she was still one of them.

Born and raised in their way.

Still fucking *Camorra*.

An eye for an eye was bred as deep into her bones as it would get, and her need for revenge came from that, and little else.

Someone had to take her, though. They couldn't find her mother. Vanna didn't feel anything about that. The Detti family it was. Or rather, Mario's parents. It was hard to want to hurt the people who also took her in and cared for her during one of the hardest times of her life.

Funny how that worked.

God had a good laugh at her expense.

"Are you almost done?" Mario asked.

Vanna nodded. "Almost."

That might be a lie.

She really didn't know.

It didn't matter. He would wait for as long as she needed on this hot Sunday afternoon while the June sun beat down on their backs, and he wouldn't say a thing about it. After all, some shit never changed, even if the world kept spinning while Vanna's felt like it had come to a fucking standstill.

Things like Mario stayed exactly the same. He still chased her like a puppy who wanted the toy being kept away from it. His crazy idea that someday, she would want him just as much as he wanted her, kept him eating out of the palm of her hand.

She never even fucked him.

He was just … *there*.

Whatever.

Vanna went back to what she had been doing before Mario interrupted. To her far right, she could see the parking lot of the church starting to empty. Mario's mother and father had likely already gone, along with the rest of the clan. Probably to their usual Sunday dinner, which she almost always attended. Other times, she just didn't care to make the effort. They never said anything one way or another.

Staring at her father's grave, the item she held at her side felt heavier. She didn't glance down at the newspaper she clutched tightly, and even Mario hadn't seemed to notice it as they walked to the grave for her to have a moment with her father.

She'd forgotten …

No, that was a lie.

Vanna *never* forgot.

She promised her father, after all.

The vendetta.

Guzzis.

The reason for *all* of this.

Even her father's death, in a way. All those years ago, when Gian Guzzi murdered her grandfather, causing her half aunt's suicide, and forcing her father to be a shamed man in the eyes of the Detti mafia … her father would never had needed to do what he did, to plan the way he had, and then to be killed at the end of it all.

She wouldn't be alone.

She wouldn't hurt.

If not for them …

No, Vanna never forgot the vendetta.

She simply had other things to focus on for a time. Wasn't that life, though? Something else was always waiting in the wings to take a person away from what should be most important.

Well, not anymore.

Not for Vanna.

Her fingers flexed around the newspaper she held as she let her father's words drift through her mind from all those years ago. She could still hear him clearly—his demands, and her promise to follow through, no matter what.

She didn't need to look at the newspaper again—once as she passed it by where it sat forgotten on a back pew had been enough. The picture of a *very* happy man, and his five sons had been more than enough to burn the image into her brain. She wouldn't soon forget Gian Guzzi's smiling face, and his boys surrounding him.

Oh, and the woman.

In her wedding dress.

No, she certainly didn't need to see the article about the wedding again, but she still lifted it to look at the picture once more. Gian stood in the middle, his arm around the groom on his left, and the bride on his right. He had two sets of twins, apparently. The groom had an identical twin, and two of the three men on the right were also identical. According to the article, Beni Guzzi was the third Guzzi son to settle down in the past couple of years.

Not that it mattered.

They were happy.

They had *everything*.

Vanna had nothing.

This—her life—was not theirs.

This wasn't happiness.

She blamed them.

The vendetta that she had left to linger in the back of her mind, simmering but never boiling over as she focused on her grief and growing up, was now forefront and sharp in clarity. It'd been years since the Guzzi name even passed the lips of someone from the Detti clan. They had little to no interest in causing problems for the Guzzi mafia, and Vanna understood why when their organization was doing just fine on its own.

That changed nothing.

A vendetta was a vendetta.

Even if it was one *woman's* vendetta.

It would mean going against the people who cared for her after the death of her father ... it meant becoming what some people believed she would be. A traitor to the clan, just like her grandfather, and father before her.

That was fine.

The vendetta was on.

Vanna's thoughts drifted to the newspaper burning a hole in her purse that she'd placed at her feet after getting in the passenger seat of Mario's car. He chatted on as he navigated the mid-city streets, returning her to the penthouse she had bought shortly after she turned eighteen and had finally been given access to the trust fund left to her by her father.

It wasn't a lot of money, but it was enough for her to live comfortably. To buy a Toronto penthouse, pay for her education when she finally settled on the fact she *did* want to be a chef, and she had a nice savings to dip into when she needed it.

The money also allowed her a sense of freedom because once it was in her hands, she no longer had to depend on Mario, or his family for anything. Not like she had for a couple of years after her father's death, anyway. She didn't have to ask them for anything, and while she was still considered a Camorra woman, and part of the clan, she came and went with little pushback from the boss, Mario's father.

Thankfully.

"Are you even listening to me?" Mario asked.

She glanced over at him, saying, "Yes."

But not really.

Her mind was on that fucking newspaper, and the

picture on the front. She considered the men and things her father told her, and what she might be able to do with the information. She had to plan, didn't she? Surely, she couldn't just *waltz* into the Guzzis' life, and tear it down piece by fucking piece. She would need time to work out exactly how she was going to ruin them … the same way they had ruined her.

Why should she care what Mario was saying?

"Anyway, about next week," Mario said, pulling a sharp left to turn into the underground garage of her building, "are you good for it, or what?"

"Depends."

"On?"

"What you need me to do."

Mario rolled his eyes. "See, you weren't listening."

She didn't bother to deny it that time.

"Dinner—I wanted you to come with me. At my parents. Their anniversary."

Vanna *should* refuse him. God knew these little *dates*— because that's what he believed them to be—only served to make Mario think they were something, or eventually would be. Really, her perceived closeness to him simply allowed her to do what she wanted with her life. No one was choosing a husband for her, yet. No one cared that she was twenty-one today, and still unmarried, never mind attending college, and living on her own without a chaperone.

All things that were no-nos for Camorra women.

Vanna bent the rules.

And sometimes, outright broke them.

Expectations came along with those freedoms, however. And they all revolved around Mario, and what he and his family wanted for the two of them. Vanna couldn't say she felt the same, but for now, she had what she wanted. Wasn't that the most important thing? She thought so.

"Of course, I'll go," she told him.

Mario nodded as he parked the car. "Good. They love you."

No.

They loved the idea of her.

They loved that Mario *wanted* her.

A prize to be won.

Very little else.

Vanna said nothing else, picking up her bag from the floor of the car, and opening the passenger door to step out. By the time she rounded the front of the car, Mario was standing there to walk into the building with her. Or so he fucking thought, anyway.

She had news for him.

"Tell your parents next week for dinner, okay," she said, "I need a nap, I think. It's been a long day."

Mario arched a brow. "It's one in the afternoon."

"And it feels like five."

"Not feeling well? You should let me walk you in, and—"

Nope.

Vanna smiled a blinding sight.

An angel with the devil's intentions.

That's what people liked to say about women who were exceptionally beautiful and could dazzle and distract with nothing more than a smile. Vanna was absolutely one of those women, and she held no shame about using it, either.

"Another day, okay?"

Mario shrugged, and nodded. "Sure, another day."

He leaned in, and she let him press a quick kiss to the side of her cheek. His hand found her side to squeeze. Both touches lingered a beat too long, but the man wouldn't take a fucking hint a long time ago, so he certainly wasn't going to get it, now.

"You know," he murmured, his lips still grazing her skin

as his words whispered into her ear, "pretty soon, this game is going to get tiring."

Vanna stiffened. "Pardon?"

"Don't play coy. This *thing*, Van. This shit you do. Dangling yourself like a treat in front of me, and then pulling it away at the last minute. Someday, I'm just going to lean in and … take a *bite*."

His hand flexed on her side.

She swallowed hard.

"But not today," she replied.

Mario took a step back and winked.

Like it was all fun.

As though her heart didn't race.

He thought she liked it.

She wanted none of it.

Vanna would do what she had to.

"Not today," he echoed. "Enjoy your nap. Call me later, yeah?"

"I will."

Or not.

The newspaper was still burning a hole in her purse, and she needed to start working out a plan for exactly how she wanted this vendetta to play out between her and the Guzzi family. That was the best part about it. Until they understood the vendetta, it was on her terms. She just had to make it work.

Vanna had her ways.

Contacts to use, if she could find the business card of a detective who had approached her a year ago when she visited her father's grave on a Sunday afternoon just like she had done today. He, too, had his own axe to grind with the Guzzis, and knowing where she came from, thought his offer to help her if she would help him would be interesting for her to consider.

Then, she hadn't cared.

Now, it sounded all too good.

"Call me," Mario repeated as he headed for the driver's side.

She didn't bother to reply.

Vanna had better things to do.

CHAPTER
3

What is that fucking banging?

Is that my phone?

Holy shit, I feel like death.

All those thoughts, and more, drifted through Bene's head as he peeled open his eyes. The white ceiling stared back at him, saying he at least made it home the night before. A burst of memory flashed in front of his eyes—he'd climbed into the back of a cab, and then stumbled into the elevator when he got home.

So, he didn't drive.

Great.

That knowledge did nothing to soothe the sudden swell of vomit he felt rising in the back of his throat. Squeezing his eyes shut again, the room stopped spinning. Visually, anyway. His whole body still felt like it was swaying back and forth, even though he couldn't possibly be moving on the bed. However, the few seconds of darkness and calm was just enough for him to distinguish what those sounds had been which woke him up.

The banging?

The idiots in the penthouse above his renovating—what were they doing this week, the floors? It fucking sounded like it. Which meant it had to be at least eleven, if not closer to twelve, because they only worked at decent hours. It should have been a good thing, except Bene didn't need to be woken up with that kind of noise while he was also hungover.

Except whose fault is that, asshole?

He ignored his inner voice.

The thing he thought was his phone ... well, Bene rolled over, cracking his eyes open just enough to see a slit of his bedside table, the clock spelling out the time—yeah, it was a little after twelve, *fuck*—and his phone blinking with a missed call. He squinted harder. *Several* missed calls, if he was to trust the ribbons covering the screen.

Damn.

The faint tune of an indie rapper he enjoyed played in the background of his penthouse. The brief flash of a memory filled his mind of him turning his playlist on through the speakers, and then he fell into bed, passed out, and heard nothing until this morning.

He drank too much.

Way too fucking much, Bene.

Again.

It took him another twenty minutes of being prone on the bed, ignoring the raging headache, and occasionally opening his eyes to test the waters—he really didn't want to puke—before he felt even close to well enough to get up. And it was then, just as he swung his legs over the bed with another bout of nausea washing through him, that his phone decided to start ringing again. He had a good mind to ignore it, but the name lighting up the screen had him reaching for the damn thing out of habit, and very little else.

Beni.

He should have known better than to take the call because his brother would know simply by the sound of his voice, and very little else, that Bene was fucked up. And yet, he was still too hungover to even realize that when he picked up the call with a, "*What?*"

"Bene?"

"Who else answers this number?"

His twin inhaled a sharp breath.

Fuck.

Did he sound as bad as he felt?

Probably.

Bene wished he cared.

That was part of the problem.

He'd sober up in a few hours—still feel like shit, though, undoubtedly—and wish he hadn't went out the night before, in the middle of the goddamn week, when he knew the morning after would be like this. When he wasn't acting crazy to keep his mind off everything else going wrong in his life, he could think clearly.

Right now, he wasn't doing that at all.

Thinking, that was.

Hell.

He couldn't *see* clearly.

Thinking was a joke.

Where had he partied last night?

The new club he liked?

Or the old bar down the street with pool tables?

"Are you listening to me?"

Bene blinked, coming back to the present, and realizing his phone was still on speakerphone, and resting in his hand. The emoji that he'd picked to represent his twin stared up at him from the contact with its funny face—something that used to make him laugh.

Now, he just … what was he even doing?

"Bene?"

"What?" he asked.

"Are you drunk?"

"Not anymore."

Or … *mostly.*

Yeah, that worked.

Mentally, he patted himself on the back for the quick attention to detail. In reality, it probably did nothing for his brother's concern.

"Where are you?"

"Why?" he asked.

Beni made a noise under his breath. "It's afternoon there, right?"

"Yeah."

"Were you drinking last night?"

"*And*?"

He didn't mean to get defensive, but it was fucking hard not to, all things considered. This was his life right now, he had to work through some shit, and this was how he chose to do that. No one else needed to be sticking their nose into it, including his twin. He loved Beni, no doubt about it, but he wasn't having this conversation when he was two seconds away from spilling *whatever* he drank from last night all over the shiny, hardwood floor of his bedroom.

That's all.

Bene dragged a hand over his face, feeling the scuff growing on his cheeks and jaw. He needed a shave, and *soon*. Or someone would speak up soon, and tell him the usual trash. *Made men don't have facial hair, so get rid of it.* It didn't seem to matter that he wasn't made yet, and he didn't have his *in* to the family business. If he wanted to be part of the mafia, he needed to act like it, no excuses.

He loved this life.

He also hated it.

Sometimes.

"You're not even listening to me again, are you?"

Bene blinked.

The call was still on?

Wow.

He needed to go back to bed.

Now.

Five minutes ago.

"Bene, are you okay?" he heard his twin ask.

"I'm *fine*."

That was all he said before he hung up the call, tossed the phone to the bedside table, and crawled back under his sheets. Fuck his whole life. *Yeah*. At least for today, fuck it all. He would handle this another time. Maybe later … maybe never.

What did it matter?

Bene didn't even know what was wrong anymore.

Not *really*.

Bene didn't manage to drag his ass out of bed until closer to four in the afternoon, and even then, it was only to dress in something suitable, so he could head to his favorite restaurant down the block that also doubled as a bar in the evenings. A business his eldest brother, Marcus, owned. One amongst many in the city that had the Guzzi name attached somewhere in the paperwork.

Not that he needed to drink again, and especially *not* mid-week, but the best way to cure a hangover was with a couple of shots. Or just chugging a whole beer. Whatever worked, Bene was up to try, and also ignore the fact he shouldn't be drinking at all. He didn't need the problem that this was becoming for him, and yet he also didn't know how to stop.

Just perfect.

He figured … at least he would get some food into his stomach, and hopefully get rid of the lingering headache. Then, he might be up to calling back some of the people whose calls he'd missed earlier in the day. Of course, nothing could ever be simple for him.

His food, and *third* shot of whiskey, had just been placed in front of him by the server when he lifted his head in enough time to watch a familiar figure pull up to the front of the restaurant. He sighed, regret filling him instantly. He shouldn't have chosen this restaurant to work through this goddamn hangover. Not when his family—but especially Marcus—had a direct contact to all of his businesses, and probably had a bead out on Bene.

Marcus stepped inside the business and took a moment to survey the busy floor and tables while he undid the buttons on his suit jacket. Bene swore it was like looking into a younger mirror of his father whenever his oldest brother was around. He often dressed the same as their father, and even carried himself with the same sway and gait, too.

"Drinking again, are you?"

Bene tried not to scowl as his brother came to stand next to his two-person table beside the large bay windows, and failed like a *fucker*. He'd hoped that if he kept his head down, and focused on the plate in front of him, Marcus might pass over him and not even realize he was there. Obviously, he hoped for too much.

Surprise, surprise.

"No, I—"

"There's a shot glass in front of you, and you smell like you spent the night bathing in … what is that, *Fireball?*"

Ugh.

"Someone spilled their drink on me last night."

"And you didn't grab a different jacket?" Marcus demanded. "You what, left the house wearing the same shit you wore the night before?"

Bene sighed, set his fork down, and proceeded to pinch the bridge of his nose in an effort to calm the headache that had come back without any warning at all. All it took was the sound of someone droning on—lecturing him, *again*—and he didn't want to deal at all. His body decided to revolt, and that was that.

"Could you … I don't know, shut up?"

Marcus took the seat across from Bene instead. "Not particularly. Beni called me earlier; said you were fucked up this morning when he called. I didn't mention it to him, or Dad … or *Ma*, but I happen to know you've been on a bender for a couple of weeks now, right?"

Bene wet the corner of his mouth with his tongue, suddenly wishing he had another shot to down right about now instead of just the one sitting in front of him. Besides, he didn't think it would be a good idea if he did pick that shot up, and down it, all things considered.

"What about it?"

"Am I right?" Marcus asked.

"I wouldn't call it a … *bender*."

But yes.

Two weeks.

"So, since Beni got married," his brother urged.

Bene let out a hard breath, and glowered at the glare of his reflection in the window. *Two weeks*. In the grand scheme, it might not seem like a long time. And hell, before Beni got married, he'd been staying in Chicago without Bene. Except for the longest time, he figured his twin would eventually come back.

That's what they did, right?

The two of them came back together.

He didn't come back.

So yeah, two weeks. That's how long he'd been trying to distract himself from, well, everything. His life. All the shit that changed. Anything he didn't want to deal with. The very fact he now lived alone, and his brother was gone—living in

Chicago with his new wife, new life, and without Bene. It just fucked him straight up, and he didn't know how to *deal*.

So, he didn't.

At all.

Was it right?

Probably not.

"Dad's worried," Marcus said. "Ma, too."

"Thought you didn't tell them I was on a bender?"

Marcus chuckled. "Thought it wasn't a bender?"

Fuck Marcus for being quick.

Or shit.

Maybe Bene was just slow today.

"Dad doesn't know the *details*," Marcus stressed when Bene didn't respond, "but he knows just enough to be concerned, and he tells Ma everything, anyway. At first, he figured you would work out your issues on your own, but—"

"I *am*."

"Are you?"

Bene's gaze snapped back to his brother, but Marcus only arched one thick, dark brow high in reply, as if silently asking, *well*? Like he was daring Bene to deny the fact that he was stepping closer and closer to trouble with every drink and night he couldn't remember.

"I'm having a … moment," he muttered, glancing down at the steak and potato mess on his plate. It was easier to focus on that than his brother who seemed to know every lie before it even left Bene's lips, and already had a response to give him, too. "It's not a problem. It's just a spell, you know?"

"Don't call it that. Don't diminish it, Bene."

"Well—"

"It doesn't matter," Marcus said in a sigh, "because that's why I'm here."

Bene's head snapped up.

Marcus met his stare, unbothered.

"What the fuck does that mean?"

"What do you think it means?"

"This isn't a *tit for tat*, Marcus."

His brother folded his arms over the blue, silk dress shirt with the matching tie and vest that he wore *under* his suit jacket. Seriously, the man didn't even leave his home unless he was dressed in his standard three-piece suit, and had his shoes shined.

Just like their dad.

Maybe that's why Bene always felt as though conversations with Marcus were like talking with their father, simply a slightly different version. God knew his brother could chastise him just the same way Gian did, if he felt up to the task.

"It *means*," Marcus said, leaning forward a bit to force Bene to meet his gaze once again from across the table, "that you just became my newest pet project for Papa, whether you like it or not. That doesn't matter to me anyway, Bene, because guess what? I know you're going through some shit, and you haven't figured out what you want to do with your life now that Beni has got his own settled, but someone needs to keep you from killing yourself while you do get it all worked out. And that someone is going to be *me*."

Bene blinked.

What?

"Like a … a fucking babysitter, or something?"

Marcus smirked a bit. "That's a tad juvenile, yeah?"

"That's what it is!"

His rising tone drew the attention of other patrons in the restaurant, but Bene really didn't give a shit in that moment. Who cared if he caused a scene here? *They owned the place.* They owned half of Toronto, for Christ's sake.

And yet, Marcus still lost that smirk, his tone cooling when he murmured, "Lower your voice, and stop drawing attention, Bene. You're not a child."

"Don't treat me like one, then."

"But am I?"

He stared hard at his brother.

Marcus didn't even flinch.

"You tell me."

"No, *you* tell *me*," Marcus bit back, "because between the two of us sitting at this table, only one of us can't be trusted to even pick up a phone, Bene. Only one of us is drinking his problems away, hoping to find a solution at the bottom of a bottle. There's only one of us sitting here right now that can't be trusted to do what he needs to do for this family, and his position. How do you expect someone to vouch for you—to get your button for this family—when you can't even stay *sober*? When you can't handle your shit?"

Bene swallowed hard.

He stayed silent, though.

That was good, right?

"Well?" Marcus demanded.

"I can," he returned.

"Except you're not right now."

"I told you, I'm having—"

"A moment, yeah," his brother replied, waving away the statement. Like it was an *excuse*, and nothing more. Bene realized in that moment this was that, too. Because he didn't want to deal with his issues, so he was excusing them, and the people around him had let him do exactly that. Until, clearly, they couldn't anymore. "What you're really doing is distracting yourself with things that either make you feel good or allow you to feel nothing at all. That's a dangerous game to play, little brother."

His defensiveness came back in a blink.

Just like that.

"Or you could just leave me alone."

Marcus shook his head. "Not likely, so here's the deal …

for the next little while, you're on my call, Bene. And when I *do* call, you answer. You do what I tell you to do, when I tell you to do it, no excuses. You want a distraction? Great, I've got enough shit for you to do that you won't even have time to *think* when you get home at night."

"But—"

"I'm sorry, I didn't ask for a response."

God.

Yeah.

Just like their father.

Marcus stood from the table, taking Bene's shot glass and the whiskey inside with him. "Don't look at this like I'm going to control your life, or—"

"That's exactly what it sounds like."

"Or you could see it like I'm looking out for you. Nothing more."

Right.

Still pissed him off.

"It's time to get your shit together, little brother," Marcus said, tipping that shot up and downing it in one go. He didn't flinch before setting the empty shot glass to the table with a grin. "You didn't need the drink, and after this conversation, I certainly did."

"Has anyone told you that you're an asshole?"

"Not lately."

"Let me be the first, then."

Marcus gestured between them. "By all means, as long as you straighten up, watch your step, and do what you need to do, Bene, then you can call me whatever you want."

"That a promise?"

"It's whatever you need it to be. Just *get your shit together.*"

Yeah.

All right.

He got it.

~

Bene had a good mind to head back to his penthouse, sleep off what remained of his bad day and hangover, and start tomorrow fresh. He had every intention of doing exactly that, too, but after an hour passed, and he'd barely touched the food on his plate, he eventually moved toward the bar where he made a home on one of the stools while he watched coverage of the Toronto Hitters during a practice. The pitcher, according to the woman on the screen, was looking at a hell of a year.

He didn't know why he was watching it. Baseball wasn't even in his top three favorite sports, honestly, but that's what the bartender had playing, so he didn't complain. He also didn't drink the three fingers of whiskey he'd ordered an hour ago, either.

God knew, he *wanted* it.

More than anything.

A couple of drinks, and he'd go home feeling good. Not even *drunk*—just buzzed, light on his feet, and unbothered. He wouldn't toss and turn all night from his lingering thoughts, or from dreams that wouldn't leave him alone. Problem was, Bene had learned he didn't do well with just a couple of drinks. It quickly turned into a few, and then blackout nights.

The whiskey held little appeal.

"He's got one hell of an arm, but a *bad* coke problem on the off season. How they're keeping him sober is a mystery."

"*Hmm.*"

Bene wasn't sure why, but the exchange between the patrons one stool away from his had him turning slightly to see who had come to sit at the bar. It wasn't as though he planned to join them in conversation, but the disinterested reply of the female had him chuckling under his breath when he looked their way.

Some women liked sports.

Some didn't give a *shit*.

"Or is someone pissing for him to keep him popping clean, do you think?"

"I don't *care*."

The guy to the woman's right held *no* interest to Bene at all. Standard suit, by the looks of him, and the briefcase under his stool. The woman, however, was a whole other story. Dressed in a light gray pencil skirt, and matching crop top, with black leather peep toe heels that showed off all kinds of tanned legs, she looked about ready to hit up a club. The black choker at her throat, simple studs in her ears, and understated makeup had him doing a double take.

Not because she was average.

Quite the opposite.

She looked like a fucking *angel*. Her dark brown hair had been pulled into a sleek, high pony with not a single strand out of place, and the ends flowed all the way down her back. It showed off her angular jaw, and the smoothness of her olive-toned skin. Heart-shaped lips pursed when the guy beside her continued to chatter on as though she was listening to him. Her brown eyes were accentuated further by, the starkest piece of her mostly neutral makeup, an inky wing that was made more dramatic by the curve of long, black eyelashes.

Yeah, shit.

Girl was *beautiful*.

How had he missed her?

It certainly spoke to Bene's distraction, and his mood when he didn't notice a woman like *that* coming to sit right beside him. The restaurant certainly wasn't *high class*. The

Guzzis owned more than enough of those types of places, and this joint was laid-back, and most were welcome which was why Bene liked it as much as he did. One could meet all sorts of people from all different walks of life just by coming to have a drink at the bar.

This chick, though?

He'd never seen someone like her walk through the doors.

And *damn* …

That was a shame.

"Are you here with—"

"Me," Bene spoke up before he could really think it through, making the woman glance up from the drink in front of her, and then over at him. "She's here with me."

The guy beside her—Mr. Fucking Suit—narrowed his gaze at Bene. "Sorry, but weren't you here before me?"

The woman, to her benefit, kept staring at Bene, never dropping his gaze even as he lied for her again so that she wouldn't be bothered further by the asshole to her right. "People can't meet up for a drink, or do they always need to come together?"

"Well—"

"I'm here with him."

God.

Yeah.

Her *voice.*

Before, she sounded bored and just fucking *over it*. As though she regretted sitting down, and one more word from the asshole beside her was going to send her straight over the edge. Now, though, staring at Bene while her soft pink lips curved in a sensual smile … her voice came out musical, and intriguing.

Just a hint of air.

Curiosity.

He smirked and pointed at her mostly empty glass. "Another one of those?"

Mr. Fucking Suit had just enough decency to roll his eyes and stand from the stool before tossing a few bills to the bar. He made himself scarce, and neither Bene, nor the woman, watched him leave, either.

"Depends," she returned.

Bene grinned. "On what?"

"Are you going to finish yours? I can't imagine drinking with someone who doesn't seem very interested in being good company. And you've been staring at that drink of yours for at least an hour now, right?"

Damn.

How long had she been beside him?

Watching him?

On another evening, that might have bothered him. Right then, he found it interesting, and her … even more so because of it. Still, he glanced down at his drink, considering her offer.

"I really shouldn't," he said, "because lately, this shit has caused me nothing but problems."

"*Ah.*"

He shrugged and watched a new highlight reel play through on the television. "I don't need to let it become a bigger problem, that's all."

What was he doing?

Why was he spilling his guts to some random *woman*? At a bar?

She didn't seem to mind. "The joy of adulting. I used to think turning twenty-one would be the best thing ever, and really …"

Bene laughed, peering over at her. "Not that great, huh?"

"All I learned about growing up was that with adulthood comes adult problems."

"Fuck, don't I know that?"

"And to think, I thought getting older would just mean *looking* older."

"You look *fine*."

He hadn't meant for it to come out as sly and deep as it did—that huskiness colored up his tone, and he wondered where in the fuck it even came from. Not that it mattered, because it was out there now, and her dark brown eyes—pools of glimmering russet—glittered from his suggestive statement.

"Thank you."

"No thanks needed. I'm sure you know how you look."

Her smile deepened, showing off perfect white teeth, and making her almond-shaped eyes lower a bit as color tinted her cheeks. Was that ... *shyness*? Shit, this woman was quickly working on making Bene lose any and all control he had. There was something about a beautiful woman—as sexy as her, dressed like she was, looking like she fucking did beside him—who also managed to be humble when paid a compliment that just did it for him.

"Do I?" she asked, leaning forward a bit.

Closer, he noticed.

And Bene, who didn't hold an ounce of shame, leaned closer to her, too. He was more than willing to feed into whatever this woman wanted as long as she kept smiling like *that* ... not to mention, at him.

Her teeth caught her fuller bottom lip when he tipped his head to the side, and asked, "Do you, what?"

"Know how I look," she said softly.

"Don't you? Do you need me to tell you how beautiful you are, and fill your head with whatever words fly out of my mouth just because? Or is the way I look at you good enough to tell you that you're—*by far*—one of the most beautiful women I've ever had the pleasure of looking at in my life?"

She dragged in a quick breath, and the color came back to her cheeks in a flash. Not that it changed the way her gaze lit up with heat all over again.

Bene nodded, and leaned back to sit straight on his stool, and put a bit of space between them. "But you know," he continued, "it's all in what you want, too, I suppose."

She shrugged, clearly trying to play off his words though he could see exactly how they affected her. He admired the way her olive-tone skin gleamed at her shoulders—he wondered what her flesh might taste like under his tongue while his hands worked between her thighs. Or *shit,* even better, with his cock filling her full and his name on her lips.

Speaking of which …

"You haven't told me your name," Bene murmured.

"Vanna. Vanna Falco."

The name rang no bells.

"*God's gift.*" Bene chuckled at the way her eyes widened at his knowledge of the meaning of her name. "Appropriate, then."

"How so?"

"My name is Benedetto—but I go by Bene. Bene Guzzi. Spelled b-e-n-e. With that hard *ay* at the end."

Vanna tilted her head sideways, his name falling from her lips far too seductively as she tried it out. "*Bene.*"

Yeah.

Hell.

That did great things for his cock.

"But how is that *appropriate?*" she asked.

Bene leaned in close to her again, just like before. And this time, she leaned into him, letting him get close enough that he could whisper in her ear when he said, "My name means *blessed.* And apparently, I am exactly that, considering who is sitting next to me."

He moved to sit straight on his stool again, but Vanna

quickly stopped him by doing nothing more than placing her hand to his thigh. A soft, *innocent* touch, sure, but those manicured, long pale pink fingernails of hers dug into his pant leg, and had his throat tightening instantly. He didn't move a muscle, not even when she turned her head to the side, and he felt the way her lips curved into a sly smile.

"*That* was quite the line."

"Did it work?" he asked.

Vanna tipped her chin up, their gazes met, and he had the pleasure of watching her tongue slide along her lower lip as she nodded. "It *definitely* worked."

She closed that bit of distance between them first, but there wasn't the slightest bit of hesitation in her actions when she kissed him. Just a soft graze of her lips moving with his before her mouth parted, and he found she tasted like sugared liquor, and pure *heat*. Sin, if it had a taste, he was sure. And she kissed how she looked, too ... sweet and *perfect* and sexy. Licking the flavor of him right from his tongue while the slowness of her kiss had him feeling like he was about to run out of air.

Goddamn.

His hands found her thighs when she turned on the stool, forgetting his place, and where they currently sat in a *very* crowded bar. Not that she seemed to mind, given her hand tightened on his thigh while she used her other to stroke those nails down his jaw.

"*Fuck*," he breathed against her mouth.

Vanna smiled. "That's totally an option, too."

Bene let out a hard, gruff noise. "Is that a promise?"

"How far is your place?"

That's all he needed to hear.

CHAPTER
4

Less than a *block*.

He lived less than a block away from the restaurant. Someone might call it divine intervention that the two of them would meet so close to where he lived, but she wouldn't. She would say it was because she had good info, and the ability to frequent Bene's haunts until the two of them bumped into one another.

And while she was happy to continue her plan—her need to fulfill her dead father's vendetta still as strong as it ever was —she would be a liar if she said the man she came face to face with in that restaurant was not at all who she expected him to be. Perhaps a part of her had simply been convinced the man would be the spoiled, airheaded privileged Guzzi twin that the media portrayed him to be. Quick to jump on whatever pretty face threw eyes his way, and easily riled when his ego was stroked.

Weren't most men the same, after all?

Bene had not been any of those things. Sure, she was a pretty thing who threw eyes at him, but that had been for an *hour*. She tried everything to turn that man's gaze away from the television, and the drink in front of him. In fact, Vanna had been just about ready to up and leave Bene's side when the man to her right started talking like she had anything at all to say to him. Whatever *finally* made Bene lift his head, look at her, and begin that conversation—simply thinking of her, and wanting to help out without any expectation of something back—changed everything.

Luck, maybe.

But when he lifted his head?

That's when she saw the *sadness*. Something haunted in his eyes and face that made her realize, no, he wasn't ignoring her ... he simply didn't see her world because he was too busy living in his own.

Then, he spoke.

And grinned.

Made her forget they were sitting in a bar, surrounded by people and noise. Somehow, he made her lose herself, and *time*, too. As though they were just two people having a conversation, that she wasn't there by her own making, *just* to run into him so that she could soon ruin his life, and his family's.

Oh, that wish was still there.

But for a time, she forgot.

He was not who she expected. He said a little less than a block to his place, and she didn't hesitate to agree. And in the time it took the two of them to walk to the large building where Bene's penthouse suite was apparently located thirteen floors high, Vanna hadn't once second-guessed what she was doing with Bene Guzzi.

Yes, she hated his family for the things they had done. She planned to make him and the rest of them pay for it without a doubt. At the same time, she wouldn't lie and say the man hadn't engaged her mind, made her wet between her thighs, *and* had her believing he truly did think she was the most beautiful thing he'd ever seen.

Until this moment, Vanna hadn't known how she would get her *in* to the Guzzi family. And right now? She had no problem with using Bene Guzzi to do it, and if she got to take the man on a ride during the process …

Vanna saw no problems.

All those thoughts drifted through her mind as she watched Bene finish up a phone call just outside the front entrance of his apartment building. He stepped away to take it, promising to shut the thing off after for the night—that was enough to make her shiver, too.

Fuck her anticipation.

It was something else entirely now.

"Yeah, I got you … tomorrow, all right."

Bene hung up the call, and Vanna leaned against the brick of the building. A couple of feet away from the front doors. The halo of light spilling out to the sidewalk and street allowed her a great view of his strong profile, the dimple that peeked in his cheek when he grinned, and how his features seemed carved from granite.

Bene was a handsome man.

From his dark hair, to his gorgeous face.

A kissable mouth.

Black slacks, and a white dress shirt rolled up at the elbows that fit his form fantastically, showed off muscular thighs and an expansive chest … not to mention the way his shoulders looked flexing under the material.

Yeah, nothing was sexier than a man with a good back— one a woman could really dig her nails in to while he fucked her to oblivion.

Bene checked every box for her.

"Sorry about that," he said, pocketing the phone, "promise it's off for the night."

Vanna laughed. "And if it wasn't?"

He shrugged. "Kind of has to be—if it rings, I need to answer. At least this way, I can say the fucking thing glitched out, and it couldn't be helped."

She arched a brow. "You mean to say a phone call could pull you away from me?"

Bene stepped forward, closing the bit of distance between them in three determined strikes. Already, he'd stopped them three times coming up the block just to kiss her. She was happy to oblige because she found kissing him was almost like foreplay for her. *Never* had she wanted to kiss a man, as though she could live from nothing more than that alone, like she did with him.

His body flattened against hers, pressing her into the rough brick and making the stone scrape at her skin. Yet, that bite of pain was quickly overcome by his weight on hers, the scent of his cedar and spice cologne, and the way his gaze looked boring into hers.

Like he'd fuck her right there.

And she'd *love* it.

"Well," he said quietly, strong hands gliding up her thighs and pushing the fabric of her gray, stretchy pencil skirt higher as they went, "that's why I'm turning off the phone so no calls come through."

God.

Her pussy was wet.

Had to be.

Since the restaurant.

Now, though?

Her thong was ruined.

"Someone might see us, you know."

Bene flashed a sexy grin. "You think?"

"Oh, are you an exhibitionist, or …?"

"Nah, I am whatever you need me to be, Vanna. That's the thing—this is all about you, now. *Your show.* You want me to fuck you slow, make you come ten times, and eat you when I'm done? I'll do that. Do you want me to fuck you where the neighborhood can watch you scream my name?

Let's go. Or how about I get you into my place, strip you naked, spank your ass until it's red, and use you like you want me to, huh?"

She swallowed hard.

Bene's hands went higher.

"Let me know," he murmured.

His thumb edged along the line of her black lace thong. All the while, he never once looked away from her. Even when she released a quiet gasp as his thumb slipped under the line of her panties, and grazed her hot sex. His lips pulled back in a satisfied smirk when his thumb found her wet. It only deepened to something wicked as her hips jerked into his touch when his thumb went higher to find her clit.

She pulsated against him.

Shuddered when his thumb pressed harder.

Trembled when he chuckled.

His head dipped lower, shrouding her face in darkness while his body covered hers from sight. Anyone passing by in a vehicle, or even walking, would think they were just a couple engaging in a heated PDA. They wouldn't see that his hand was up her skirt, and he was thumbing her clit with enough intensity to make her ready to come.

"What do you need me to be, Vanna?"

Air rushed out of her, just like her words. "Just make me *come*."

Bene flashed his teeth in a sinful smirk, thumb circling faster at her clit. "Give it to me, then."

She did.

Breaking all apart, and barely stifling her moans until his hand left her hip to slip two fingers into her mouth. She sucked on his digits while she came, before he pulled them free and kissed her again.

She hoped he fucked the same way he kissed.

All in, owning her, and hot as hell.

She'd soon find out.

~

"You have a twin, huh?"

Bene made a dark noise under his breath as he came to stand behind her in the hallway.

She'd stepped out of the bedroom, fully naked after he'd undressed her and only then realized that he didn't have any condoms in his room, to look at the pictures hanging on the wall. Sure, she was on the shot, but it didn't hurt to be extra safe even if she hadn't slept with someone in a long time ... the last time hadn't ended well when Mario found out, and she hadn't been looking for a repeat of that.

She felt him slip in closer, the heat of his naked chest pressing against her when his lips dropped down to find the crook in her shoulder.

He'd quickly realized she liked that.

A kiss there.

A *bite*.

Sucking.

God, yeah.

It'd make her shout.

"I do," he said simply.

If he heard the lack of surprise in her voice at her declaration about his brother, he didn't say. She knew he had a twin from the picture in the newspaper. She knew exactly how many brothers he had—how long his parents had been married. Hell, she knew Bene Guzzi's birthday, and even his middle name.

Contacts went a long way.

"Is that strange?" she asked.

"Hmm?"

"Having someone who looks just like you? Does he sound the same, too? *Act* the same?"

"In many ways."

She hummed under her breath, considering that. "Was it a little sad?"

"What?"

"I don't know," she mused, taking in the grinning brothers in the picture. Nothing about the two men seemed *sad*, not like her words implied, but she still wondered ... "Was it sad that you couldn't really be an individual when someone else was just like you for your entire life?"

He stilled behind her.

She wondered if she might have crossed a line.

"I never thought about it, really. But you're not here for the pictures in my hallway, are you?" he asked, teeth grazing her throat while his hands drifted down her sides.

For a split second, her heart stopped. She was sure it did. He posed a question that made her wonder if he knew her true purpose for seeking him out, but his tone gave away what he *really* meant. Just like that, she was reminded of the fact she had work to do here, but also that she planned on having every bit of fun that she could while doing it.

"Not interested in the pictures *at all*," she whispered.

Bene was already lowering to his knees, rough palms sliding across her ass before slapping hard down on each cheek. The sting was enough to make her hiss, but when his fingers dug into her ass, and he pushed her against the wall ... all she could think about was the feeling of his breath pulsing between her thighs.

A tease.

A *promise*.

It was the only warning she was given before he spread her ass wide while her hands found purchase on the wall, and he buried his face into her pussy. He ate her like he was starved, and she'd just given him a feast. All she felt was his tongue diving into her pussy, and then his deep moan that vibrated his approval against her heat.

His fingers flexed.

She'd have *bruises* on her ass.

Surely.

And yet, nothing else mattered to her except the way his mouth felt working against her sex. That fast beat of him lapping at her slit quickly went up to her clit, beating a steady pace that had her shaking and whining.

She couldn't breathe.

"Oh, my God, oh, my *God*," she breathed.

Louder and louder.

Her moans started to *echo*.

And then she was falling off an edge she hadn't even realized was there until she flew. Maybe it was the bite of his fingers against her ass again, or the way he sucked her clit between his teeth, but she saw fucking stars.

And screamed his name while she did it.

"*Fucking perfect.*"

That's what she heard whispered against the curve of her ass.

"What do you want me to do to you, huh?" Vanna breathed through the bliss still dancing in her veins as Bene rose to stand behind her, his weight pushing her into the wall while his wet mouth glided over her throat. "Tell me what you want, and I'll give it to you."

Her words were air.

"Use me."

He still heard them.

"*How?*"

She didn't even have to think about it.

"Fuck me like you don't *care*—make it worth it. Use me

to get you off, it'll get *me* off. Fuck me hard until I can't breathe, and then fuck me even *harder*."

His hand found her pony, wrapping it into his fist before he tugged her head back. His lips found her jawline, teeth sliding along her heated skin. "What, do you want to be my slut tonight?"

"God, yeah. So much."

That was all he needed. He pulled her away from the wall without care or concern, and yanked her into the bedroom. Thing was, they didn't even make it to the bed. He pushed her knees down to the white leather bench that rested against the foot of his four-poster metal framed bed covered in a black duvet that was now scattered with her clothes he'd pulled from her earlier.

"Hands on the footboard," he demanded.

She raced to comply, hearing the tug of a zipper as a hand curved across her ass. His palm slapped down, surely leaving her pink and hot, but all she could do was moan. The shift of fabric echoed in the room, and the tear of foil.

Anticipation curled in her gut, hot and heavy, when he fitted in behind her. Her fingers curled tighter around the metal curve of the footboard when the blunt head of his cock pressed into her slit. He worked in slowly, at first, stretching her open with every short thrust, and letting her feel every single inch of his girth.

God.

He was thick.

And long, too.

She saw heaven when he finally filled her.

Vanna would swear on it.

His slowness only lasted as long as his control. And that only remained until she begged him over her shoulder to just *fuck her.* Then, he was really fucking her. Fast and deep and *wild.* Making the bed shudder, and then drawing out whine after whine from her when his hands curved around her throat, and drew her back as far as he could get her while he pounded into her.

"Jesus, you better make me fucking come, Vanna," he uttered, voice husky behind her, "you better make me come when you milk me, babe."

He held nothing back, and when that need of hers started to grow all over again, he fucked her even harder until her throat was raw, and all she could do was shake through yet another orgasm.

"*Yes*," he praised, bending over her to taste her shoulder when he added, "now do it *again* for me."

She didn't know if she could.

He seemed determined to make her do it.

Best way she spent a night in a while.

Vanna slipped out of Bene's bed when the sky gleamed black through the large floor-to-ceiling windows covering half of one wall. He didn't stir as she climbed from the bed, plucking her crop top and thong from the floor to slip on quickly before she left the bedroom with her purse in hand.

She shot his sleeping form—shadowed in the moonlight and looking all too inviting in the bed—a glance before leaving the room. Without an idea as to what she needed to look for, or where to even look, she padded through the moderately sized penthouse. She didn't have time to admire the state-of-the-art kitchen, or the decor of the living room, although both seemed nice enough as she passed.

Instead, she needed to find something to *use*. Something in this man's home that was attached to the criminal side of his life—his *Guzzi* blood. He was a Guzzi son. One of many heirs to an entire criminal empire. His father was a Cosa

Nostra *Don*. No one would tell Vanna that Bene wasn't somehow involved or connected to the mob.

It was in his blood.

His purpose.

Like she was Camorra.

There was no *out* from this life.

Surely, she would find something that she could use to fulfill the vendetta ... or get a start on something even bigger. She wouldn't know if she didn't look, however. That was her purpose for being here, after all. Even if her body just wanted to be used by that man again.

Soon, Vanna found herself in the small office that seemed far too tidy and put together for a man of Bene's age to use often. It was stylishly decorated in dark colors, richly-stained hardwood floors, and furniture that looked both inviting and productive with all the leather and wood.

She knew before she even stepped behind the desk, however, that it was highly unlikely she would find anything to use in this office. Simply because it seemed as though this space wasn't very *personalized* to Bene Guzzi. Not like the rest of his place, or even his bedroom that had all sorts of little knickknacks and flavors of his personality and life.

The one personal thing she did find in the office came in the form of a picture resting at the edge of the desk. At first, she overlooked it in her perusal of the office, but then she took a second look, and fury burned hot in her heart.

Gian Guzzi.

And his wife.

His second wife, the mother of all the man's boys. Not Vanna's dead half-aunt who had apparently been so abused by this man that after the murder of her father, she killed herself. Gian at least had a bit of decency and gave it time before he remarried, although everyone knew he'd been fucking Cara—his current wife—when his first wife was still alive, not to mention, his first son was born in that time, too.

In the photo, the man seemed happy. His gaze locked on his wife as though she was the only thing in the world he cared to look at for the rest of his life. *His world*, Vanna thought. He stared at Cara—that was his wife's name, and Bene's mother—like she was his entire world.

Vanna couldn't wait to ruin it.

Forcing her attention away from the photograph, she dug through the drawers in the desk. She snapped pictures. Nothing screamed *organized crime* or *made man*.

It didn't matter.

She sent the pictures off.

The person who received what she *did* manage to find—some information on a few businesses scattered throughout the city, bank account numbers, and one off shore account paperwork—would do what he could for it, and let her know what else she should look for in relation to it.

If it was even useable.

Those were things to handle at another time.

As it was, Vanna had risked a lot doing what she did tonight. Seeking Bene out, then willingly going home with him to hookup, and now *this*, too. She almost felt as though she was playing with fire in a way, and she wasn't quite ready to be burned yet.

She left the office in the same condition she found it. Returning to the bedroom to pick up her things, she had to wonder what the still-sleeping man might think to find her already gone from his place before he even woke up in the morning.

He hadn't asked her to stay.

She couldn't afford to, either.

Still, her mind warred. The part that wanted to ruin this

man and his family … and the part that wanted to see him another time to do this with him again.

Thing was … to ruin him, she might just need to get closer. She might have to come back again.

Vanna left her number scrawled on a piece of paper that she sat on his bedside table before she left. And her signature underneath.

Or rather, her signature *V.*

Let him make of that what he wanted.

CHAPTER 5

Bene woke up to the sound of his landline phone ringing. *Because of course, he did.* A part of his brain managed to remember that he shut his cell off the night before as he stumbled from bed, and that was likely the reason for someone calling directly to his penthouse phone. Another part of his brain was just pissed that he had been taken from a good slumber, forced to trip over the pants he discarded the night before, just to grab the phone on the other side of his penthouse before it went to voicemail.

And *shocker* …

Marcus answered Bene's mumbled, sleepy greeting with a, "Why aren't you answering your phone?"

It took Bene entirely too long to reply. He blinked for a while, staring out his living room windows that faced the corner of another skyrise, and a part of the streets down below. Sunshine filtered in, making streaks across the floor.

Shit.

At least, it wasn't still dark.

He gave Marcus that.

Very little else.

"Are you even awake and dressed?"

"What?" Bene asked.

He glanced down at himself, deciding it was probably better *not* to answer Marcus's question with the truth. He didn't think his brother would appreciate the information that no, he was neither entirely awake considering his vision blurred, nor dressed in any kind of way that was respectable to leave his place.

In fact, anyone looking into his windows was getting a *great* view of his morning wood that was now starting to go down. Shit, he hadn't even bothered to pull clothes on before he jumped into bed, which wasn't his typical style. Usually, he'd beat the hard-on out in the shower, grab a coffee, and get on with his day.

Not today, apparently.

Perfect.

"What did I tell you last night when I called?"

Bene searched his brain to come up with an appropriate answer. He blamed that on the fact clearly, he had been woken up before it was the right time. What else could he do?

"Uh …"

"The *Capo* … Johnny," Marcus snapped. "That's where you're supposed to be today *working*. This morning. In a half an hour, actually."

Fuck.

Fuck, fuck, *fuck.*

"I'm on my way," Bene lied.

"I called the *penthouse*. You haven't even left yet. I told you not to fuck this up, right? That you were going to be busy for the next little while? Lucky for your ass, I actually set up your meeting with the Capo for noon, so you really have an hour and a half, now. Just thought I'd screw you a bit before I told you to get your ass in gear and get to work. Time to get yourself straight, Bene."

Bene squeezed his eyes shut and rubbed at his jaw. Memories of the night before flooded his mind—a beautiful woman with an angel's face that fucked and tasted like sin. He barely had time to enjoy those thoughts, or the semi-erection it caused, promising he might get to enjoy his time in the shower after all, before Marcus spoke again, and he lost that small joy.

No surprise there.

"You're on *my* time now, little brother," Marcus said, "and you answer to my rules. Don't take offense, I'm just keeping you out of trouble."

"Marcus—"

"That wasn't the opportunity for a conversation, Bene."

Jesus.

His brother wasn't fucking around.

"I'm on my way," Bene said.

Even though Marcus hadn't told him what work he would need to do for one of their father's favorite Capos. In fact, he had no clue what he would be doing at all while Marcus controlled his work for their family. It could be anything. Normally, he handled payments from dealers, rackets, and other business. A go-between for his father, and older brothers who were made men. Whatever they needed, he was there to do.

Now, he was under Marcus's thumb.

Or so his brother said.

Thing was, he wanted his button.

His *in* to the family.

Bene needed to be a made man.

He'd do what he had to.

"Better be," Marcus replied, "and don't show up smelling like a fucking brewery, either, because Johnny will let me know. You hear me?"

Bene cleared his throat. "I didn't drink last night."

"Good."

"What will I do for the—"

"Whatever the Capo wants, and whatever I can dream up."

"What does that even mean?"

"It means," Marcus said, "don't fuck this up, Bene."

That's all Marcus said.

Then, he hung up the call.

Bene was left staring at the dead cordless phone in his hand, wondering *just* how much trouble he would get in to if he beat the hell out of his older brother. Not that he *could* ... sure, Bene could handle himself in a fight fine, but he also grew up with Marcus, and they had gone on a few rounds together more than once.

Might be worth it.

Right.

He ignored his taunting brain, knowing he had to get a move on, or he'd surely be hearing it from his brother once again. Heading back to his bedroom, he didn't even have time to put the shower to use considering he was already running late, and with traffic, it would take him a good hour to get to where he needed to go.

He yanked clothes from the floor, tossing them aside to find his car keys, and whatever else he left in his pockets from the day before. In the walk-in closet, he grabbed a clean pair of slacks, and a pressed shirt along with clean underwear, and a pair of shoes. It didn't matter that he was a criminal, or that his family was full of them, he didn't have to dress like it, too. Or, that's what he had always been told.

He eyed the empty bed when he came back out. Messy sheets, indented pillows, and the room still smelled like whatever sugary sweet perfume Vanna had worn the night before. He didn't have time to be pissed that she up and left his place before he could even wake up. In fact, he wasn't mad about it at all considering it was usually him slipping out of a woman's bed before the sun rose in the morning.

He did, however, notice the handwritten note on his bedside table when he plucked his watch from the glass bowl resting on the far corner. Her number. That's all she had written.

That, and a simple, swirled *V.*

Well, then …

Bene wasn't a second-round type. He wasn't the kind of guy who led women on, either, just to get them into bed, but a one-night stand suited his needs fine considering he wasn't looking for much more. And yet, he found that he was willing to see Vanna again as long as she was up for it, and he had time.

He stuffed the note in his pocket.

Another day.

Two fucking weeks.

Marcus had Bene running non-stop for two entire weeks. From one job, to the next. The first Capo he had to see was just the beginning, and by the end of that first day, Bene was already exhausted, and over whatever trick his brother was trying to pull.

Some of it wasn't even *work.*

Gian wanted take-out from his favorite hole-in-the-wall diner in the middle of *Quebec City*? In a whole different province? Bene was called to go and get it. And the thing was, he knew that he couldn't complain about it. Not one negative word could leave his lips every time he was sent on yet another wild goose chase for his father, one of his brothers, or any other made man who suddenly now had his phone number.

Because yeah, that was another thing.

Made men kept calling.

All the made men of their family.

Or rather, the ones with enough position and status that

they could order Bene around and get away with it. He couldn't complain or refuse an order or a job because that wasn't how the life worked. *Mafiosi* ran the show, and as Bene wasn't yet a made man, but *wanted* to be, well, that meant he had to do whatever they wanted him to do, whenever the fuck they wanted him to do it, no questions asked.

Oh, someone needed a pack of smokes at two in the morning? Bene dragged his ass out of bed, drove to the closest convenience store, and then delivered the cigarettes to the Capo—or whoever—with a fucking smile on his face while at the same time, asking if the man needed something else from him.

Someone needed an extra pair of hands on a crew for the day to do some manual labor in a stuffy warehouse that was better suited to be torn down and cemented for a parking lot than for working? Bene wasn't the type to roughen his hands up with shit like that or blacken his lungs, but he didn't get a say, and so he did what he was told without a word.

It didn't stop.

At all.

One thing after another.

Yet another person with a new task or job for Bene to do. In two weeks, he maybe slept in his own bed a total of eight hours, *if that*. Sometimes, he just slept in his car while he waited for his fucking phone to ring again.

Was he eating three times a day?

Fuck no.

Unless one considered fast food *eating*.

Bene sure as fuck wasn't drinking.

He didn't understand what in the hell was going on, but he was quickly growing tired of it. Not that he could say that, or even *stop*. He couldn't because he'd done this—he asked for this life, and sometimes, shit just wasn't easy. Not being made meant Bene had to answer to every single man in the organization that was a made man. And they could use him for whatever they wanted, as long as the boss agreed.

Apparently, his father did.

Up until this point in his life and working toward getting his button for the Guzzi Cosa Nostra, Bene had been spoiled. Privileged, really, because of his last name and the fact he was one of the youngest sons of the Guzzi Don. Unlike others, who worked their way into the family from the ground up, Bene had only answered to his father and older brothers, most of the time, with a couple of Capos thrown into the mix as a mentor to him.

His right, he was told once.

At the same time, he'd been warned this would happen, too. That at some point, he would be all or nothing in this family and business. That his status as a Guzzi son would afford him little to nothing compared to others trying to get their in, and he would have to earn it the same way every other man did, too.

Bene hadn't been ready.

He blamed himself for that.

A part of him wondered if that was Marcus's point. To keep him so busy that he didn't even have time to worry about his problems or trying to find the solution to them at the bottom of a goddamn bottle.

But who knew?

Not Bene.

He didn't get to ask *questions*.

Not anymore.

Bene drummed his fingers against the leather-wrapped steering wheel of his Lambo—a car he'd painted bright red so that everybody and anybody would see him coming, and know it was him just by the distinct color and car alone. His father had been quick to point out the car was a little ostentatious, and drew too much attention, but he never said to get rid of it, and Bene considered that a win.

It was also serving him well when Marcus called to demand Bene drive all the way across the city to meet him at the back of a barber shop—one he'd never heard of before— in a time frame that would have been impossible in any other vehicle except his Lambo. He was thanking that goddamn upgrade he had done to the engine shortly after he bought it for that extra fifty horsepower under the hood.

Still don't know why I'm coming to this place tonight, though.

Yeah, his thoughts were still hell.

That couldn't be helped.

Bene pulled his vehicle into the rear parking lot of the barber shop that … well, didn't look like it had been open in years, if the plywood covering the windows was any indication. Even the red and white pole—no longer spinning in its cracked glass case—seemed as though it was on its last legs.

What is this place?

And why was he here?

Bene noticed the cars parked in the lot first, and his brother standing at the doors second. Marcus, that was. He recognized the vehicles, too, as belonging to Capos of the family, an enforcer or two that were lucky enough to get their *in* to the family, and his brothers', Marcus and Christopher, as well.

Not to mention, his father's coveted, custom Rolls-Royce.

The second Bene stepped out of the car, Marcus arched a brow, and smiled faintly from his position on the sidewalk. He'd be a liar if he said a part of him didn't want to wipe that fucking smirk from his older brother's face.

If only because …

"Do you enjoy making me run all over the city like a *cafone*?" he asked.

Marcus shrugged one suit-covered shoulder. "My right, no?"

"Well—"

"And their right. The boss thought you needed a reminder about what this life was *really* like, and just how lucky you had it, Bene."

He understood a lot of things then.

First, his brother called Gian *the boss*. Not dad, or papa, like he usually would when they had a conversation about their father, and words *mattered*. Right now, words mattered more, and calling him the boss meant only one thing.

This wasn't family time.

This was business.

"What's going on?" Bene asked.

"We needed to make sure you could clean up your act, and get back to business before someone vouched for you. Do you understand what I'm saying?"

He thought he did.

Was this … "Am I getting my button tonight?"

Marcus lifted his hand to show three cards he held. *Saints.* Even from Bene's position ten feet away, he could see the different religious figures on the cards, and he knew he had been right about his assumption.

"Pick your saint before we enter, and you speak the *omertà*."

"That's why you had me running like crazy?"

"Part of it."

Bene had another thought, then. "Am I getting my button because Dad's worried someone might kill me otherwise, or is it that he thinks I earned it?"

Marcus didn't answer right away.

He didn't like that.

"Well?" he demanded.

"Is being a made man what you want, or not?" Marcus asked.

"Of course, it's what I want."

"Then, pick your saint, Bene, and let's get this night started. The boss has places to be this weekend—we're handling *famiglia* business, it's *the boss*—so let's not make him wait, so that he can finish this, and take his wife out of town for the weekend like he promised her."

Well, then …

"Saint John the Apostle," Bene said.

Marcus smiled. "The saint of loyalty. Smart choice. Keep making those, and you're going to be just fine tonight, little brother."

His palm *stung*.

Like a motherfucker.

In Cosa Nostra, it was tradition for a man's hand to be sliced with a knife chosen by the boss as he spoke his oath, and after the patron saint he'd chosen burned to nothing but ash in his palm. Symbolic, in a way, speaking to the oath they all had to take for this life.

The *mafia* came first.

La famiglia was held most important above all else.

Family.

Friends.

Love.

Even God.

Hence, the saint.

It was Bene's only thoughts when he finally got home— the watch on his wrist said it was only five, but hell, it felt like *one*. In the morning. Maybe that was because the past two weeks finally caught up to him, and he now realized what it was really about and what it meant for the rest of his life.

The cut on his palm? Dried with blood? Dirtied with burned ashes from the picture of a saint he'd picked for his initiation into Cosa Nostra?

It only meant one thing, now.

He was made.

Bene walked through his penthouse in a haze, of sorts, seeing different things he had left scattered and forgotten while his life was upended for two weeks. A bag of chips on the counter. Unwashed dishes in the sink. His bathroom had turned into a hurricane, and his bedroom didn't look much better, either.

Clothes strewed across the floor from just changing when he needed to, but not having the time to properly put things away. He hadn't made his bed in two weeks, and the sheets needed to be washed. He had a pile of shit that needed to go to the drycleaners, and he just had *zero* desire to clean anything. Not after the day he had.

Couldn't he just … *enjoy* this moment?

This milestone?

Bene didn't know.

So, while he tried to figure it out, and settle everything that had happened over the course of an evening, he did attempt to clean up his penthouse. At least now, he had the time to do so, and no one would be calling him away as soon as he started something.

Maybe it was time to hire a maid.

Besides, after today, there would be no more running to do odd jobs or answering to whichever made man had his phone number. He was now set to work as his brothers' right-hand man, for whatever Chris or Marcus needed. Considering Marcus was the underboss of the family, Bene knew he'd be making his brother's life easier as the go-between for Capos controlling the men on the streets.

Work he *liked*.

By the time Bene made it back to his bedroom to pick up the clothes strewn all over the floor, and strip the bed of the dirty sheets, he was ready to call it a night. And yet, when he picked up a pair of pants he hadn't worn in two weeks, and a piece of crumpled up paper fell to the floor—writing side up —he hesitated.

Her number.

That signature *V.*

Christ.

Why could he still taste that woman on his mouth? How did she make him hard when he hadn't even seen her in weeks? Not to mention, why did his exhaustion suddenly disappear at the idea of calling that number, and seeing if he might be able to celebrate this night with her?

Bene had no intention of questioning it. He simply grabbed that paper and pulled his phone from his pocket. He was already dialing the number before he even left the bedroom.

Surely, he earned this.

Right?

CHAPTER

6

"This is *delicious*," Senior praised.

"Isn't it? Wasn't sure what she was doing at that college, but this is a good sign," Mario replied to his father. "Might even dare to say it was worth it."

Senior turned his gaze on Vanna, and nodded. "Not sure how much longer you'll be attending there, but while you do, I need you to cook for me more."

Across the table, the man's wife—and Mario's mother, Gemma—did her best to keep a straight face, and not roll her eyes. *Barely.* Vanna might have been offended about that on another day, but she kind of got it.

Men were praising another woman's cooking at her table, and no Italian woman took very kindly to that. To her bene-fit, Gemma was *attempting* civility, and politeness. Vanna couldn't say she would do the same if she were in Gemma's position. Not that anyone gave her a choice. Mario called the week before, said his father wanted to spend more time with her, and he agreed with the promise she would cook them all something to eat the next week.

Well, that turned into this. A table *full* of people from their Camorra clan. Vanna killing herself in the kitchen. And now a woman across from her who looked like she had finally found her limit with all the compliments going around that were not directed toward her, or her cooking.

Just perfect, really. This night couldn't get any worse than it already was, surely.

She would usually enjoy someone praising her cooking considering the effort that went into her attending George Brown College for their amazing culinary program. A program that would, essentially, guarantee her success in her chosen field once she finished, and went on to apprentice under a chef in the city.

Unless, someone else stopped her dreams.

Considering some of the offhanded remarks Mario made over the course of the dinner, to his father and the other Camorra men attending, Vanna was beginning to think he intended to do exactly that. Cage her into this life, *somehow*, and keep her with him.

Across the table, Mario watched her with a smile playing at the edges of his lips. She could tell without him even needing to say it that he was enjoying this night. It was almost as if he had been able to show her off, like some trophy he'd been keeping hidden from the rest of his family and his father's people. As if they hadn't known Vanna her entire life, and now they were getting a fresh look at her on Mario's arm.

Up until now, Vanna had felt forgotten by a lot of the clan. The little orphan teenager who had been taken in by the boss and his wife but had never really been *favored* or put on display for the rest of the clan like Mario had been as their son. In that moment, during the dinner, it felt like every-thing changed, and Vanna hadn't seen it coming.

She *hated* it.

All of it.

And yet, the only way she could continue to have the freedom she did, like going to college, living on her own, and more … was to feed into Mario's nonsense. It was his word in his father's ear, after all, that allowed her all she had and could do.

Vanna didn't want to play with fire.

"Thank you," Vanna said to Senior when he stared at her expectantly, waiting for a reply to his earlier praises. "I love cooking."

And she did.

Before her father died, cooking had been a way she spent one on one, quality time with her dad. Because she didn't have a mother to teach her any useable skills, like *cooking*, the job fell to her dad, and it was just her luck that he enjoyed it, too.

Then, after his passing, cooking became the way Vanna coped a lot of the time. Baking cookies at two in the morning when she couldn't sleep because she kept dreaming of getting the news about her dad … well, it got her through it.

The people at the table didn't care to hear that, though. Nothing about her father, or her life *then* mattered because then they might look at her as though she was nothing more than Adam's child. His blood, determined to ruin their clan and life the same way he and his father had once done, even if that had never been her plans.

"Back to business," Senior said, waving a hand as Vanna stood to clear the plates with Gemma's help. Just like that, the men at the table went back to discussing their plans to take over several road construction rackets the following year after a few deals they'd pulled in this summer. "And bring me in a drink, love."

Gemma nodded to her husband.

Mario looked Vanna's way expectantly, clearly wanting the same. He didn't outright ask, but the raise of his brow when all eyes turned on the exchange between the two of them, and his quiet, "If you wouldn't mind, of course."

Yes, she minded.

She wasn't his.

Nor was she a maid.

Vanna still smiled. "Sure."

The men had no issue with discussing business while the women milled about, even a few of the wives of other men attending the dinner. So was the Camorra way—not entirely unheard of for a woman to control, or even head, the family should the time call for it. That didn't mean women weren't highly controlled in the Camorra, because they were.

Far too much.

Women were held to a far higher standard than any man. And things a woman would be punished—or even killed for —a man would be praised for doing the same. Funny how that worked, except it wasn't really funny at all.

Vanna listened to their conversation as she helped to clean the table, and then proceeded to load dishes into the dishwasher. Gemma barely spoke to her at all, but that wasn't anything unusual. The woman never held much affection or care for Vanna, even when she agreed to bring her into the home after her father's death.

She didn't take offense.

It wasn't *personal*.

It just was.

After they brought the drinks to the table, Vanna excused herself to the kitchen to finish cleaning, even though there wasn't much left to do, if anything at all. She busied herself with wiping down the counters while watching through the entryway.

Occasionally, Mario would look her way, but mostly, he watched his father, and engaged in the conversation at the table. A little king in waiting, or so he thought. She used to think his strange infatuation with her would die once he figured out she didn't feel the same, but if anything, the man seemed determine to prove she would someday be sitting at his side at the table with the rest of them.

Vanna didn't think so.

But one thing at a time.

She had other shit to focus on right now.

Finishing her work in the kitchen, Vanna washed her hands as a familiar ding echoed. She darted for her purse to find the phone hidden inside and checked the screen to see the contact that lit up the ribbon with a text.

It was an unknown number, but the text explained it clearly enough. *Bene.*

Vanna smiled.

Well, well, well …

Hey, it's Bene. You free tonight?

That's all his text read.

She shouldn't leave the Detti home yet.

She had other things to do.

And yet, the vendetta …

That man.

Those thoughts warred. She needed more on the Guzzi family to have anything useable to ruin them, and nothing she had now would work. That much had been confirmed by the man who received her initial findings from Bene's place. Not to mention, she would be a damn liar if she said she hadn't thought about Bene *a lot* in the last couple of weeks. It was memories of him that helped her find relief in too-hot showers with only her hand between her thighs.

Vanna didn't hesitate to reply, *I can be—give me a time and place, we'll meet up.*

That was that.

Vanna stepped out of the cab to find Bene leaning against the brown brick of a small bar that wasn't very far away from his place. "Was that intentional?"

He arched a brow. "Pardon?"

"Did you get me over here so that we were closer to your place when the night is over?"

A laugh answered her back.

And *damn*.

The man looked sexy doing it.

She took a moment to admire the leather jacket and dark-wash jeans he'd thrown on that fit perfectly to his strong thighs, and the tall, dark, and handsome appeal of the rest of him. Everything about this man seemed to be dangerous for her body, considering the only thing she seemed to feel around him was the strongest lust of her life.

It made things hard.

"Nope," Bene eventually said, pushing off the wall to step closer to her, "it's just the only place I like to play pool, and it happens to be close to my neighborhood."

"Mmhmm."

"Not your scene?"

Vanna eyed the entrance to the bar, taking in the gold detailing around the doors, and the sign hanging above. "Not really, but if you can make it fun …"

Bene grinned. "I can make *anything* fun."

"Oh?"

"That a challenge?"

He was *a lot* closer now.

Just a foot away.

In a blink, before she had even been able to take in a breath, he closed the distance between them. One of his arms wrapped around her back, hugging the loose fabric of her t-shirt tight to her body as he dragged her into him. His head tipped down, and those smirking, sexy lips of his met hers.

The kiss was soft at first.

Seeking.

Testing.

And then he found it.

The answer she gave back to him—the way her lips parted for him to get that *taste*. She didn't even think about it, simply wanted to have him kissing her because she swore no one ever kissed like this man did, and she wanted more of it.

Even if a part of her still hated him because of the people he came from, and the last name he sported. It didn't matter. A kiss wouldn't have her handing over her heart to him—*surely not*. She had more self control than that, didn't she?

Well, it was hard to say.

And she didn't have a proper answer when he was still kissing her like he was. As though he couldn't get enough of the way her lips worked against his, and how she was more than willing to let him dominate her with a kiss on a sidewalk in the middle of a city where *anyone* could see.

Fuck anyone else.

They could look.

She was still getting hers.

All too soon for her liking, Bene pulled away, that smirk still playing at the edges of his lips while his dark eyes looked her over. *My God*. His face was just as bad for her body as the rest of him, honestly.

"Was that too much?" he asked.

Vanna grinned. "Why would it be?"

"I didn't ask first."

"You don't have to *ask*."

"I should, though."

Vanna shrugged. "I wouldn't have come tonight if I didn't plan on having fun, Bene."

"Good to know. Do you play pool?"

"A few times. I'm sure you're better at it than me, though."

He chuckled. "I'll let you whoop my ass, if you let me take a bite of yours later."

Yeah.

Hell.

That's where she was going. Straight to hell. Because a part of her liked this man. Another part hated him. She was making him like her, too. And yet, she would also ruin him when her plans finally came together.

Vanna pushed those thoughts away.

At least, for now.

Pushing up to her tiptoes, she kissed him and winked. "That sounds like a deal."

~

Vanna leaned over the pool table, feeling Bene's gaze firmly stuck to the way her pert ass lifted a bit over the wood edge as she readied on her next—and hopefully, *final*—shot. He was such an ass man, and she didn't mind using that to her advantage while playing this game of theirs. After all, she'd just used his attention to her ass to her benefit for his last shot, making him miss to give her the next round which left her with one final ball to sink.

"Eight ball to the far right," she said, "and that's game."

Before Bene could reply, Vanna took her shot, easily sinking the eight ball into the pocket she called. He let out a low whistle behind her as she stood from her leaning posi-tion, resting the pool cue to the floor as she stayed looking over the table still scattered with Bene's solid-colored balls.

"Played pool a *few* times—wasn't that what you told me?"

Vanna laughed lightly, the sounds of the bar fading in the

background as she spun around to face Bene. His heated gaze met hers, and she couldn't help but grin. "There was a billiards table in my father's basement. Apparently, he used to play a lot when he was younger, and instead of getting rid of it, it just found its way into the basement. He taught me how to play, and a few tricks. We used to play a couple of times a week."

Bene's stare softened, and she saw that *dawning* flash across his face as he leaned forward a bit on the pool cue. "Used to, huh?"

Shit.

"Yeah," she said, knowing she should lie but finding that she didn't want to, "my dad passed away just before I turned sixteen. I buried him on my birthday."

"That must have been hard on you and your m—"

"Don't have a mom."

Her tone came out clipped, and a little strained, despite the fact that she tried to hide it. It was almost impossible for her not to have that reaction when it came to talking about her estranged—*missing*, too, because she had no idea where the bitch was—mother. It wasn't Bene, and it definitely wasn't fucking *personal* to him. It just was.

Bene's brow lifted high. "Sorry."

She shook her head. "Don't apologize just because you pity me or anything."

"Nah, I'm sorry I asked. Wasn't my business unless you wanted to tell me, you know?"

Vanna swallowed hard, shifting in her tall, strappy heels. She could have gone for something simple to dress in, and comfortable. She seriously doubted Bene would care seeing as how he looked at her the same in her t-shirt, strappy heels, and boyfriend-style jeans that were rolled up at the ankles, as he did her sexy two-piece, crop-top dress from their first meeting. But she didn't *do* simple, and if heels were always a choice, then she would forever pick them.

"I …" Vanna sighed, glancing over her shoulder and across the bar to stare at the gleaming bottles lining the cedar shelves behind the bartender. It was easier to admit something when she didn't have to look someone right in the face while she did it. "Sorry, it wasn't you or what you said that made me sharp—just my mom does that, in general. She was gone before I could even sleep through the night, I guess."

"So when your dad died … *shit.*"

"Yeah." Vanna chewed on her inner cheek, wishing it hadn't been as easy as that just was to spill some of her deepest secrets—even if they weren't the kind of secrets Bene could use to hurt her—to tell him that. She looked back at him, arching a brow and offering him a small smile. "Can we just … get back to talking about pool, or literally *anything* else but all that? A little too deep for a second date, is all."

Bene chuckled. "Anything?"

She nodded. "Yep."

"What were you doing when I texted?"

That was random.

It kind of made her smile, too. It wasn't the question she expected him to ask, but it shouldn't really shock her at all that Bene could keep her on her toes. He consistently did that, right from the moment they met. She expected him to be one thing, and he turned out to be something different. Even if he *was* still a Guzzi.

She couldn't forget *that.*

"Cleaning up after a meal I cooked, actually. Showing off what I learned last year at George Brown College."

Something appreciative and approving colored up his handsome features. "A *chef?*"

"That's what I'm trying to be."

Another one of those low whistles split through his lips.

"And she *cooks* …" He pressed his hands together in front of his chest as though he were praying while glancing upward. "Killing me here, *Jesus*."

Vanna's laughter lit up their small corner of the bar again, and Bene grinned lazily as he moved to drop his hands to his sides again. It was then that she noticed the bandage on his right palm, covering most of the surface.

"What happened there?"

Bene didn't even glance down like she did. "Nothing."

"Doesn't look like *nothing*."

He used the injured hand to grab the pool cue he'd rested against the wall before doing his fake prayer, nodding to the table as though his next words would make her forget that she had even asked her question. "So, since you whooped my ass, and not the other way around, does that mean I still won't get to take a bite out of yours later, or …?"

His tone dipped suggestively.

Vanna blanked.

Damn him.

His words did make her momentarily forget about her question, but only because her mind was suddenly filled with the image of this man biting her ass before he ate her pussy on his knees like a king kneeling for a queen at her throne. It was quite the picture, and she gave her mind credit for its efforts.

Bene smirked as he pushed away from the wall, the one stride between them closing in a blink as he leaned forward to put one hand somewhere behind her on the pool table. It was kind of hard to know what he was doing with him close enough that his chest pressed against hers, and the slight scruff on his jaw tickled her cheek when he tipped his head down to let his lips brush against her skin.

Then, she heard the telltale sound of the coin slot on the

pool table being pushed in after he'd tossed in a couple of quarters.

"Another game?" he asked.

Vanna let out a shuddering breath. "Who's killing who here?"

Because *this man* ...

He was something else.

Bene winked when he straightened. "Good to know I'm not the only one, then."

"Definitely not."

And she hated that was the case.

Even if she would never say it out loud.

Right then, though Vanna had no doubt it would be bad for her—if not for her body, then for her *heart* later—she stood up on her tip toes and pressed a kiss to his lips. That's all it took—one soft, innocent kiss for his hands to find her waist, the wood of the pool cue biting into her hip as he pushed her against the edge of the pool table. His tongue darted into her mouth, slashing against hers in the best way while she was once again made to forget where they were because they'd simply *kissed*.

She didn't mind it at all.

Until, of course, she heard someone mutter, "If you're gonna do that, could you fucking move it outside to the alley like every other bitch that'll get on her knees does, and give someone else the table?"

Vanna stiffened the second Bene's lips stilled against her own. She physically *felt* the change in his posture, and sensed it, too. Like his playful, sexiness had left him just like that, and the heat in his gaze suddenly burned with more rage than it did lust when his stare met hers.

She didn't know why she thought to speak to defuse the situation, but she still did. Or at least, she *tried*. "It's fine. Just ignore him. It's o—"

That was all Vanna managed to say before Bene pushed away from her. He spun sideways, as though he had just known the asshole came up to his right without even looking that way when he had been distracted with her. His fist was already flying, crashing into the face of the man before Vanna even had time to think about what was happening.

And then as fast as it happened, it was over. Bene spun on his heels, a dark grin tugging at his lips when her wide— slightly amused, but also *terrified*—gaze met his. *Yes*, she'd seen a man hit another man over her before. But no, she had never quite liked it the way she did right then.

The man hadn't even hit the floor before Bene's hand found hers, and he pulled her off the pool table, grabbing her bag from the floor at the same time, and moved them toward the back entrance of the bar. She peeked over her shoulder in just enough time, right before they darted out the back doors, to see the bartender coming around the bar.

They were already gone.

It was over.

That's how fast it happened.

Her hand stayed tucked tightly with Bene's as he pulled her through the back alley behind the bar, and through the maze of another three. He didn't stop until they were one block down, and she recognized the familiar brick design of his building. Except it was the side, and not the front. Not that it mattered to her when he pressed her into the brick, his body crowding hers in the best way, leg slipping between her thighs to give her pussy something to grind on while he kissed her harder than ever.

Until her lungs burned.

And all she saw was him.

His hands skimmed over the front of her jeans, unsnapping the button and pulling down the zipper before sliding underneath. She stared down the alley to the busy street where people bustled on by. Not to mention, *all the windows around them*. What were the chances that this alley would be empty at this time of night? And still, anyone could see them there, if they just thought to look.

Vanna still didn't care.

"That was crazy," she breathed against his mouth.

Bene chuckled, lips curving with hers. "*Worth it.*"

"Shouldn't make a woman run in heels, Bene."

"Can I fuck one in them?"

Vanna groaned. "*Yes.*"

That was all he seemed to need. Her *consent*. Like the fact she was willing to say—out loud, and clearly—*yes, you can fuck me in this alley*, almost got him off. He wasted no time turning her around to face the brick, while yanking her jeans down her thighs until they pooled at her heels. His hot left palm drove up under her shirt, smoothing over her spine while his other worked at the zipper and button on his jeans.

She saw stars when he finally freed his length, asked if she was good with bare, and then stretched her full with that first thrust. There was no mercy, no slowness, in the way he fucked her. Just rough, fast flexes of his hips snapping against hers while her palms scrapped against the brick.

He tucked in closer behind her, hands flattening to the roundness of her ass, so he could clench his fingers into her cheeks while his teeth grazed her jawline. "Fucking love that cock, huh? That hot pussy of yours can't get enough, Vanna."

He wasn't wrong.

And his dirty words only edged her along.

The funny thing was ... the guy at the bar hadn't been wrong. She was doing exactly what he said in an alleyway with a man she'd only met once before in her life. It was fucking *crazy*. And yet she didn't care that nothing about this was sane.

She just wanted to come.

Even better that Bene would make her do it.

Was that a betrayal to her cause?

Probably.

Vanna would deal with it later.

"Come on, come on, give me what I want, baby. Fucking *love it* that you'll let me fuck you like this, yeah."

His harsh moan filled her ears, and she swore she felt that right in the center of her bones. Deep in her stomach. Aching in her pussy. Even her damn toes curled because *God* … this man was sin to her. Pure, but so good, sin.

She came hard.

And it was *bliss.*

Bene followed soon after, his lips sucking against her throat and then his teeth biting into the same spot as his hips stilled against hers. He was quick about pulling out, and fixing her pants, but he didn't seem to care about moving them away from the wall, or even turning Vanna around after he'd fixed himself.

Instead, he nuzzled his face against the side of her throat. "What are you doing this weekend—anything important."

Vanna cleared her throat, trying to let the emotional war inside her head calm as she replied, "Nothing, really."

"What if I asked you to spend it with me?"

"Oh, where?"

"I don't know. How about a mansion?"

Vanna smiled over her shoulder, and he grinned back when he tipped his head up to stare at her. "Really?"

"My penthouse is a mess, that's all."

"You know, I didn't really mention that you clearly have money, but now you say *mansion* … and I don't want to make it awkward by *not* acknowledging it, but also it might because I say something and—"

Okay, now she was rambling.

Vanna stopped that abruptly.

"You don't have to mention it at all," he said, "I'm just used to wealth … was born into it, basically, so it's never me showing off as much as it is me just stating my life."

"It's not the wealth … well, not really. My dad left me money, not a lot, but enough to give me a few comfortable years, and it bought me a penthouse."

His dark laughter soothed her overheated skin. "Oh?"

"But you said *mansion* and it took a second to sink in."

"I get it. Point is, I want you to spend the weekend with me if you want to."

Vanna didn't even have to think about it.

She knew it was crazy.

Stupid.

Mario would probably wonder where she was … he liked to stop by on the weekends. She barely even gave him a thought, though.

No, she didn't think at all when she said, "I would love to."

CHAPTER

7

"Is this yours, or—"

He put the Lambo into park. "My parents' place."

Vanna nodded slowly, her appreciative gaze taking in the Swedish-style eaves of the mansion before drifting to the large trees lining either side of the driveway. "They're not home, right?"

Bene laughed. "Hell no. My father would kill me for bringing someone here like this."

Not a lie.

Gian had rules.

For the most part, Bene tried to follow them. One of those rules centered around the Guzzi brothers bringing home women. To which, they *shouldn't* bring one to their parents' home unless she was the type of woman they intended on keeping. *The respect of the matter*, his father would say, as if that made any fucking sense at all.

Thing was, his father and mother headed to their vacation home in Quebec for the weekend, wouldn't be back until Monday, and Bene knew just enough about his parents' security system to make sure everything was deleted from the security cameras. Any enforcers that stayed posted at the house while his parents were home always left when the owners did, usually to follow them to wherever, not that one of them would say anything, either.

It wasn't the first time one of the brothers broke the rules. They simply didn't talk about it when they did it.

Plus, why not?

Bene felt reckless.

Time to have some fun.

"Come on," he said, unlatching the driver's door of the Lambo. "I'm sure you want to see the inside."

Vanna laughed, following his lead. Outside of the vehicle, he rounded the front, and met Vanna in the middle. She took his hand with her own, letting him lead them toward the grand entrance of the mansion, its sloping roof hanging overtop a large outdoor fountain more than big enough for cars to drive under and park.

She stopped to admire the fountain while he went for the front door, and the panel right beside it. The only way his father wouldn't get a notification for the security was if he punched in the correct code, and the fingerprint reader scanned a print it recognized—like his, or any one of his other brothers'—and only then could he put the key into the lock. He was sure his father hadn't given his sons the codes and ability to get inside for Bene to do what he was doing, but he would deal with that at another time.

"Are you coming?" he called to Vanna.

She came his way as he unlocked the front door, following him inside. If one didn't get to see anything else but the grand entrance of the Guzzi mansion, it would still be more than enough to amaze them. As large as most people's homes, with two curving staircases on either side, and with a large indoor fountain featuring a naked statue to give it just that extra bit of … *excessiveness*, it was quite a sight.

White marble floors clicked under Vanna's heels as she walked in ahead of Bene, her eyes wide as she looked all around, taking in the paintings hanging on the walls—probably ten of *hundreds* in the place—although some of the most expensive rested in this hall.

"Wow."

"Yeah," he said, "it's a little much."

Her laughter colored up the space, echoing back to them.

"But is it, though?"

He grinned, saying nothing.

Frankly, he hadn't been sure *what* she would think about the mansion. Sure, he could have just as easily grabbed them a hotel in the city for the weekend, but it wouldn't be quite the same as *this*. Besides, he liked familiar spaces. This home was certainly that, and if it meant he got to spend the weekend with a beautiful woman in bed with him, then he didn't see a problem. His father might, but if all went well, then Gian wouldn't even know when they left on Sunday.

Simple enough.

Bene kicked off his shoes at the door—habit from hearing his mother repeat the order for him to do it for as many years as he had been alive—while Vanna walked over to the fountain. He watched her as she leaned over the side, admiring the sight of those boyfriend jeans hugging her pert backside, and remembering how good it felt to dig his fingers into her ass as he fucked her deeper. She really did look like an angel, with the body of a sinner. He didn't have the first clue what he was doing with this woman, but he liked it.

Wasn't that good enough?

Vanna let her fingers drift through the sprinkling, dancing water while she peered back at him with a sly smile. Clearly catching him looking at her ass, but he didn't have shame, and she didn't seem to mind, either. He winked when she just shook her head.

"Was this your childhood home?"

Bene nodded, now shoeless and heading for her. "Yeah, we used to have the *best* games of hide and seek in this place."

"I bet. You must have loved growing up here with your twin, and other brothers."

He blinked, taking in her words. His mind flooded with a dozen different memories, most of him and Beni running after one another through the house, or across the large back property. From sliding down the banisters to putting a slip and slide in the upstairs hallway which had *not* impressed their parents in the slightest. They even had their own hiding spots and things they liked to do together in the mansion that they'd never told anyone else about because well, twins had to have *some* secrets, right?

It made him smile.

For a brief second, Bene realized that was the first time he'd thought of his brother all day. In fact, the last two weeks had been so busy for him, and he was enjoying himself so much right now, that all the shit he'd been dealing with his brother getting married and moving to Chicago had become nothing more than an afterthought.

Oh, his chest ached *now*.

Was that a betrayal?

To not think about his twin?

Bene didn't know.

Now was not the time.

"Bene?"

He hadn't realized it until she spoke, but he had come to stand right next to her beside the fountain. Entirely lost in his thoughts and the memories he shared with Beni, his entire demeanor and mood shifted just like that.

Except all it took was her calling his name. A pretty smile curving her sexy lips, and a glimmer in her eye that said they were about to have some fun together.

Just that.

And his mood was gone.

"Hmm?" he asked.

Vanna flicked her hand in the water, making droplets fly up and splatter across his chest and face. Her laughter echoed all around them again as she turned and darted away from the fountain. She'd said earlier that he shouldn't make a woman run in heels, but *fuck* … she was damn good at doing it. He supposed his distraction at watching the way her hips swayed gave her a decent head start to run from him.

Worth it.

He found himself saying that a lot about this woman. And he didn't even know anything about her. He had to wonder if that was part of the draw—that she didn't know fuck all about him, and he knew less than zero about her life, too. It made this thing, whatever they were doing together, easier than if both their baggage needed handling, too.

Instead, they could just have fun.

Enjoy all of this.

There was no need to get deep.

Right?

"You can have me wherever," he heard her say as she headed for the left staircase, "but only if you can *catch me*."

Well …

Bene did like a challenge.

He managed to finally catch Vanna on the third floor of the mansion, crowding her against the decorative table while he kissed the air right out of her lungs. She didn't seem to care a bit that she had lost their little game, not when her hands slipped into his pants, and under the line of his boxer-briefs to find his hardening cock.

All it took was tight stokes …

Her fingertips gliding over the head of his dick …

And then her getting to her knees.

She took his pants down with her, the head of his cock finding its way between those pink lips of hers to find the heat of her mouth, and *fuck*. He couldn't breathe, but he could see. It was a hell of a sight, too, with her on her knees, surrounded by so much fucking wealth, and sucking his dick like it was the only thing in the world she wanted to do. His fingers tangled into her hair, holding tight while moans of her name fell from his lax mouth.

Yeah.

Perfect.

~

"Have you picked a room to sleep in, yet?"

Vanna didn't turn around from the painting of his mother and father that she was currently admiring just outside the hallway on the second floor. "The one at the end here, I think."

"Good choice. The *principessa* room."

She did turn to peek over her shoulder at him, then. "The princess room?"

"You speak Italian?"

He didn't miss the way her throat jumped at that question, but her gaze remained calm and unbothered as she shrugged. "It's not hard to guess what *principessa* means, is it?"

"Your last name is also Falco—that's Italian."

He wasn't stupid.

And he could push the line until she snapped.

"I know a little."

"Catholic, too?"

Vanna smirked a bit. "Of course."

Goddamn.

Who was this woman?

She was perfect in every sense of the word.

She turned her attention back to the painting of his parents, tilting her head to the side a bit as she took in the plaque underneath it that stated the artist, and people featured. All the paintings in the mansion had that little plaque.

"Your parents have a lot of art."

"One whole hall is dedicated just to pieces of our family."

"And a lot is just … expensive art, Bene."

He nodded, coming to stand beside her. She wasn't wrong. Paintings decorated the walls of the mansion. Statues and different pieces his mother and father picked up along their travels over the years filled every nook and cranny. That was before he got into everything else. From the imported rugs to the custom tapestries. Or his mother's library—filled with rare, first edition books. His father's *three* garages, brimming with custom vehicles.

Guzzis had expensive tastes.

It came with the lifestyle.

Never was there a better show of their wealth, however, than inside their homes. None of his brothers were quite as showy as his parents, but they were still pretty … excessive. Yeah, that was as good of a word as any.

"A good way to hide vast wealth is in material things, or that's what my father always says. Sure, we've got a lot of money in the bank, and spread across investment portfolios, but you'll find the real money in my parents' properties, and what's *inside* those properties."

"Like the art," she replied.

"Exactly."

"Why, though?"

Bene cleared his throat, shifting from foot to foot. "That's … not an easy answer."

Because it had to do with his legacy.

Their family *name*.

The business.

Mafia.

A lot of his father's illegal business brought in more money than any person would know what to do with, and so to hide what he couldn't launder to make clean, Gian often *spent it*. He donated money, too, but Cara was the one who chose which charities their money would go to at the end of the year. Mostly, money just got spent. New homes. Lavish vacations. Pieces of art. Renovating. *Things*.

It was easy to hide it.

Easy to liquidate.

"We have a lot of money," he settled on saying.

Lamely, too.

It didn't matter that he liked this woman, or that for whatever reason, being with her seemed easy even though they barely knew each other at all. None of that factored into this for him.

He couldn't tell her the truth.

Simple as that.

Vanna, of course, surprised him. "Is what they say about the Guzzis true?"

His gaze darted sideways to her, but she didn't look away from the painting. "And what do *they* say about us, huh?"

"Sorry—did I touch a nerve there?"

Bene arched a brow when she finally met his gaze. That was one of the things he found he liked about her, though. She wasn't afraid to outright say the things that were on her mind. Like when she stated about his wealth, or that day in the bar.

Vanna was frank.

Straightforward.

He respected it.

Even if it made conversations tough.

"What do they say?" he asked again. "And you never thought to mention to me that you recognized my last name when I introduced myself?"

She shrugged. "What difference would it make? I clearly wasn't interested in your last name, was I?"

Well ...

He gave her points for that.

"You haven't answered my question."

Vanna's expression didn't change. "I haven't figured out how to phrase it."

"Try anything."

"Your whole family is all over the society rags."

"As much as we try to avoid it, sure."

She smiled a bit, murmuring, "They only *hint* at things."

"Because my father has a team of lawyers that will sue them into their graves if they try to state something about us as though it were a fact."

Even if it was a fact, and Gian would eventually lose in court, it didn't matter. His father had more than enough money to just *throw* into lawsuits with magazines that tried to spread information about their family. More disposable cash than the society rags had, anyhow. He didn't mind spending more than enough to bankrupt them in the process, even if he would fail at winning his case, and that's what mattered the most. The rags knew it, too. The game of the wealthy was not for the faint of heart.

Bene learned that lesson well.

"But the hints ..."

"Mmhmm," he urged.

She sighed, turning back to the painting. "They make it seem like your family isn't all that it seems, I guess."

"We're not."

Vanna continued staring at the painting of his parents. "Oh?"

"No, we're far more."

And that was all he would say about it.

She didn't seem to mind.

"So," Vanna said, spinning on her heel and heading down the hallway with Bene following after her, "the bedroom at the end, then?"

"If that's the one you want to use."

She grinned over her shoulder, as if their previous conversation hadn't happened at all, and she moved onto something else entirely. "I noticed speakers everywhere—can you turn music on, or connect the system to my phone?"

He arched a brow. "I can. Why?"

"I want to dance."

Bene groaned.

Fuck, yes.

"I would love to see you do that."

"You know, I do have to feed you."

Vanna, wearing nothing but his shirt from the day before, peeked over her shoulder at him as she raised up on her tiptoes to reach for a book on a higher shelf. She looked like absolute sex and sin standing there in the library, hair still mussed from the way she'd let it dry naturally after jumping into the shower with him that morning.

Instead of heading to the kitchen with him, she asked if she could explore. He didn't see the issue, simply said to stay out of the rooms that were closed, like his parents', or his brothers' old rooms. She didn't mind agreeing.

"Do you *cook*?"

Bene chuckled. "Well, I can try."

"You said feed me. Not make me cook for *you*, Bene."

"I can make a mean bacon and eggs."

She grinned. "Is that all?"

He was a little distracted by the way his shirt rode up over her bare ass, and how he could see just a sliver of flesh between her thighs when she leaned forward a bit. Teasing and tantalizing him like nothing else ever had.

"Pardon?" he said, meeting her gaze.

Vanna's smile deepened. "Am I really *that* good to look at?"

Didn't she know?

"*Donna*, you drive me crazy. Yes, you are that good to look at."

A sweet pink tinted her cheeks, and even with the shyness she dared to show, a heat still lingered in her stare. He'd bitten her plump lips a sexy red that morning when he woke her up already hard between her thighs, and ready to go.

The shower was round two.

He was looking for round three *any fucking time*.

Let's go.

Vanna looked ready for it, too.

She finally found the book she wanted on the higher shelf, and pulled it down to flip it over as she turned around to face him. Leaning against the bookshelves in his mother's large library, she turned pages, and while he couldn't see what book it was from his position in the doorway, that didn't mean he couldn't enjoy the sight of her smiling over whatever she was reading on the pages. One could always tell a bookworm simply by the way they stared at an opened book in their hands. *Pure joy.*

"Was this a room I wasn't supposed to be in?" she asked.

"Was the door open?"

Vanna shrugged, peeking up at him. "Yeah, but it's … different in here."

"What does that mean?"

"Well, for starters there's a wet bar near the window and a whole wine fridge. Also, there's a glass bowl with a bunch of bracelets in the reading nook. Someone must like Lindor chocolates because there's a whole selection to choose from in the corner. A journal, too, but I didn't look inside."

"Not so much a journal," Bene replied, glancing at the leather-bound notebook his mother kept on her stand, "as it is something for my mother to keep notes of what she's reading, and what she thinks about it at any given time. She goes back to her notes sometimes—anonymously reviews for a newspaper twice a month, actually."

Vanna's eyes widened. "For the Toronto Tribune?"

"I don't read them."

"Are you *serious*?"

Bene laughed. "What?"

"It's like the *only* book reviewer in a newspaper anymore. At least, in Toronto. Everything is online now, and that's one of the only papers still thriving. The fact she gets two entire columns for her reviews is amazing. And she's anonymous, so it isn't even her *name* drawing in readers for her reviews. An actual, *physical* newspaper. I read it every second Sunday just for her reviews on the latest releases."

He smiled. "Small world."

Something changed in Vanna's gaze—he couldn't tell exactly what it was, but he didn't miss the way her stare darkened a bit, a tiny knot forming in her brow as she glanced down at the book in her hands again. It hid her face from his view, but he decided not to ask her what was wrong because she spoke first.

"So, this library is your ma's?"

"My father uses it as an office sometimes, even though he works more in the one upstairs. But yeah, it's hers, and no, she doesn't mind someone else enjoying the books in here. No worries on that, I promise."

Vanna nodded, but continued staring down at the book in her hands. "You love her a lot, huh?"

"My mom?"

"Yeah."

Bene wondered if that was a strange concept for her … considering how she reacted to talking about her own mother the night before. "I mean, we all love our ma. Growing up, our dad kind of put Cara on a pedestal, and nothing less would do except the very best for her. She was always there, too, didn't matter if she had shit going on, or was sick … none of that mattered to Ma, she was just there for us when we needed her. The first person to tell us to go and get something, if we wanted it. How can you not love that?"

"Yeah, I get that."

Now, her voice turned faint.

Her head stayed turned down.

Bene wondered *why*.

"Anyway," Vanna said, closing the book and looking up with a bright smile. All that strangeness was gone, and in its place was the sweet, but sexy woman who caught his attention, and had yet to lose it, even if he wasn't willing to dig into the whys quite yet. "Food, you said?"

He could have pressed on her behavior.

Or the change in demeanor.

Instead, Bene just said, "Yeah, let's get some grub."

CHAPTER

8

The mansion was wired to the nines. Every single light in the place could be shut off with a press of one button from Bene's phone—or any of his other family members, he explained. A camera rested in almost every high corner, keeping watch on hallways and main rooms. The security in the place was top notch, no doubt about it.

Yet, even knowing that, Vanna didn't hesitate to slip out of the bed she shared with Bene for the weekend once he was passed out, to take another walk through the mansion. After all, he promised he would clear out all the footage of their time in the place, and he didn't even have to look at it to do it, just select dates he wanted to wipe from the memory. Which meant, for the most part, she had free reign when he fell asleep to do what she wanted.

And *needed*.

Apparently, his parents wouldn't appreciate them being there when they ... well, weren't, basically. Bene had been quick to explain that wouldn't even matter once he got rid of the footage of their time there. Vanna found that amusing.

A little.

Vanna only felt the slightest tinge of guilt when she headed past the library about what she was doing. Mostly because she had never felt any connection to the Guzzi family except through the stories she'd been told, and the moments she shared with Bene.

Other than that, her hate fueled by the past and memories of her father kept the vendetta well and alive for her. Nothing else factored into it—she never considered the fact that the family shared a whole life that they wouldn't want destroyed by someone like her. That behind the private walls of their lavish homes, hid stories of … well, a family.

Love.

Kids.

Marriage.

More.

So yeah, she felt a little bit of guilt as she passed the library, remembering that for the last several years, she had bought a newspaper every second Sunday just to get a peek at the anonymous reviewer's take on recent book releases. Reading, like cooking, had been a way she forgot about the loss of her father, and it helped her to get through tough times. She *loved* books, and the fact that she had enjoyed reading a column that Bene's *mother* wrote—a fucking Guzzi—had her doing a double take.

Not to mention, the way he spoke about his mom.

And his dad.

His *brothers*.

All of them.

He spoke about them in a way that almost made her want to *like* them—as though meeting them would be easy because they seemed like likable, interesting people through his point of view. She didn't want to give them much time in her mind for that shit because nothing good would come of it, she was certain.

After all, she was here for one reason.

She might enjoy fucking that man.

It meant nothing.

She was still here for a damned *reason*.

Vanna couldn't afford to forget it. Her stupid heart

couldn't get in the way of her end game, and neither could her conscience. She wasn't supposed to have one of those, anyway. And what really were the Guzzis or their love worth to the fact that because of them, her father died. *No*, they didn't pull the trigger, but they also didn't have to.

It only took one pebble to make a landslide.

Decades ago, Gian Guzzi was the pebble.

Vanna would be their landslide.

Palming her phone, she climbed the stairwell to the third floor of the mansion. Down the hall, and to the left, facing the entire front of the Guzzi property, rested Gian's office.

The door had been closed.

One of those *off-limits* rooms.

Vanna pushed the door open, and for a moment, simply stood in the doorway. She couldn't help but notice how there weren't any cameras in the top floor hallway in this wing. There weren't any cameras inside the office, either.

Not surprising.

No criminal wanted his acts on tape.

Vanna took in the richly stained wood of the oak desk that dominated the middle of the office, and the built-in shelves that matched behind it. A large, wingback office chair with studded detailing along the sides sat proudly behind the clean, yet still personal, desk. A few pictures of the family rested on the top, and a bowl with a few knickknacks, a lighter, and even a money clip with a few hundred-dollar bills sat inside.

A laptop sat on one side.

A desktop on the other.

In the middle, a pile of folders.

Windows across from the desk overlooked the entire front of the property, giving the man who sat behind the desk a good view of anyone coming near his home. She doubted that was done in error, but rather, purposefully.

Vanna took a single step in the room, hitting the home button on her phone to turn it on before typing in the passcode. It took no time at all for her to get the camera running on her phone as she crossed the space, and went to the desk first.

Surprise.

The drawers all had locks.

And they weren't budging.

She focused on the folders instead, flipping the first couple on top open to look inside. She didn't really understand what stared back at her, except it was something about a maple syrup farm, and the fact that it made *a lot* of money.

But why the off-shore accounts?

Because those documents were right underneath.

Attached to the farm.

She could clearly see deposits into the accounts on the paperwork, too, and not ones that came from the farm. It looked more like transfers from other accounts. Like someone was using the maple syrup farm to hide other cash flows.

It took her a second.

Money laundering.

And wire fraud.

Vanna started snapping pictures.

She'd send them off once she left.

The office was a fucking gold mine. Surely, she could do something with *this*. Especially, if it was exactly what she thought it was.

Only time would tell.

～

"Where have you been all weekend?"

Vanna's head snapped up, gaze darting to the end of the

hallway instead of the phone in her hand that had taken her attention while she headed up to her penthouse. She'd been distracted, replying to Bene's text in one window asking if she got up to her place safely—he'd driven her home, but she promised she was fine to head up alone, even though he offered.

In the other text chat, her contact asked if she thought she would be able to get inside the Guzzi mansion again for another round of her spying. According to his message, he needed more info on the maple syrup business to hand over before he could guarantee anything would come out of her findings.

Fucking perfect.

Fuck her whole life today. Because in her distraction, she totally missed the man waiting at her front door looking like he had been standing there for way too long. Damn, he probably did, too, knowing him. Had his car been parked downstairs? Because she missed that, too.

Mario gave her a look when she didn't answer right away. "Well?"

"Quebec," she lied.

She didn't even know why she said that.

Just did.

It was the first thought to pop into her head, and apparently, she was too fucking stupid from spending the weekend under a gorgeous man that knew how to play her body like nothing else to care about thinking up a good lie for Mario when she returned home. This had been inevitable, and even she knew that.

This asshole was too attached.

Always nearby.

She couldn't have him ruining her plans.

"Why?" he asked.

Vanna quickly turned off the screen of her phone and dropped it into her bag as she came up to her door, keys in hand. God knew he didn't need to see *either* of her chat windows. That wouldn't be good for her end goal. "To see a new restaurant one of the previous graduates opened up last year—she's looking for someone to apprentice under her, and my name was suggested."

All lies.

She pulled it out of nowhere.

Thing was, Mario had never been very interested in her schooling, the fact she wanted to be a chef, and he didn't have the first idea what it would take for her to become one. Like the fact that she would need to apprentice under someone for a set number of hours before she could get her seal.

As she turned to slide the lock into her deadbolt, Mario slipped in beside her. His hand landed to the door right by her head, making Vanna still as she tilted her head to the side, staring at him. He looked back, a smile curving his lips, but a fire burning in his eyes.

It meant nothing good.

"What?" she asked.

"You didn't think to tell me you were going out of town for the weekend? You just dropped off the radar, Vanna. Hell, you didn't even stay long enough to say goodbye to my parents on Friday night. I had to apologize to my parents for you. Do you even realize how fucking stupid that makes me look to them?"

Oh.

Was that the problem?

He needed to make things good with Senior, and his ma?

Vanna wished she cared.

"Didn't think I had to mention it," she replied.

Hoping that would be the final say on the matter, although she knew that was a pipe dream in and of itself, she unlocked the door, and reached for the knob to twist it open. Mario's hand dropped to hers, his fingers tightening almost painfully.

It stopped her from opening the door.

"You didn't think to mention it to me?"

That nice smile of his was gone.

Mario wasn't even *pretending* now.

This man could ruin everything for her—beyond just the Guzzi family, and her plans ... he could screw her entire life with a single conversation. All he would need to do was go to his father, say Vanna had stepped out of line, made the clan look bad, and best-case scenario would be that she was put under lockdown by the boss. Given a chaperone to follow her everywhere, to the point she probably wouldn't even be able to piss alone.

Worst-case scenario?

His patience for this game he thought he'd been playing with Vanna for years suddenly ran out, and instead of locking her down ... he just ended her. It was the Camorra way, after all, but especially for women who didn't stay in line.

God knew Vanna walked a thin line for a long time in this life.

She searched her brain for *something*—anything—to focus Mario's attention elsewhere, so that he dropped this line of conversation. If he started looking too deep into her business—more than the asshole already did—her plans would come crashing down before she could properly get started on making them work.

"Do you want to go out for dinner?" she asked.

He blinked. "What?"

"Dinner. You and me. Right now, because I'm hungry and I don't feel like cooking."

"We're talking about something right now."

"I get it—let you know where I am. Sorry, next time I will. So, dinner?"

She wouldn't call it a date.

He might, though.

That's all Mario wanted.

Just the *idea* they were something.

His smile curved his lips again. "*Fine*, woman, dinner."

Battle won.

She was sure it wouldn't be the last, either.

Vanna tapped her ballet flat against the tiled floor of the college's hallway, trying to settle the way her nerves suddenly decided to make themselves known. It didn't seem to matter how many times she had these meetings, or the fact that they had *never* gone badly—never mind that she hadn't even been caught doing it—she still became terribly nervous.

Classes at the college were over for the day, and since it wasn't unusual for Vanna to hang around for a bit after she finished, no one ever thought twice about the fact that for the last month … she had stayed an extra hour every Friday.

The squeak of cheap shoes against the tile had Vanna sighing. She glanced up, but stared at the white brick wall across from her position, instead of the man she knew was approaching her from the left. Soon, he was sitting on the bench to her right, and swiping at the screen of his phone while she waited for him to speak first.

It always went this way.

Never failed.

She thought it was stupid sometimes—*anyone* could see them having a conversation, so why did they need to make it seem like they were just two random people sitting in a hallway of a college that the man with graying hair *clearly* wasn't attending?

One look at him, and everyone would know.

Cop.

He looked like one.

Smelled like one.

Walked like one.

All cops were the same.

They simply wore different badges.

"How was your week?" he finally asked, never looking up from his phone.

Vanna rolled her eyes. "Could we not?"

His head tipped up, giving her a good look at his aging profile, the lines speaking of years past etched on his features, and the almost gray eyes that seemed cold whenever he did stare at her. His jawline had softened, but she could still tell that once upon a time, he had probably been a very handsome man.

A long time ago.

Probably before his partner, who once thought to take down the infamous Gian Guzzi, had failed, ruined his career as a detective in the process, and then proceeded to drink his life away. Then he decided hanging himself from his stairwell would be the best option.

Vanna learned, with nothing more than a conversation at her father's grave with this cop, that vendettas didn't stay with *only* Italians. Sometimes, a person's need for justice when it came to something that just wouldn't let go of their very soul, and they were willing to do anything to get what they wanted.

Like this man beside her.

Jacob Keefs. A constable in the Royal Canadian Mounted Police. A detective who had been moved from several divisions after several upsets in his earlier career—including a failed attempt to take down Canada's biggest crime family, the Guzzis. He'd worked with her father for a time, according to him. Just enough for her father to trust him, and for him to trust Adam. A cop that was willing to be dirty to serve his desires to end a criminal empire ... was it justified?

She didn't know.

Didn't care.

This time, it was all about her.

Her vendetta.

"How about," Vanna said quietly, peering down the hallway to check for anyone at the other end, "you just tell me what I need to look for next, and we'll go from there."

The man grumbled under his breath. "Your father at least gave me conversation during our meetings. Passed the time a little easier."

Yeah.

Well, she wasn't her dad.

Her father might have been fine with justifying his reasoning for working with a cop—dirty or not—but she certainly wasn't the same. Even Adam had told her that cops couldn't be trusted, all the while he worked with one, and now here she was ... doing the same thing. The difference was, Vanna didn't trust this cop to save her life.

She didn't doubt for a second that if it helped him get what he wanted, then he would quickly throw her right under the bus. It was the one and only reason she kept a tab on this man for her own purposes, just in case she ever needed to use it.

It was a good thing to do.

"Again, anything you want me to look for?" she demanded.

"You certainly hit on *something* with the last bit you sent to me. Took it higher to my superiors, without mentioning the name of my source, of course, and he jumped on the chance to tell me to go ahead with it. Whatever I needed, he was willing to make it happen. Seems he thinks the Guzzi family's money laundering and wire frauds using their maple syrup farms could really lead to something huge."

"One business of many, probably."

"They control a good portion of this city, areas of Quebec, and beyond. Their reach is—"

"I know who I'm dealing with," she muttered, "I don't need the rerun, Mr. Keefs."

She understood better than anyone.

He couldn't tell her differently.

Vanna risked *everything* to see this vendetta through. The career she hadn't even been able to start yet, her freedom, and even her life. Yes, she understood very well the kinds of people that she was working to take down, and what it would mean if something fucked it up. She didn't need his reminders.

Besides, now they were just wasting time.

"I have to leave soon."

"Right, right." He cleared his throat, sitting back on the bench to rest his leg over his right knee while he pocketed his phone. "Anything relating to the maple syrup farms would be good—even better if you can find documentation of any imports for their businesses. I have reason to believe they're also smuggling their drugs, illegal cigarettes, and more through those businesses, and if so … maybe you can find something. If we could catch them at a port of entry, it'd be a heyday."

"His office was clean."

"You found the folders."

"I found things that *suggested* something wasn't right. Bank accounts. Documentation of transfers. Nothing that says that cash came from illegal means, or otherwise. You told me that yourself—it's enough to suspect that's what it is, but they have to find the *source* of the cash, and what's making it for them, before you can prove they're laundering it."

"But this is enough to get excited over."

Right.

But it wouldn't take them down.

She heard what he didn't say.

Vanna already knew.

"So, you need more," she said, swallowing hard.

"Exactly."

"A lot more."

Perfect.

To her, that spelled bad things. More risks she would have to take, and time spent with Bene. Not that time with him bothered her, as it was quite the opposite. The more time she had with him … well, the stranger her feelings about him became.

Playing with fire, Vanna.

"Has the twin figured out who you are yet?" the detective asked. "Because that would be bad, and you'd have to step back immediately. If he does, tell me. I can get you into a program, as long as we have enough information to lawfully go against the Guzzi organization, that will keep you safe. It could mean starting over … from everything, including Camorra."

Yeah.

He'd made that offer before.

Did she want to take it?

"He hasn't figured it out, right?"

Vanna pushed away from the wall. "No."

"Then, you're all set."

Was she?

Vanna didn't know about that.

She left the detective sitting alone on the bench.

Her thoughts kept her company.

CHAPTER
9

Bene's father had a habit of calling his men together just to remind them that he could do it, for no other reason than he wanted to. Oh, sure, business was always had at these meetings with Gian leading the conversation, but it was more a flex of his father's power and position as the Don of the family than anything else.

Sometimes, Bene had attended the meetings before just because he could, or his father extended an invitation. Now that he was made, however, he didn't have a choice but to attend even if he was supposed to be across the city, picking up payments for a Capo.

While his father chatted on with one of the family Capos, discussing the recent takeover of yet another maple syrup farm that they would use to launder money, as well as *make* money, Bene stood between his brothers. He stayed quiet because he didn't have anything to add to a conversation he didn't know very much about, and like the other made men around his father's office, he hadn't been invited into the discussion.

Between Mafiosi, it was all about knowing one's place.

Respect was most important.

"How's Beni doing in Chicago?"

Bene tipped his head sideways toward Chris, an acknowledgement that he did, in fact, hear his brother's question. "Good, I guess."

"You guess?"

"He's busy; me too."

Out of the corner of his eye, Bene didn't miss the way Chris's brow dipped before he shot Marcus a questioning look. Marcus, to his benefit, only shrugged as though he didn't have anything to say. "Corrado runs back and forth between Vegas and New York every other week, and my wife is pregnant ... we still find time to call each other once a day."

Huh.

It seemed Bene had missed a lot of things happening around him while he was stuck inside his head, trying to deal with his problems. A part of him felt like shit about it, sure, but the other part simply felt like he should just move on, and be done with it. Do better now because nothing could fix the past. *Right?*

"How far along?" Bene asked.

"Six weeks," Chris returned.

He nodded. "Congrats. Nobody thought to tell me?"

"You've been ... not yourself lately."

Not a lie.

Bene sighed. "I get it."

To say the least ...

Hell, he'd only seen Corrado's kid—Caroline—a couple of times since she had been born eight months ago. It wasn't by any fault of his brother, or Les or Ginevra, but rather, himself. They brought the baby to Toronto regularly enough to visit with his brothers, and parents. Usually once a month, but sometimes twice. Bene always found an excuse to be doing literally anything else because sitting down for dinner with his family typically meant someone pointing out how much he was partying lately, or whatever else.

No, it wasn't their fault. Only his. Because he didn't make the effort when he was too busy being involved with his own issues—fucking selfish—instead of focusing on what was important.

Like family.

Bene needed to do better.

He made a mental note to do exactly that.

"Besides," Chris added, shooting Bene a small smile, "don't feel badly. We haven't told anyone outside of the family. Waiting a bit before we do, just to be safe."

"Nothing is wrong, right?"

"Everything is perfect, man."

"Good."

After everything Chris's wife had been through, Bene figured she deserved to be happy. Especially while she was pregnant.

"What's Maria think about that?"

Valeria's daughter, and Chris's adopted child, looked at her mom and dad like they were the moon and the stars of her very small universe. She was a good kid—sweet as could be, really—but she did not like to share her parents' time with other kids.

"So far so good."

"The bigger issue is having control of all the production across Canada for maple syrup, not to mention the distribution and sale of it, means we run the risk of being called a cartel when we jack up the prices, boss."

The Capo's reply to whatever Gian had said brought Bene back to the business at hand. His brother didn't seem to mind because now, their father was also looking their way. Not that their conversation had been loud enough to detract from Gian's talk with his man. And really, his father was looking more at *Bene* than his brothers.

"And?" Gian asked, never looking away from Bene.

The Capo in question sighed. "Well, it might have us being audited year after year by the CRA—they'll be so deep into our books and accounts that it'll be almost impossible to hide anything."

"Or we buy that farm that consistently bleeds cash, and make it *look* like it is turning profit with all the other farms helping out a bit. Falsified records that can't be proven otherwise means we can dump as much cash into it as we want to hide it while it's cleaned, *oui*?"

"Well—"

"There's really only one answer to that, Greg. It's not an opportunity for a discussion, or debate about how you want things to go, considering this little scheme was *my* idea, family money went in to making it work, and you were just the lucky prick I put on it. Anything else is still for me to decide, as I am sure you're aware. And so, your answer to me is …?"

"Yes, boss, we can make that happen."

"Good, good." Gian's gaze darted back to the man, and he nodded. "That's what I want to hear. Marcus?"

"*Sì*, boss?"

"I want you working with Greg on this venture—I'll feel better about it knowing you're there to keep an eye on things, and to run it the way I prefer."

"I can handle the farms—"

"The *business* side," Gian interjected fast, pensive stare drifting back to Bene and making him feel like his father was searching for something in his son. "Marcus will handle the paperwork and getting the right accountants on everything. And if he wishes to overlook the work you're doing there, Greg, then he will do that, too. Underboss's right, no?"

The Capo cleared his throat but stayed quiet.

Gian, seemingly satisfied with the way the conversation had gone, gave Bene one last look before turning his attention to the men in the room once again. If anyone except him noticed the fact his father kept checking on him like he wanted to be sure he was still standing there, no one said a thing.

Not that it mattered now.

They were on to *money*.

Tribute was coming up.

"What's all that about?" he asked.

Marcus, who had been quiet for the most part at Bene's left, checked his watch. "Pardon?"

"Papa—"

"Boss."

Right, right.

Bene was doing better about that whole thing—you know, differentiating between his father when they weren't doing business, and Gian as the boss when other made men were around. Someone should give him credit for that, but Marcus just liked to correct his ass.

"He keeps looking back at me," Bene muttered. "And he only does that when …" *I've done something wrong, and he knows about it.* Gian used to pull that shit on Bene and his twin when they were teenagers, and thought they were pulling one over on their parents. It never worked. One might think Bene would learn his lesson, but apparently not. So was his fucking life. Where was the fun if he wasn't getting into a bit of trouble now and then?

Besides, Vanna was *harmless*.

Sexy as sin.

Looked good in his bed.

Fucked like nobody else.

To them, though, she was harmless.

Bene didn't say any of that out loud because he knew that if he did, Marcus would undoubtedly hear the oncoming lie on the tip of his tongue. His follow up of *and I didn't do anything wrong.* Except he had—by bringing Vanna to the mansion the previous weekend when his parents were away

—and Bene was not a good liar when it came to his brothers. They all knew the difference, so it was better if he didn't even bother to try.

"Hmm?" Marcus asked.

Bene scowled. "Nothing."

"You sure about that?"

He gave his brother a look.

Marcus raised his brow right back. "Good weekend?"

Fuck.

All he needed was that simple question from his brother —as innocent as it seemed—and Bene's mind was thrown back to the previous weekend, and exactly how he'd spent it. Which meant, mostly between the thighs of a woman using her pussy to sustain him like it was the only thing he wanted to eat for the rest of his life.

To be fair, her pussy was *heaven.*

Didn't matter if he was fucking it, eating it, or watching her play with it ... that woman could start wars over her pussy, and Bene knew it. Besides that, there was just something about her that he liked, and he wouldn't apologize for it, either.

"Well?" Marcus pressed.

"Don't know what you're talking about, Marcus."

His brother chuckled. "Sure, you don't."

"We're supposed to be having a meeting here, not—"

"Did you think Gian wouldn't get suspicious that there was no camera footage *all* weekend?"

Bene chewed on his inner cheek. "No, I just figured he wouldn't look at all since he usually doesn't unless he has a reason to. And since the digital recordings start over every five days, by the time he did look, it wouldn't even matter."

"You're fucking terrible."

Yeah, well ...

"And you forgot that the cameras on the entrance gate are on entirely different servers, Bene," Marcus added.

Ah, shit.

They saw him come in and out with Vanna, then.

There would be no hiding that.

Now, he understood perfectly fine why his father kept glancing his way even though it was clear he had better things to focus on in this meeting than what one of his youngest sons had done the previous weekend.

Perfect.

Bene was more than willing to keep pretending like he didn't know what in the fuck his brother was talking about—at least, until he couldn't anymore—but the vibration in his pocket stopped him from saying anything at all. Knowing he could get away with checking his phone while his father's attention was on the discussion of the upcoming tribute, Bene pulled it from his pocket, and kept it hidden in his palm while he glanced down at the screen.

V the contact said.

Contents Hidden, the message read.

That usually meant someone sent him an attachment, like a picture or something. He didn't even think about his older brothers standing on either side of him as he unlocked the phone, and clicked on the ribbon to bring up the text message.

Holy fuck.

There it was.

Or rather, there *she* was.

Part of her, anyway.

All he could see in the picture Vanna had sent was the image of her legs in fishnet, thigh-high stockings, the stark red heels on her feet, and the tiled floor beneath her. The photo had been cropped up near the fucking promise land, keeping what was between her thighs hidden from him, but *damn* … this had been more than enough.

Because now his throat was tight.

His cock perked to life.

And he was in no position for any of it.

"Damn." Marcus whistled low.

Bene clicked the home button quickly. "*Shut up.*"

"That the same one? Kind of hard to tell when you can't see her face and—"

"Shut the fuck up."

Chris chuckled on the other side of him. "Whoever she is, she better be worth bringing her to the mansion when Ma and Dad weren't home to meet her, Bene."

His father looked their way again.

He did his best to look innocent.

Except he wasn't.

Not at all.

"More than worth it," he muttered.

"Yeah, tell Dad that."

Right.

"Bene, feel free to close the door once everyone leaves, and take a seat."

With his back turned to his father as he was just about to leave the office, Bene cursed inside his head. He thought he might be able to skip out of the meeting before Gian even realized he left, and then perhaps they could have the discussion about bringing a woman to the mansion at a later date. Or better yet, over the phone where his father wouldn't be looking him right in the face when he tried to lie about it.

Bene couldn't be so lucky.

"Sure, boss," he said, still refusing to turn around.

Marcus gave Bene a smirk over his shoulder, as he was the last man to leave the office—not unusual, considering he was Gian's underboss. Bene responded in kind with a flipped up middle finger that only his brother could see before he closed the office door after him. Marcus was getting too much out of this, the asshole.

"Pick a seat," Gian said once the door was closed.

Bene sighed. "Could I stand, or—"

"That wasn't an option, no."

Awesome.

It was going to be one of *those* talks, then. It was also how Bene knew that now, he was dealing with his father again, and not the boss of their *famiglia*. Gian was always careful about how he had discussions with his sons, but especially when it was in the form of what someone might consider discipline. He never stood over them—never made it seem like he was talking over one of his boys. Instead, they all sat down, eye-level, if possible, like they were equals to have their chats.

Bene avoided the heavy stare of his father until he took one of the two wing-back leather chairs across from the desk, and sat his ass down. His father's face, void of amusement or anything, really, gave him a good indication about how this chat was going to go today.

"Would you like to start, or not?" Gian asked.

"Well—"

"Let me pose it a different way, son. You can tell me what you did last weekend, *here* when I wasn't home, or I can do it. Feel free to make a choice."

Bene sighed. "You already know what I did, clearly."

"Yes, but I'm starting to wonder about what *you* know."

"What?"

"Rules, Bene." Gian leaned back in his large chair, steepling his fingers as he peered out the windows that overlooked the front property. "The same rules you grew up with here—you know them, I have repeated them time and time again. Those rules are in place not just because I don't want you or your brothers to disrespect our home, but because it keeps us all safe. We don't bring *strangers* here—that's never, nor will it ever, be tolerated. So, go ahead and tell me why you decided to bring a woman who none of us know to our home for an entire weekend when no one else was here. Go ahead, I will wait."

Well, when you put it that way …

"I didn't really think about it," Bene admitted.

"You're doing that a lot lately, hmm?"

"Pardon?"

"Making choices without thinking."

"Low blow, Papa."

Gian smiled faintly. "And yet, not entirely untrue, either."

Bene shifted in the chair under the intense weight of his father's stare. He didn't need Gian to verbally cut him down, not when the man's gaze did it for him. He knew what he did was wrong, and now it was just a matter of admitting as such and apologizing. That was really all his parents asked of their sons when one of them stepped out of line.

Still, Bene stayed quiet.

Gian didn't miss it.

"Who is she?" his father asked.

"Does it matter?"

"Matters to me, if you're willing to bring the woman to my home and go as far as erasing my video footage to try and hide her."

"It wasn't *hiding* her."

"What would you call it?"

"Avoiding this situation," Bene returned.

Gian chuckled. "Because you didn't want us to know you were seeing someone, or—"

"I wouldn't call it that. It's just ... she gives me something to do, instead of focusing on all the other shit going on. It's not that deep, you know."

"Oh."

His father's quiet proclamation had Bene lifting his head to meet Gian's gaze. He shrugged when his father waited for Bene to say something else. He wasn't sure what he should say.

"But would you like it to be something else?"

That was a tricky question.

"I like her," he said simply.

"Hmm."

"Could you give me something else?"

Gian grinned. "Well, that's not for me to do now, Bene. *You're* the one who is apparently seeing a woman you liked well enough to bring to my home when you know you're not allowed to bring anyone here that you don't want to sit down to chat with your mother or me. And you know, that's the only reason why I haven't chewed your ass off over this yet. Because you brought her here, and you do know the rules. Which means ...?"

He intended for them to meet her.

Some day.

"Her name?"

Bene dragged in a quick breath. "Vanna."

He didn't bother to give her last name because he didn't think it was that important for the time being. None of those details mattered more than the fact that his father simply wanted to know *who* the woman was that Bene dared to break their very clear rules for.

Funny how that worked.

"Lovely," Gian murmured. "I will give you a chance to

correct what happened last weekend. Your mother is having her thing for the shelter in a couple of weeks, which means there'll be lots of people here to act as a buffer … no awkward conversation."

Cara frequently threw dinner parties for the many organizations she either had a direct hand in, like the women's shelters around Toronto, or the ones she had interest in when it came to donating money. Bene didn't usually attend them, but it didn't sound like his father was giving him a choice this time around.

"What do you think?"

Bene hummed under his breath. "And what if she says no?"

"Yet another one of those things that I can't help you with, son. Bring her to your mother's party, *if* she agrees to come, and we can properly greet her. Then, if you want to bring her back around when the rest of us aren't here, I don't see the problem."

"No promises."

Gian shrugged. "Then, she isn't welcomed back here when we're not home."

Seemed simple enough.

Bene wondered if it would be.

"Oh, and call your twin," his father added when Bene stood up from the chair, "he's worried that we're lying about whether or not you've gone on another one of your spells."

"I'm not—"

"Tell him that."

Jesus.

"Fine."

"And say hello to your mother before you leave."

Bene waved a hand over his shoulder as he headed for the door, but Gian didn't seem to mind his lack of a verbal response. At the end of the hallway outside of the office, he already had his phone in his hand, bringing up the contact list.

At first, he planned to call his brother.

Like his father said.

Thing was, Bene knew Beni was good, and had his own shit to focus on with work in Chicago, not to mention his new wife—he didn't need to be worrying about his twin. No doubt, a phone call from Bene would only get his brother worked up again because he wasn't here to confirm everything that they told him.

Bene was doing fine.

Beni had to trust that.

Instead of calling his brother, he finally replied to that *very* sexy picture from Vanna that still had him sporting a semi-erection, even if he had been doing his best for the last hour to ignore it. That was a pointless effort, considering nothing about that woman could be ignored.

You home?

Vanna's reply to Bene's text came almost instantly with, *Yeah.*

His fingers flew over the screen of his phone, replying, *Mind if I stop by?*

Up until that point, he'd not been to her place other than to drop her off at the front entrance. He never asked to go further, and she didn't invite him. And yet, it was seconds before her reply came across his screen. As though she hadn't hesitated at all in her answer.

Sure. The penthouse has its own elevator in my building. The girl at the front desk will let you in to come up once she calls through to the penthouse.

That was that.

⁓

Bene surveyed the clean, modernly decorated lobby of Vanna's building while the girl behind the front desk finished her phone call. A resident upstairs wanted someone to deal with his noisy neighbor, by the sounds of things. The man at the front door had let him in with a kind greeting, and a nod.

"Sorry about that," the girl said, smiling widely as she hung the phone up, "what can I do for you today?"

"The penthouse—Vanna Falco."

"What about her?"

"She said you would call up, and then let me into the private elevator."

"Sure, I can do that. Your name?"

Her words said one thing, but her tone said another. Bene tried not to get too strange about it, if only because the girl looked no more than nineteen years old—how had she gotten this job, anyway?—and it *was* her job, after all.

"Bene Guzzi."

"Just give me a sec."

"Sure."

In no time at all, the chick had called through to Vanna's penthouse, and with the confirmation that he was a welcomed guest, she handed over the key to the private elevator. "Drop it off when you come back down, please."

"No problem."

With the key in hand, Bene headed for the elevator with the plaque labeled *Penthouse* right above the closed doors. Shoving the key into the pad beside the doors, he waited for the beep that signaled the elevator had been unlocked for him to use. He hit the button and waited for the doors to open which only took a couple of seconds before he stepped inside.

Hitting the button for the penthouse—the only button on the wall, other than the emergency stop or the call buttons—he couldn't help but notice how the girl across the lobby was talking on the phone again behind the front desk. Which wouldn't be something that concerned him, except she was clearly looking right at him while she spoke.

And she said his name.

Not *loudly*.

He didn't hear it.

But he saw it.

Watched her lips move to form his name perfectly. *Bene Guzzi*.

What was that about?

The doors closed before he could think on it.

Soon enough, the rising elevator lurched before coming to a stop, the doors sliding open to reveal a long hallway that led to a single door on the right. He passed a plant resting on a decorative table, sitting across from a large painting of Toronto on the wall right across from it. Vanna already had her door opened wide when Bene came to stand in front of it.

"Hey," she said.

Her grin had his own growing.

"Hey," he murmured.

She still wore those fishnet thigh-highs. Only now, he was fully able to appreciate the rest of her outfit, including the skin-tight black dress that stopped a good six inches above her knees, and showed off all kinds of leg.

In fishnets.

The low cut of the dress gave him an ample view of her cleavage, and instead of her usually understated makeup with the dramatic wing, she'd smoked out her eyes and painted her lips a dark, stark red that had his mouth going dry.

"Going out?" he asked.

Vanna shook her head. "Nope."

"You dress like this just because?"

"I like to look as beautiful as I feel."

Huh.

Well, he wasn't complaining.

"Are you coming in?" she asked.

"As soon as you invite me."

He had a good mind to ask about the chick at the front desk downstairs, but he figured … not his business. The two of them weren't in that kind of relationship, and it wasn't his place to be asking things unless she offered. Simple as that.

Vanna took a step back, widening the door further while her heels clicked against the tiled floor of the entryway. "Come on in—wasn't expecting anyone tonight, but I *am* cooking enough for a small army, and I've got my favorite show ready to binge, so …"

"Sounds like my kind of night."

And even if it wasn't before, it certainly was now.

With *her*?

Looking like she did?

As she stared at him like she was?

Fuck yeah.

Absolutely his kind of night.

Vanna winked, and Bene stepped into her place. He gave the white walls, decorated sparingly but still stylishly with black and chrome accents in the entry, a brief second of his attention. He could admire her place later. Right now, the woman living in it had way more of his focus. And wasn't that the most important thing?

Bene figured so.

She let the door go, and he closed it behind him. Once the hallway was shut out, he closed the space between them. Vanna was already smiling a sexy sight when he tugged off his jacket at the same time he leaned in for a kiss. He didn't give a single shit that her red lipstick was likely going to leave stains on his mouth. How could he when she kissed him as though it had been *far* too long, and she was finally getting a taste of what she wanted again?

Before he'd even realized it, Bene had her backed against the wall, and his hands were fisting into the tops of those fishnets around her thighs, ready to pull them from her body. She stared up at him, lipstick only *slightly* smudged, but looking damn good. Her heat soaked into his body, and he breathed the scent of her in.

Sugared sex.

"That was nice," she whispered.

Bene laughed darkly. "Feed me, and put me somewhere I can get you horizontal, and we'll see just how nice I can get later."

"Promises, promises."

"That I'll absolutely keep."

Vanna swallowed hard. "Hope so."

"I had a reason for coming here … not just this."

"Oh? But I was liking this."

Yeah, him, too.

Still …

"Would you, uh, want to go to a thing with me?" he asked. "Something my mother is having at the mansion in a couple of weeks. It's like a dinner party. Nothing big, but—"

"Are you asking me on a date? A *real* date?"

Was he?

"Is that what you want to call it?"

Vanna arched a brow. "Does it change anything?"

"Not if you don't want it to."

"Are you still going to fuck me tonight whether I say yes or no?"

Bene's fingers tightened in her fishnets, and he heard the telltale rip of the fabric. Just a little, not too much. Her shiver said she felt it against her skin, and heard it, too. "After that picture you sent, you should have expected me to show up to see what else you had waiting for me."

"Well, that *was* the point."

"So, you answered your own question."

Vanna smiled slyly when his fingers trailed higher on her thighs, skimming over hot, silky flesh until he was between her legs and found her *bare*. "I guess I did."

"You're not wearing anything under this dress."

"*Nope.*"

And she was wet.

"Is that a yes on the date?" he asked, fingers skimming over her waxed, slick sex.

Vanna let out a shuddering breath when his fingertips found her clit as she widened her stance a bit for him. Her words came out trembling, just like those red lips of hers, and her dark eyes danced with lust while his fingers circled faster and faster. "That's a yes on the date, Bene."

Good to know.

CHAPTER 10

A black car waiting for Vanna on a Friday when she stepped out of the college after her final classes never meant good things. She only knew the town car idling on the curb was meant for her because she recognized the muscle leaning against the passenger side door. She didn't call him *muscle* for it to be derogatory but given his large size, and the job he held for the Detti Camorra as a personal guard for Senior, and occasionally Mario, when the time called for it, the title fit just fine.

His severe features—he didn't earn his nickname, The Pitbull, for nothing—held no warmth when he looked her way, and without a word, she still sensed his silent command for her to come closer. Better she went to him. It never ended well when he had to go to someone else.

"Dante," she greeted, "something up?"

He raised one thick, black eyebrow at her question. "Why do you assume something has to be wrong because I'm here?"

She didn't really have to think about an answer—it was already on the tip of her tongue. He often delivered bad news to people of their clan, a personal messenger from the boss. Besides that, he had been the man standing down the hallway with Senior the day she found out about her father's murder.

Vanna said none of those things out loud. Instead,

settling on, "Why are you here, then? I usually take an Uber home, and no one sends a car for me."

He smiled thinly.

If that could be considered a smile.

"Someone sent a car today," he replied.

"Someone as in—"

"Senior, of course. The only one who gets to throw an order at me that I will follow through on. Now, if you're finished questioning me, because I don't answer to you and I'm becoming bored with this conversation, then you should be asking what is expected of you, as good clan women *do*, Vanna."

Right, right.

She constantly forgot her place.

That despite having a sense of freedom, her own place to live, and a life outside of the Camorra, she was still a part of their world. Still one of theirs—*in the clan for life*. Once in, born to it or otherwise, there was no out.

Maybe that should have been a sign.

One with a giant red flag.

She didn't belong.

"Get in the car," Dante said, "and I will take you to dinner at Senior's."

"I have to study for—"

"It's not a request."

That was that, she supposed.

Vanna didn't need to be told a second time because she knew better than to argue with Dante, or any other man inside their Camorra clan. Unless she was a woman that held any sort of power over them within their confusing structure, they didn't—and wouldn't—listen to anything she had to say, nor did they care about what she might want.

It was always what the *boss* wanted.

She wasn't the boss.

Dante said nothing long after Vanna took a seat in the back of the car. The silence echoed as they drove through the city, just skimming the late-day traffic rush, thankfully. She bet that was purposeful because Dante, like the rest of them, knew far better than to make his boss wait for anything, including an excuse like traffic.

She didn't bother to ask more questions because she wouldn't get the answers, that was, if even Dante knew them. The man got orders, but rarely was he given the reason for them. Plus, she just wasn't in the mood to talk.

At least, not to the man in the front seat.

Instead, her attention dropped to the phone in her hand, and the text she had been starting to reply to when she came out of the school, and saw Dante waiting for her. A message from Bene; her fingers hovered over the *send* button for the reply she'd already typed out.

Busy later?

Vanna hit send on her new reply after she deleted the old one that had confirmed she wasn't busy, and was up for anything he wanted to do. Plans changed, it seemed, even if she didn't want them to. She didn't even know what Bene's plans for the night had been, but she bet it would have been a lot more fun than what she was going to do.

I'll get back to you, she told him.

Bene's response came a few minutes later with, *Let me know.*

She typed back a confirmative reply, but quickly dropped the phone into her purse when Dante glanced into the rearview mirror. Not that he would care she was on her phone, but she didn't feel like pushing her luck today.

An hour later, and Dante opened the rear passenger door for Vanna to step out onto a familiar driveway after he parked the car. He said nothing as she glanced toward the house, noting the only vehicles parked in front of the large three-door garage of the suburban home belonged to the boss, his wife, and Mario's sleek, black Mercedes.

That was unusual.

Entirely.

Rarely did Vanna get an invitation to dinner with the boss, his wife, and Mario unless something was going on with the rest of the clan, and they had been extended an offer to join, as well. It didn't matter that Senior and Gemma had taken on the responsibility of giving shelter and raising Vanna for those two years after her father's death, before she turned eighteen and was able to move out on her own ... she had never really been a part of the family.

Not like *that.*

The lack of other vehicles—other *guests*—should have been her first clue that something was definitely up here. Instead of letting her thoughts linger for too long on things she couldn't control, Vanna headed for the house without as much as a goodbye to Dante over her shoulder. No doubt, the man didn't care, anyway.

Quiet conversation drifted down the entry hallway from the dining room as Vanna took off her coat and shoes. She tried to keep up with the conversation Senior and Mario were currently having between one another in Italian, but with how fast they spoke, it was practically impossible for her to understand more than a couple of things. She'd never picked up on the language as well as her father wanted her to, much to his displeasure.

Not that it mattered now.

Vanna came to stand in the doorway of the dining room, finding Mario's, and his father's, gazes already locked on her, as though they expected her to arrive at any time. *Bad sign number two*, she thought.

Why?

She couldn't say, really.

Didn't have anything to put her finger on.

It just *was*.

Maybe because they'd been waiting on her, and it made sense now why no one else was here for this *dinner*. Because hell, even the table was empty. Where was the dinner?

"I thought we were eating," Vanna said.

Senior smiled, but it was tight.

Not unusual for him.

Still ...

Vanna just felt cold.

"Oh, we will," Mario's father replied, "and more will join us."

"Ma is working in the kitchen. You can help her after," Mario added.

Vanna's brow lifted. "Oh?"

She was just *expected* to help?

Not even a question.

"Yes," the boss said, heaving his large body from his chair. An intimidating man in size, Mario Senior Detti was not a person that one might want to meet in a dark alley, and Vanna had never been more aware of his presence then when he left the table and crossed the room to come and stand in front of her. He still wore that smile, sure, but something changed in the aura around him, electrifying the air, though it made it felt chillier than ever to Vanna all the same. "I thought you and I should have a chat before the rest get here, though, because I figure ... well, I *am* the man heading your household in this clan, aren't I?"

Her jaw clenched.

Vanna did her *best* to hide it.

"Are you?" she returned.

Senior nodded. "After you father died, I took you in, by default—"

"Your father ordered the murder of mine."

"Vanna," Mario warned quietly from the table.

"Your father was planning against my father's life. This is how Camorra works, child. You know that, so do not pretend otherwise."

Child.

Twenty-one, but against this man, she was still just a *girl*.

Nothing less, nothing more.

His reminder, as gentle as it was, changed nothing for her. And this was exactly why Vanna didn't like to get into these discussions with anyone. She would always have her opinions about those things, and how this all came to be. Her father was the traitor, sure, and she was the blood straight from his veins. The more she reminded them all of that fact, it became far more likely that they wouldn't allow her to continue walking and living among the rest of them.

"You're at an age now," Senior continued as though Vanna weren't glaring daggers at him, "as my son reminded me this week, where other women of your status and position have been handed different expectations, and acted accordingly."

Vanna straightened on the spot.

Her spine as stiff as a board.

"And what does *that* mean?" And then she had *another* thought, one that made her glance around the side of Senior's large form to stare right at Mario still sitting at the table. "*You* reminded him of something about me?"

"Well," Mario started.

Senior held up a hand, quieting them both. Anyone with an *ounce* of brain matter, that had seen this man get angry on at least one occasion, knew better than to test his very short patience. It took nothing at all for him to go from zero to one hundred, and he had no problem with making very violent and rash decisions when his anger took over.

Vanna wouldn't be caught in the crossfire.

Not at all.

"Vanna," Senior murmured, drawing her gaze back to him as he readied to put the final nail in her coffin. She just *knew it*. Felt it in her fucking bones for what was coming next. Those words didn't need to leave his lips for her to already be aware, and yet … they still felt like knives slicing across her skin when he said it. "It's time for you to serve your purpose as a woman in the clan—for the greater good, as they say."

"The greater good."

It wasn't even a question.

And why was her voice so faint?

"We—this *clan*—have given so much to you, haven't we?" he asked.

God.

She wanted to say no.

She knew that wasn't what he wanted, though.

"Yes," Vanna whispered, "it has."

And it took, too.

A lot.

They took *so much from her*.

They weren't done taking, either.

Senior confirmed it, saying, "Mario brought it to my attention that at your age, and he's right, you should be focusing more on the family—the clan, and *your* life."

"I am focusing on my—"

"Marriage, family … *business*."

She sucked in a sharp breath.

Her eyes burned.

Still, she held back those tears.

"You and Mario are to be married soon."

Yeah.

There it was.

Vanna wanted to be surprised.

She wasn't.

Her heart *screamed* to fight the news.

Her brain knew better.

This was Camorra.

The boss spoke.

The rest of them listened.

That didn't mean she was happy because a rage like never before curled around her heart, squeezing with heat that damn near stopped the beats altogether. She didn't know if Senior could see the hatred in her stare, but she didn't really care, either.

"That so?" she finally asked.

Senior nodded. "It is."

"How soon?"

"Ma thought an October wedding would be nice," Mario said.

Vanna did her very best to stay still, and not cross the room to claw out his eyes when he finally stood from the table, and Senior turned just enough for the two of them to face each other. *Her future husband.* Fuck him.

He was finally getting what he wanted. That was the thing here. It's why he never pushed before. He didn't *force* Vanna. Not her feelings, or her physical choices. Mario didn't have to. He knew what he would eventually have.

Her.

"Three months," she said quietly.

Mario smiled. "Yes, and we'll announce it to the rest later at dinner."

Well, *he* would.

She had nothing to say now.

~

"Hey."

Vanna outright ignored Mario's call behind her as she loaded the tray with clean glasses to take upstairs to Senior, and his men. She wasn't even asked to do it—simply *told* to by Gemma, because apparently that was going to be her life now.

Mario's wife.

A woman who *served*.

No fucking thank you.

"Are you listening to me? And could you drop the fucking silent treatment for five goddamn seconds?"

Oh, was he mad?

Poor him.

"I'd rather not speak to you at all," Vanna replied, picking up the tray and turning to face Mario with a sardonic smile, "never mind *look* at you, but if you're going to insist on me doing it, then maybe you shouldn't complain about the attitude you get in the process, yeah?"

He blinked.

She took *great* satisfaction in that.

It was all she had, now.

"Vanna—"

"Excuse me," she muttered, not even giving him the chance to speak before pushing past him in the kitchen entryway, "because I have people upstairs who want clean glasses for their drinks. And you know they don't like to be made to wait by a woman."

He didn't let her get past him entirely before his hand struck out, and he grabbed her. He wasn't easy about it, either, his fingers tightening around her wrist painfully, making her hand flex against the tray to the point that she almost dropped it.

"Let me go," she said quietly.

Vanna didn't even look at him.

The *warning* should have been enough.

Except it wasn't.

Shocking.

Mario didn't let go, and if anything, he just held tighter. In fact, he tugged on her arm, pulling her a little closer to him in the process so the side of her body pressed against the front of his, and she was forced to smell that *spice* cologne he seemed to prefer that reminded her of men like his father. *Old men.*

Nothing young, and fresh.

Nothing *attractive.*

"Stop it," he hissed, his first show of nastiness to her in a *long* while. The last time it had been when he caught her with a guy she'd been sleeping with in high school during her senior year, and he had possession and jealousy issues to handle. "You knew this was fucking inevitable, Vanna. I've been telling you for years what I wanted. How is it *my* fault that you just continued to ignore me, huh?"

"Because *no* wasn't enough? Because me saying *I don't like you* wasn't a good answer for you, or—"

"You don't get a choice, that's the problem."

Vanna laughed.

Bitterly.

Yes, it was a problem.

For her.

Not him.

"You've been comfortable, you know," he said, head tilting down so he could murmur those words in her ear. "Comfortable thinking you were *free* … that you could do whatever the fuck you wanted; that you weren't *one of us*, Vanna, but surprise, you are. All that shit you wanted? The life you thought was yours? That was an illusion, and I let you have it as long as I could, but now I'm tired of waiting, and I want what's mine."

Right.

Yeah.

Because that's all she was to him.

Just a thing.

Something to *have*.

A trophy.

With the title *wife*.

"I'll never love you," she breathed, "never *want* you. There isn't one single part of you that makes me need you, and you'll know it for every single day we're together. If you're going to force me into a marriage with you, then I will make sure you suffer for it, too. I hope you know that."

"Is that a threat?"

His grip on her suddenly took her breath away. Vanna almost dropped the tray *again*. Still, she held her composure, refusing to show Mario how much he affected her, and not in a good way, either. Sure, he didn't *scare* her, not really. If he thought he could beat the compliance into her, then she had news for him.

It still bothered her, though.

"Not a threat," she replied cuttingly, sneering up at him before she yanked her arm right out of his hold, and before he could stop her, took a step away from him. Out of his reach entirely. "It's a *promise*."

"You were always meant to be mine."

"Only in your mind."

"But who is the one getting what they *want* here, Vanna?"

Yeah.

And she wouldn't soon forget it.

Mario would ruin everything for her. She'd known it from the start. All of her plans, the vendetta—something she struggled with for reasons she wasn't quite ready to admit—and just her *life*. This man would ruin all of it. But damn him if he thought she wouldn't fight for it.

"I'm still my own woman," she told him, "and you'll treat me like it until a marriage certificate says differently."

Mario tipped his chin up. "And what does that mean?"

"Nothing changes, that's what it means."

"You're going to be my *wife*."

"And until then, I am still *Vanna Falco*. I will do what I want, when I want, and *how* I fucking want, Mario. It's the least you can give to me after all this."

"Like what, going to the stupid college?"

God.

He called it stupid like he understood.

As though he knew her hopes and dreams.

"Or my penthouse," she replied. "Nothing changes until it has to. Otherwise, I'll make your life a living hell."

"Don't threaten me."

"You keep using that word."

His gaze narrowed.

She smiled.

"But it doesn't mean what you think it does," she added quieter, "now excuse me."

She left him fuming behind her.

No doubt, she would pay for that.

Eventually.

Vanna made it through the night of the dinner—and Mario's *news*—and then Saturday. *But barely.* She was still trying to process; still trying to figure out how this changed her plans, the vendetta … her entire fucking life.

And then she just didn't want to do anything.

She didn't want to think.

Or feel.

Or *be*.

None of it.

So, instead of wallowing in her penthouse for another lonely night, she decided to do the exact opposite. Something that might very well get her into trouble, if Mario found out, but hadn't she been playing with fire a lot lately, anyway?

What did it matter?

Vanna was ready to be *burned*.

What better way than Bene Guzzi?

No questions asked, she sent Bene a text, asked him to meet up with her at a café a few blocks away from her penthouse, and he was there within the hour.

He took one look at her.

Saw the *sadness*.

Asked, "What happened?"

"Nothing," she lied.

He didn't press.

She adored him for that.

Instead, he asked, "What do you want to do?"

"*Anything.*"

That was how she found herself flying down the highway in the passenger seat of Bene's Lambo while they sped out of the city going fifty over the speed limit. His hand skated across the seats, finding its way to her thigh, and squeezing tight.

Heat lit up her body.

Pain squeezed her heart.

"Ever been to Maggie's Falls?"

Vanna looked over at him, enjoying the way the shadows of the car darkened his handsome features. "No, never even heard of it."

"You'll love it."

Why didn't she doubt that?

"Good," she whispered.

Bene quieted just long enough for Vanna to think he wasn't going to say anything else. Of course, he surprised her. He always did. From the jump, this man hadn't been what she expected.

It was still a goddamn problem.

For more reasons than ever.

"Whatever's going on," he said, "it'll be okay."

Vanna didn't know how to tell him, but …

No, it wouldn't be.

Not for him.

For her.

Or for anyone else.

Had she made a mistake?

Was trying to finish her father's vendetta the biggest one yet?

Vanna didn't have those answers, and she no longer knew what to do to fix all of this mess that surrounded her. All by her own making, too.

Sweet justice, maybe.

God.

Instead of answering Bene, she asked, "How long until we get to … that place?"

"Another hour, maybe."

"Okay."

They drove the hour in silence, but Vanna didn't mind, and neither did he. As long as he was touching her, it didn't seem like Bene cared about anything else. It was almost strange how she felt the same way, but for now, she refused to indulge those feelings.

Nothing good would come from it.

It was easier this way.

Bene had said *Maggie's Falls*, but Vanna didn't think anything of it. She certainly didn't think he meant a place way out in the fucking *woods*. Literally, three miles into the woods, off the highway, on a dirt road that eventually ended, to where they had to get out of the Lambo, lock it up, and walk another twenty minutes before the two of them stood on a rocky ledge that overlooked a small waterfall that dropped into a swimming hole. A rope hung from a tree on the other side; one people clearly used to swing and drop into the water.

"It's twenty feet deep, that hole," Bene said, "so it's safe to jump from here."

Shit.

"We're like … twenty feet high."

"Yep."

He started shrugging off his clothes.

Vanna laughed.

"How did you even find this place?"

He shot her a wink. "Bored with my twin one summer."

"Really?"

"Yeah, kind of stumbled on it." He looked her up and down. "Are you going to jump in with me, or …?"

Damn.

She loved the way he was looking at her.

It was also *really* high.

"The water is probably cold," she said.

Bene stood straight, pushing down his pants at the same time to let her know he was wearing *nothing* underneath. She noticed that—sometimes he went with boxer-briefs, and sometimes he wore nothing at all. Like his moods or the weather, it changed depending on the day. He did nothing to hide the way his cock hung against his thigh, semi-hard and inviting to her.

"I'll warm you up," he promised.

Jesus.

Behind her, she heard the ring of her phone muffled inside her purse. A familiar ringtone. She hadn't heard it in a while, but she knew what it meant. The detective was calling —they had another meeting coming up, and he probably wanted to make sure she still had all the details for it settled out so it was safe.

Vanna had *every* reason to answer that call. To ask the man for *safety* in exchange for her info. To take his offer of a program that would put her underground, and out of sight of the Camorra for the rest of her life. Now, she had every reason to do that.

And yet, she continued staring at Bene.

He gave her every reason to stay rooted to the spot. To wish she'd never known about the vendetta. He made her want to turn back time, so things could have been *so different.*

Vanna felt like a failure.

A fraud.

Traitor.

She truly was her father's daughter. Just not the one he wanted.

Bene closed the distance between them, his kiss finding hers in the darkness, with the canopy of trees up above hiding even the stars and the moon. The sounds of the water surrounded them and took her away to a different place while the man pressed against her seemed determined to pull the soul from her body with nothing more than his kiss.

So fine.

Fine.

She'd just give it to him.

He could have it.

If only she could fix this.

"Are you getting in, or not?" he asked, words teasing the seam of her lips.

Vanna pulled off her dress when he backed away.

Her panties went next.

Then, her bra.

He jumped in first, cutting through the water, and coming back up with a swing of his head that tossed the water from his face as though he'd done it a million times before.

The phone kept ringing behind her.

Vanna jumped in second.

Free falling.

Twenty feet below.

Bene's knowing, sexy laughter surrounded her as adrenaline rushed through her bloodstream, and she swore it felt like she was flying as she cut through the air. She hit the water, slicing through it as it took her breath away.

She was *right*.

It had been cold.

Bene was right there to make her warm when she came up for air, though.

CHAPTER

11

Bene grabbed Vanna the second she came up for air, dragging her to him in the water until her legs wrapped around his waist, and his lips found hers. She tasted like the clean water of the falls, of the droplets falling on his face from the waterfall overhead, and of the air all around them.

Clean.

Clear.

Crisp.

Her mouth parted for him, giving over to his teeth scraping against her bottom lip, a silent demand for her to open. She knew his kiss well, now. Her tongue warred with his, something that had his cock hardening *more* than just the sight of seeing her naked standing on the rocks above had done for him. Oh, he loved that sight sure, and his dick felt like it would be able to pound through rocks, but now it was almost painfully hard from wanting her.

Their kiss never broke as Bene moved them backward in the small pool of deep water. Closer to the rocky edge at the bottom of the small waterfall the water was far more shadow, and he was even able to sit on it with his legs hanging over into the deeper portion.

Vanna didn't hesitate to straddle him on the ledge, her bare pussy under the water grinding against his cock in the best fucking way. Enough to think he might blow his load if she didn't chill the hell out, and that was *not* what he wanted.

Not then, anyway.

"Safe, *safe*," he mumbled against her lips, "tell me you're safe."

"Yeah, the shot."

God was so good to him.

Bene did a lot of crazy shit, and undoubtedly took more risks that he ever should in his young life, but fucking raw wasn't one of them. And yet, this wasn't the first time he'd done exactly that with Vanna. Had he ever brought home a chick pregnant before he was settled, his father would have throttled him for the first and only time in his life. And sure, he might be stupid, but he wasn't quite that stupid.

Until this woman, apparently.

Because he was absolutely willing to ignore the fact he didn't have a backup here, and he knew it was going to be a hundred times better because of it, too.

"Jesus fucking Christ," he muttered against her rough kiss, hissing after from the sensation of her manicured nails dragging lines down his chest, "you're gonna fucking kill me here, *donna*. Is that pussy of yours aching that bad for me, or what?"

Her response was a breathy whisper of, "*God*, yes."

He thrust his hands into her wet locks of hair, shoving the darkened strands back from her face and pulling her away from his kiss so he could get a good look at her face. At the bliss and wildness turning her into *something beautiful* for him.

"You gonna ride me?" he demanded.

She nodded.

"Fuck me 'til you can't breathe?"

"*Yeah.*"

He leaned in, hands sliding down to wrap around her throat while his teeth grazed down her jaw to get the taste of her skin on his tongue while he asked, "Fucking get on my cock and fuck me dry, then."

Her hands slipped into the water between them, grasping the base of his cock to steady him before she dropped down on him. All at fucking once, too. She stretched out around him, the heat of her sex yanking a hard moan from his clenched teeth.

His hands flexed on her throat when she started riding him. All her soft, "*Holy fuck, holy fuck,*" driving him even crazier.

She was so loud, this woman.

He loved it.

Needed all her sounds and the way she sighed his name when she started to come, all breathy and lost. It was pure sin —total bliss to his senses.

Her thighs trembled when her fingers dug into his pecs, her pace coming faster and faster. He knew it was coming when her pussy started tightening around his cock, and what she wanted while she did it.

Vanna just seemed to love it when he took away a little bit of her air when she came. He swore it dragged those orgasms out of her for longer, and there was nothing quite like the sight of her with those pupils blown wide, and his name on her mouth while his hands wrapped her throat like a collar, and she broke all apart for him.

"Almost, yeah?"

She whispered. "Yeah."

"Get it, then."

Vanna stilled above him, coming down hard on his cock one last time before a shudder raced through her entire form. He was right, too—all it took was the flex of his fingers, her eyes blew wide to find his, and he got to feel the thrum of her pulse under his fingertips go on for what felt like *forever*.

"Oh, my God, Bene," she gasped.

He gave her exactly a breath to recover from that orgasm before he let go of her throat, and his hands found her ass. He grabbed tight to her backside, sure he'd leave marks behind that he would be able to appreciate later, before he used *her* to get himself off. Dragging her up and down on his length with deep, hard strokes that had her whining again until he felt that familiar tightening in his balls.

The heat shot up his spine a second before he held her tight to his cock, and *yes*, it did feel better to come like that. With nothing to hold him back, feeling the aftershocks of her orgasm milking every fucking drop from him that it could.

"*You, you … you*," he said, not knowing what else to say.

Because what was this girl doing to him?

How and why?

Vanna laughed, her eyes shutting as she lifted from him. His cock slipped out of her still clenching pussy, but he was caught staring at her in the darkness, really, and the way she looked like this.

Wet and shivering.

Hot from him.

Ready for another round.

She hovered above him, pussy flashing him over the water as her hands drove down the front of her body. He watched those deft, delicate fingers of hers drift past her navel, over the damp flesh above her sex, and then between her thighs. She stroked herself, entirely unashamed that he was still panting from the aftereffects of his orgasm, and his cock was already starting to go limp on his fucking thigh.

Although, watching her let his cum fall onto her fingers before she used it to stroke fast circles into her clit until she was coming again with loud cries … well, that was enough to get Bene hard again.

"*Fucking look at you*," he said, tone thick with a groan.

"Are you?"

"For as long as you want me to."

She grinned, her lashes fluttering open for their gazes to meet. "Good."

This woman?

She was absolutely going to kill him.

But damn.

What a fucking way to go.

~

"See, told you."

Bene grinned at Vanna when she turned, wearing his shirt from earlier, her shivers wracking her whole body for a second before he covered her in the blanket he'd grabbed from the back of the Lambo. It wasn't unusual for people in Canada to keep a blanket in their car, but especially in the winter, in case one went off the road and needed to stay warm until help arrived. His precaution came in handy tonight.

Vanna had been perfectly fine in the water until they had to get out. Then, the shivers started. And her chattering teeth. She was barely even able to pick up her own clothes, let alone put them on. Bene quickly pulled his shirt down over her head and asked if she could stand to wait for ten minutes while he ran to the car for something better.

The blanket, that was.

Her happy sigh at being warm was all he needed before he gathered her in his arms, she tucked the ends of the blanket around him, and the two of them stood like that next to the bottom of Maggie's Falls. He rested his chin on the top of Vanna's head while he watched the water pour down from overhead on the rocks.

"You're happier now," he murmured.

Her shivering stilled, before her head slowly tipped up. Bene met her gaze, raising an eyebrow as if to dare her to deny his statement. She didn't even bother to try.

"You helped with that."

"Still don't want to talk about it?"

Vanna smiled, but it didn't quite reach her eyes. "Or it just doesn't matter now."

"It matters to me."

"Okay, so maybe it doesn't matter when I'm *with* you."

Huh.

And her smile was more *real* now, too.

He took that for what it was and dropped a quick kiss to the tip of her nose. The way her face scrunched up, all sweet and cute, and how her eyes crinkled at the corners, had something warm growing in his tightening chest.

Fuck.

He wasn't the type for soft and sweet.

Didn't care to snuggle.

Couldn't be bothered.

What was this chick doing to him?

Vanna made a soft noise under her breath when he leaned in to kiss her again, only this time, it was his lips meeting hers. God knew he had gotten more than enough of his fill of this woman over the evening—still had the flavor of her in his mouth, too—but that didn't seem to matter to his brain, or his cock. He just wanted *more*.

Except their kiss stayed soft, and slow. He didn't move to deepen it, and neither did she. He liked that just fine, too.

"How much convincing would it take for you to jump off the top rocks again with me?" he asked, pulling away from the kiss.

Vanna shook her head. "You're *crazy*. Once was enough."

"Come on, that was awesome."

"Until you realize you're jumping twenty feet down into

a six-foot-wide pool of water, and if you jump too far, you might hit the rocks. Which, you know, if it doesn't kill you … it's *really* going to hurt, Bene."

"And?"

Vanna smacked his bare chest with her hands. "*And*? Are you serious?"

"Yes. Absolutely."

That was basically his whole life in a nutshell. His mantra should be *but did it kill you?* He didn't think it was the right thing to say to her right now, however. He was a little crazy sometimes—still wasn't stupid, though.

Bene squeezed her tighter. "But you *didn't* hit the rocks, and it was fun, right?"

"That's really what it is for you, huh?"

"What?"

"*Fun.*"

He thought about that. "I mean, yeah. What's so great about life if you're not actually *living*?"

Vanna nodded. "You're not entirely wrong."

"But?"

Because he could hear it.

Even if she didn't say it.

"But I am not jumping off those rocks again."

Bene smirked, his hands sliding down the damp fabric of his shirt she was wearing overtop her shivering spine. Those shudders of hers picked up when his palms found her bare ass, palmed the plump flesh, and squeezed. He pulled her harder into his body, letting her feel the firm length of his erection under his jeans.

"You *sure*?"

She smirked right back at him. "Oh, is the promise of your dick supposed to make me risk my life?"

"It might …"

"Let's be honest, I can get that dick whenever I want it, and all I have to do is tell you I need it."

Bene's mouth went dry.

She wasn't wrong.

God, he loved that.

How she threw his shit right back at him.

Vanna cocked a brow at him. "Well?"

"Fine," he half-heartedly grumbled.

"Are you always like this?" she whispered against his grinning lips.

"Hmm?"

"*Fun*—wild?"

Bene laughed. "My family would say yes."

"Oh?"

"Usually, it was Beni and me together, though. Always looking for the next thing to chase after—whatever might get us into trouble, but would be fun, too."

Vanna's gaze glittered with amusement. "I have no doubt."

"I miss my twin all the fucking time."

There.

He said it out loud; he actually told someone instead of keeping it inside his head where no one would know the truth, and he could keep lying to them, and himself, that everything was okay. It was out there. He couldn't take it back. Maybe he didn't even want to.

Vanna stilled in his arms, her smile fading as their stares met. "You don't see him often?"

"Used to. We lived together—fucking woke up in rooms right next to each other for two decades, and then it just changed. He met a girl, got married, stayed in Chicago, and I had to figure out how to do everything by myself. I wasn't very good at it."

"*Hey.*"

His gaze darted back to hers.

Vanna lifted one shoulder under the blanket. "I don't really know anything about him—just you, Bene."

"Yeah, I know."

"And I think you're pretty good at being *you*. I mean, without him, and all."

Was he?

"With you, maybe."

Vanna's brow dipped. "What's that mean?"

"It's easier with you maybe because you don't know him, or my family … any of it, really. I only need to worry about being me with you—you distract me, it's easy."

Her pink lips pursed.

Bene let out a heavy breath.

"Or maybe it's just me," he muttered. "Everybody keeps saying I need time without him to just be me … but I keep wondering if all they see is *us*, and I'm busy trying to prove I can be okay, anyway. Fake it until you make it, kind of thing."

"But are you?"

"Hmm?"

Vanna stood up on her tiptoes, the blanket falling a bit on her shoulders when her lips pressed to his, and those fingernails of hers dug into his chest in the best way. "Are you okay, Bene?"

He didn't even have to think about it.

Not really.

"I'm getting there."

It was better with her.

She was only part of it, though.

"Good."

She grinned against his kiss. He forgot he was also cold, and still damp, when her hands slipped under the waistband of his pants. *Wicked woman.* That's what she was, and her smile was just as sinful, too. Especially when those teasing fingers of hers wrapped around his shaft, and her words whispered along his lax lips.

"Maybe I lied."

"About what?" he asked.

"*Maybe*," she said, pulling away a bit and winking, "you can convince me to jump off the rocks one more time."

Bene chuckled. "*Knew it.*"

Bene drummed his fingers against the steering wheel while eyeing the phone in his other hand. Parked in the underground garage of his building, he should have entered the place a half an hour ago when he first arrived. Instead, his mind just ran *crazy*.

On the woman he dropped off well over an hour ago. The kiss he gave her before she got out of his car. Her smell still lingering on him.

All of it.

He only thought about the fact that as soon as he took her home, and then arrived at his place alone, the first thing he wanted to do was go right back to her. Make sure she was still smiling because something *that* beautiful didn't ever need to be sad.

And then he wondered …

Was it like that for Beni, too?

When he met August, and it was like his brother suddenly did a whole one-eighty with his direction in life, and everything else … had it been *that*?

Bene never thought to ask, and he kind of felt like a shit about it. Mostly because the first thing he wanted to do was call his twin, and tell him all about the woman he met. This *chick* he was so fucking on for all of the sudden, who just came into his life by chance, and now he didn't know where to go next with it all.

Thing was, Beni would answer.

He'd *talk*.

And let Bene talk, too.

No questions asked.

It still made Bene feel like shit, though, because for all this time, he'd just been trying. *Barely getting by.* His twin worried about him all the time, and he knew it. Everyone told him. Instead of calling his twin and letting him know he was okay, Bene just pushed it aside.

Lied to himself.

Said it would be *fine*.

It wasn't.

Or it hadn't been.

Yeah, his brother would answer, and they'd talk like everything was fine because Beni would never admit how much it bothered him that Bene never asked about August back then—only acted like a prick—never mind how he'd been acting lately.

Those thoughts, the doubt, and his self-loathing was almost enough to keep him from calling his brother, but Bene turned on his phone, and brought up his brother's contact before he could think better of it. Beni had already tried making *several* first steps to fix this shit between them, but Bene kept holding them back.

He would stop that.

Starting now.

On speaker, the call rung three times while Bene stared at the clock on his Lambo's dash. Chicago was an hour behind Toronto, and it was already a little past one in the morning his time. Chances were, his brother was fast asleep next to his wife, unless someone had him out doing business for the Chicago mob.

And even then, he might not pick up the phone.

Business first.

Everything else second.

Beni did pick up on the fourth ring, though, right before it went to his voicemail. "Yeah, *fuck* … hello?"

"Sorry, I woke you up, huh?"

It took a second.

Then, *two* …

"Bene?"

"Hey, man," he said quietly. "Uh, if you're not up for talking, I can call you tomorrow or—"

"Now is fine."

It clearly wasn't.

He'd obviously been asleep.

And *still* …

It had been so long since the two of them talked that Beni didn't even seem to care his twin was calling *way* too late for it to be normal.

"Everything good your way?" Beni asked.

Bene cleared his throat. "Yeah, I mean, it's good. A lot of shit's changed, and—"

"Yeah, Marcus mentioned you got the button, huh?"

His laughter filled up the car.

"Can't say it was because I deserved it, or anything."

"You did," Beni replied quietly, "you just had a moment for a bit, that's all."

Right, right.

"How's August?"

Beni sighed, proud and pleased. "Great, man. Loves her job. You know, her articles made her more famous in this city than *I* am back home."

Bene chuckled. "I know, I'm subscribed to Manic Media's online edition. Swear she could write about a polar bear eating snow, and it would somehow be interesting."

He wasn't even lying.

August was an amazing writer.

"Tell me about it."

The silence stretched on between Bene and his twin, but it wasn't uncomfortable. He broke the silence first, if only because he just needed to talk to someone about Vanna, and maybe then he could go upstairs to his penthouse alone, instead of rushing back across the city to spend the rest of his night with that woman.

God.

He felt fucking crazy.

"I met someone," he said.

Beni sucked in a lungful of air on the other end of the call. "Did you?"

"Yeah, man, she's … *perfect.* She's great."

"Huh."

Bene chuckled. "That all you got to say?"

"Well, no."

"What else, then?"

"I mean, does she have a name, or …?"

"Vanna."

"Has she met Ma or—"

"Not yet."

"But? Because I can hear that in there."

"But I think she'll love her, you know?"

Beni whistled low. "Well, *damn.* It's like that, huh?"

"It's not like anything right now. It just … is."

It sounded lame.

It was still the truth.

Or, that's what Bene would keep telling himself.

For now.

"Is that why you called?"

"Pardon?" he asked.

"To tell me about her," Beni clarified.

"Uh, yeah. Just needed to talk to someone."

"All right," his brother murmured, "so tell me about her. I am all ears."

He did.

He told Beni *everything*.

CHAPTER 12

"Of course, I am getting ready right now for dinner," Vanna said.

She carefully balanced the phone between her shoulder and ear as she slid a diamond stud into the lobe. It complimented the thick rope of clear diamonds that hugged her mid-throat like a choker. The only two pieces of jewelry that she wore to compliment her floor-length black gown made up of silk and chiffon with an off the shoulder neckline, and a deep plunge in both the front and back. Not to mention, the slit up her thigh that showed off her sky-high, pointed-toe stilettos and the gleaming skin of her legs with every step she took.

"Just finishing up, and I will be on my way," she added.

On the other end of her call, Mario continued muttering on about the fact she wouldn't let him send a car to pick her up, and how that would look on him. His voice droning on in her ear was beginning to get tiring, and she just wanted to get him off the phone as soon as possible. Especially considering her other guest would be there soon.

"The engagement has been announced already," he continued bitching as though he was going to get a real response from her. "You don't think someone might assume things based on the fact you don't have a chaperone, or—"

"Never had one before now."

"*Yes,* but because I talked to my father."

"And you can say that now."

"Doesn't mean it looks *good*, okay?"

Right. Because it was all about fucking appearances in their life. It seemed to now be the most important thing on Mario's mind, but especially where she was concerned, and this ridiculous engagement. She wished she cared to listen to him, but vanity *was* one of her flaws, and she would willingly admit it. So, instead of paying attention to his nonsense, she found more pleasure in admiring her reflection in the mirror.

Besides, regardless of what she told *him*, she wouldn't be going to the dinner with his mother and father in the city at one of their favorite restaurants because she had better things to do. And yes, it was absolutely going to get her in a world of shit, but she couldn't find a single ounce of her that gave a damn at this point.

Her life had been decided.

Her future, written in stone.

Vanna didn't get a say.

She wasn't afraid of what they might do next. At worst, he would kill her for the things she was doing behind his back. At best, they would continue down the same path they were already on with her being forced into a marriage with him that she didn't want. At this fucking point, Vanna had nothing left to lose. She didn't even know how to protect herself, *hell*.

"Listen," Vanna said when a familiar ding sounded through the apartment, letting her know someone was coming up the private elevator to her hallway for the penthouse, "I need to finish up here, and then I'll be in a car on my way to you, okay?"

"Don't make me wait, Vanna. You know how much I hate that."

Mario's warning went right over her head.

Oh, well.

"You won't," she lied smoothly. "And besides, I am always worth the wait."

He cleared his throat on the other end. "Sometimes, yes."

All the time, you fucking asshole.

Not that it would matter to him if she said that out loud, or not. He didn't give a shit about pleasing her, making her happy, or giving her the things she wanted to make what would eventually be their life better for her. To him, her only purpose now was for her to look good on his arm, act appropriately, and give him whatever he wanted.

Vanna had no intention of doing any of those things, but she had yet to figure a way out of this goddamn situation she found herself in. So, for now, she had to do what she had to do. And tonight, she was doing what she wanted.

The ding sounded again. Someone was in the hallway, coming down to her penthouse. Now, she *really* needed to get Mario off the goddamn phone. There was no way in hell he would appreciate hearing a man on the other end of the line when she went to answer her door. That would really mess with her plans, too.

"Okay, you're keeping me from finishing up here," she said.

Mario sighed harshly. "*Fine*, but you're using drivers after this, Vanna. I can't have the future wife of the next Camorra boss going around unattended. That will never be acceptable to the clan, and you know it."

Of course.

"Sure, whatever. Revisit it later, okay?"

"You know we will."

If it let him sleep at night …

Vanna waited just long enough for Mario to say goodbye before she hung up the phone on him without saying the same in kind. She didn't have the time, or give a damn for pleasantries with him, and she was just about done pretending like she did.

Tossing the phone in her clutch, Vanna swung away from her reflection in the mirror to head out of the bedroom. Despite what she told Mario, she was finished getting ready for her evening, it simply wouldn't be to go out with him. Her smile grew wider as she headed through the penthouse, the ding of the doorbell echoing throughout the space when she came closer to the door. Maybe she should have prepared to see the man who would be standing behind the door when she swung it open, but she was too excited to see him to worry about anything else.

Bene grinned in the hallway, his hands pressing to either side of the doorjamb when she opened up the penthouse for him. And *goddamn*. He looked like sin melted into a tailored three-piece suit with a silver vest and tie with a matching silk square tucked into his breast pocket. One of his leather loafers tapped against the floor, while his fingers drummed to the wood. A watch encrusted with diamonds on the face glinted under the hallway lights.

He screamed *wealth*.

Good looks.

Total fucking heartache.

Vanna knew it now.

And how did she know that?

Because instead of considering the phone in her clutch, and the fact that tonight was supposed to be yet another opportunity for her to use in order to get information on the Guzzi family to deliver to the detective she worked with … she was more concerned with seeing him. *Spending time with him*. Everything about him.

And nothing about the vendetta.

Bene whistled low, drawing Vanna from her thoughts as his dark gaze looked her up and down. He didn't move an inch, but the slow perusal of his gaze lingering on her form, the way the fabric clung to the shape of her breasts, giving a peek at her cleavage, and the slit in her thigh, *almost* showing off the lace thong she wore underneath … well, it had her shivering on the spot in those sky-high heels.

It never failed to amaze her how this man could make her feel like the only woman in the world with nothing more than a glance thrown her way. Never mind the things he dared to let slip past his lips that were more than enough to have her wet between her thighs, and ready for yet another round in bed with him.

She was sure he knew it, too.

"Got something to say?" she asked.

Bene's tongue peeked out to wet his bottom lip. "*Well …*"

"Hmm?"

His stare darted up to meet hers. "I am a lucky fuck to have you on my arm tonight, huh?"

See.

How hard was that?

For a man to say *he* was the one honored to have her at his side? To put her first before himself? To make an *effort*?

Bene did all of those things.

And more.

Her guilt kicked up a notch, reminding her all over again that she had no business being anywhere near this man anymore. Not after the things she did, and planned for him and the rest of his family. Except she was selfish, so she wouldn't be turning him away.

Not tonight.

And not on another.

"Can't wait to show you off," Bene said, finally dropping his hands and stepping forward. "And they're going to love you."

"Who?"

"My family."

"*Oh.*"

Vanna hadn't even considered that was who he meant, even if tonight would mean she was going to be front row and center for his family at their party. Before she could even take a breath, he was on her. She didn't worry about her makeup, or the stark red lipstick she'd put on earlier because all of that could be fixed.

Instead, she was just happy to have his lips find hers. The familiarity in their kiss was something she craved, now. Like him, because God knew she needed him more than she ever wanted to … but she couldn't find it in her to be sad about that, either.

With his hands curving along her jaw, the warmth of his palms seeping into her skin as he kissed her with a hunger that promised good things were coming later, Vanna forgot about everything else. Her life. The world. Everything she was supposed to do, and the things she thought she wanted.

Bene came into play.

Everything changed.

Vanna hadn't planned for this.

Never mind … fixing it.

"God, yeah," he said, pulling away as his thumb roved over what she was sure were her smudged lips, now, "they're gonna adore you."

"You think?" she asked softly.

Bene smirked, lax and lazy. "I know."

She had a strange feeling, then.

One she hadn't expected.

Vanna wanted to meet them, too.

Not *Gian*, the man who apparently ruined her family's life and legacy. But *Gian*, the father who raised the man in front of her. She wasn't interested in meeting Cara, the woman who took her dead aunt's place, and was handed the keys to a kingdom that should have been theirs, but rather … *Cara*, the mother who Bene talked about with love, and total adoration.

His brothers.

Their people.

She wanted to know them.

And not the people she thought she knew—not the stories she had been told, but *theirs*. The things she didn't know. All of that, she wanted to know them.

That was a problem.

Did it need to be fixed, though?

That was the better question.

If he noticed her strange change in mood, Bene didn't say. "And hey, we've got a little bit of time before we need to head out … and you need to fix your lipstick now, so."

Vanna grinned, hearing the suggestive tone in his voice clearly. She started taking steps backward, and he was quick to follow, slamming the door behind him as he moved after her. "Oh, really?"

"Mmhmm."

Her fingers curled into the fabric of her dress, pulling up the skirt just enough for the slit to give him a peek of that thong she wore underneath. His gaze flicked downward, his lips curling up at the edges in a satisfied grin before his attention was on her face once more when she asked, "And what do you think we should do with that time, Bene?"

"Find a place to let me bend you over, say my name like that again, and you're going to find out."

Yes.

Absolutely, yes.

~

They were late to the dinner party because the one round where Bene had Vanna bent over the couch just wasn't enough, and somehow, they found themselves naked in her walk-in closet when she attempted to fix her makeup in front of her vanity.

Shocker.

No one said a thing about the fact they were late, though, and by the time they arrived at the Guzzi mansion, dinner had started to be served. She felt *all eyes* on them as Bene pulled her closer to his side when they came into view of the dining room entry. His fingers drifted through her loose waves, pushing the hair out of her eyes before he pressed a quick kiss to her forehead. His lips were just drifting away from her skin, their gazes meeting, as they walked into the room still tightly together, and seemingly forgetting about the room around them.

Still, she felt those eyes.

The stares.

And how it all went quiet.

Bene grinned her way, and Vanna felt an unfamiliar sensation kicking up in her stomach. *Butterflies.* How long had it been since something like her nerves took over, and reminded her that she was just as human as everyone else?

Too long, apparently.

She wasn't used to this.

She did her best to focus on him as they rounded the large table filled with numerous faces, she didn't recognize for the life of her. Not that any of the people staring back at them as she smiled and nodded at the ones they passed looked as though they recognized her, either, or as if they didn't think she was meant to be there.

They all smiled.

They all greeted them with kindness.

It settled her nerves.

And kicked up her guilt.

Fantastic.

"A bit late, Bene?"

He had just found them a spot to sit at the table that literally filled the whole room and looked as though it was easily sitting thirty people. Was it a custom piece, or had they bought it that way? He pulled out the chair for Vanna to sit as they turned to the man at the far-left end of the table, sitting in a large captain's chair.

A recognizable face to her.

Gian.

Bene's father.

Vanna hadn't known what to expect the first time she came face to face with the man—or for now, just a few seats down at a table from him—but the welcoming smile he wore was not it. Maybe she thought he would be the same as every other man within the life ... cold, almost, detached in his stare, but kind because appearances were everything.

Instead, he watched her with a hint of curiosity, but also a warmth that said he was glad to see her there, but especially with his son.

God.

Would he feel the same if he knew the truth?

Or would she finally see the coldness she'd expected?

"We can do proper introductions after the dinner," Gian said to Bene, and giving a nod to Vanna before adding, "but you can apologize to your mother for being late, hmm?"

"*Oui*, Papa," Bene quickly replied.

The first time she ever heard him use French. Even if it was only one word. It was shocking.

He dropped a kiss to the top of her head before helping her push in her chair, and then he left her to sit alone. He headed down to the other end of the very long table to greet the woman sitting in a chair that matched Gian's opposite to hers. She looked every inch a queen sitting in her throne with her red hair let down in soft waves, and the buttery, cream-colored dress hugging her feminine curves as she smiled up at her son.

Cara.

Even as Bene's mother reached for him to take his kiss to her cheek, and whatever apology he gave for being late, her gaze still drifted down the table to Vanna. There was a warmth in her gaze, too, but her stare didn't linger as long when she went back to her son, hooking her finger as if to silently ask him to bend down again.

Bene did.

Cara murmured something that had him grinning. Then, he nodded, and that had his mother mouthing the words. "Ah, I see."

It was clear the woman adored her son. It showed in every action—from the gentle pat of her hand against his cheek, to the smile on her face filled with pride. Even the glimmer in her eye, as if Bene was the only person in the room while his attention was on her, couldn't be hidden. Not that it seemed like his mother wanted to hide it.

The love.

It was so painfully clear.

She looked Vanna's way with a sly smile.

What was that all about?

Vanna didn't have time to find out.

Bene made his way back down to her, and Gian addressed the table with a clap of his hands that had servers coming in through three different entrances. While the table was already full of food, and some even had plates filled in front of them ... the servers held pitchers of water, juice, and one held a tray of wine glasses.

"Time to eat," Gian said.

Across the table, one of the men that Vanna recognized

from the newspaper picture at the wedding smiled at her. Christopher, was it?

Another Guzzi twin.

"Dad might be good with waiting for introductions," he said to Bene beside Vanna, "but I don't care about politeness, so …"

Bene laughed, waving a hand between his brother, and Vanna as a server came up to them with plates ready to sit in front of them. "Vanna, this is Chris, and his wife, Valeria."

"Val is cool, though," the pretty woman to Chris's left replied, although her attention was more focused on the young girl sitting next to her that was trying not to spill sauce down her sweet dress. "Here, let me put a napkin on you, Maria."

"Nice to meet you," Vanna said.

Chris nodded. "Fair warning, it's going to get loud … it always does. And no worries, nobody is going to get offended if you forget our names tonight. There's a lot of us."

"Too many, sometimes," a man—another she did recognize from the newspaper—to Chris's right muttered.

"Marcus, my oldest brother," Bene filled in, confirming what she already knew.

She laughed.

"I'll remember that."

"Eat, eat!"

The shout echoed down the table.

Bene gave her a wink.

Food it was.

~

"Vanna, is it?"

Vanna turned away from Marcus who had been showing her the long corridor in the mansion that was dedicated solely to portraits of the Guzzi family. Currently, she was admiring one of Cara surrounded by her boys when they were younger in a forest setting where she sat on a chair that seemed more like a throne, staring head on at the artist painting, proud as could be over the empire around her.

An army of principes.

And a queen leading them.

The woman in the picture was the same one walking toward her now. Marcus dropped Vanna's hand that had been tucked into his elbow with a smile, but only long enough to greet his mother with a one-armed hug, and kiss to her cheek.

"I'll give you two a minute," he murmured.

"*Grazie, mio ragazzo.*"

"Be nice, Ma."

Cara laughed, winking Vanna's way as she asked, "When am I *not?*"

"Never, of course."

Marcus gave Vanna a smile and nod before he headed down the hall. Cara waited just long enough for him to disappear from the corridor before she turned to face Vanna, and the portrait behind her. Well, she stared more at the portrait than she did at Vanna, but that was okay, too. It allowed her to admire the beauty of Bene's mother, but also the almost *regal* aura around her. She'd always been able to sense those things about people, but it was so much stronger in this home with these people.

"It is, right?" Cara asked.

"Pardon?"

Cara's gaze flicked to hers. "Vanna, sweetheart."

"Yes. Vanna Falco."

If the last name rang a bell to the woman, she didn't say. Then again, her attention was back on the painting on the wall. Vanna turned to stare at it, too. It really was a perfect representation of the woman, and her sons. Realistic in more ways than she could explain with careful brushstrokes that brought the people in the portrait alive.

"I'm always worried people might think this corridor is a bit pretentious, considering ..."

Vanna shook her head. "I thought it was ... well, a beautiful tribute to a legacy."

"The legacy of a name, or a bloodline?"

"A family, actually," Vanna murmured, "I only saw a family."

And *she did*.

Standing in this corridor as Marcus explained portrait after portrait, and each Guzzi in every single frame, she heard the pride in his voice, and the love he held for his family. Ones no longer with them, and those still on earth.

It made this night, and the choices she would have to make after it, harder. Not that she would tell Cara Guzzi that, however.

"I'm glad to see you came," Cara said.

"Why is that?"

Cara shrugged, smiling softly again. "Bene gives me a lot of things to worry about ... I would like it if one thing in his life didn't, that's all."

Something like her.

Vanna met the woman's stare—they had a conversation earlier, during the dinner. And a short one after before Bene got called away by Christopher to help with something upstairs while they had time, and an extra pair of hands on deck. However, their chats had been short, and not very deep. Not that this one was anything amazing, either, but it felt different.

Things unsaid clung to the air.

Vanna was fine with that.

"You seem familiar to me," Cara said.

She stilled next to the woman. "Do I?"

"Somehow. It's your face, I think. As if I've seen it before."

Vanna cleared her throat. "I can't say we've ever—"

"Cara, one of the shelter's managers is getting ready to leave, and I know you like to see them out, *mia bella*."

At the end of the corridor, Gian Guzzi darkened the entrance and stared down the way at his wife with fondness. *Clear love*. Like Cara with her son earlier. And with her other sons throughout the rest of the evening.

The Guzzis loved.

All of them.

"Sorry about that," Cara said.

Vanna shrugged. "It's okay. I can find Bene."

"He's still busy." Gian took a couple of steps into the hallway, turning his head a bit to stare at some of the portraits as he passed. "But I can keep her company until he finds his way back to her."

"Perfect."

Not wanting to intrude on Gian and Cara's moment as the two met in the middle of the corridor, the man already leaning in for a kiss from his wife, Vanna turned around. Her gaze fell on another portrait, one she had looked over previously, but now seemed to take center stage.

Featuring Gian in a chair fit to be a throne, he dominated the painting. His fingers curved around the intricately carved wooden arms of the chair, and his left ankle rested on his right knee while his head turned slightly to stare off at something that one couldn't see in the painting. His profile, showing off the strong line of his jaw, and the curve of smirking lips reminded her of the man's sons … but especially Bene.

"Which one is your favorite in here, hmm?"

Vanna's heart stopped.

She swore it did.

"Sorry," Gian said, chuckling as he came to stand beside her. "Didn't mean to startle you, Vanna."

She didn't bother to lie and say he hadn't. "It's okay … and I'm not sure."

"On your favorite, you mean?"

"Well, that's a lie. I like the one with your wife and sons."

"Ah." Gian turned a bit, eyeing the portrait three spaces down where it proudly rested for everyone to admire. "My favorite, too."

"Really, not all the ones or any of the ones that you're featured?"

Gian chuckled, his handsome features softening as he turned to meet her gaze. "Not at all … see, I love my wife more than anything in the world. She's an angel and I am only a well-dressed sinner standing next to her. And since this," he said, waving at the hall and his home, "was the world she gave me, it only seems appropriate that I make sure everything in it revolves around her. I made a lot of mistakes in my life, but Cara wasn't one of them."

Truth.

That's what stared back at her.

Guilt.

It's what killed her.

Vanna saw a man who loved his family.

She heard another man in her mind.

A *vendetta*.

Her promise.

The war raged on.

A silent battle.

Vanna was losing.

Or was that her heart?

She didn't know anymore.

CHAPTER
13

Bene figured Vanna wouldn't be in the kitchen of the mansion, but since he was passing it on his way back to the dining room and grand entrance his parents were using for the dinner party, he decided to check just in case. When he'd left her earlier to help Christopher move something upstairs from one room to the other, because their mother refused to allow Gian to lift a finger, Marcus had been giving her a tour of the downstairs.

As though he didn't already know she'd been here before.

Funny thing was, the weekend she spent with Bene here hadn't given Vanna much insight to the mansion, or the history within it. He had been far more interested in getting her back flat to any surface that he could, and enjoying it, rather than giving her a grand tour. She hadn't seemed to mind, so …

Unsurprisingly, Bene found the kitchen to be organized chaos. Not unusual when his parents threw a decent-sized dinner party like the one tonight. The catering company his mother favored—one that had no problem with signing nondisclosure agreements and regularly having their staff checked when inside the mansion—moved all over the space, passing each other like ships in a very crowded harbor.

And yet, they didn't bump into one another. Hands tossed high in response to the orders the head chef threw out to her people, and there in the middle of it all was his mother, helping right along to keep everything on track, and making sure everyone knew what they had to do or go to next for the evening.

"We need those bottles of champagne ready, Kassie," Cara told the head chef.

"Working on it, ma'am."

"Thank you. *Oh.*"

His mother's gaze fell on him in the doorway, and while Bene had a good mind to slip out of the space, and let her get back to work, he didn't. Instead, he smiled when she grinned his way, and moved toward him.

"Did you get that done upstairs?"

"All moved," he assured.

"It looks better in the hallway, doesn't it?"

He shrugged. "Makes sense to put the cabinet there, sure."

"Because it looks *nicer.*"

Bene laughed, knowing better than to argue with his mother over something like decorating. Sure, she had a whole team that regularly came in to decorate her spaces, but they always worked with her to do it. She had an eye for that sort of thing, and frankly, Bene had very little interest in it. He was fine to just do what he was told in that case.

Cara reached up to stroke his cheek with her soft fingertips. The same action she used to do to him when he was a child, and she wanted him to know she was giving him special attention even when the room was full of his brothers. Her fingers would drift over the side of his face, up into his hair, and then she'd give him a little smile from the side. She didn't do it nearly as much as she used to when he was little, but it still reminded him of that every single time.

Her soft smile had him reflecting the same thing back.

"Looking for her, are you?" his mother asked.

As though she just *knew.*

Bene tried to play it off with a, "Well, I was going back to the party, but—"

"Yes, you were looking for her."

"Do you like her?"

Cara lifted her brows, as though she was actually contemplating his question. And just as fast, she let out a light laugh. "I see how much *you* like her, that's for sure."

"What does that mean?"

"It means you're happy. A lot happier than you have been, yes?"

For a moment, he forgot that he was standing just beyond the kitchen entry. A room full of other people who could undoubtedly hear their conversation just fine. In that second, it was simply him, and his mother.

He could always be honest with his ma.

It was the love she fostered for them.

"She helped a bit with that," he admitted, "but I just needed some time to figure things out on my own about shit, too."

Cara rolled her eyes at his choice in language. "She makes you *smile*."

"Does she?"

He wouldn't notice.

It always felt like he was smiling with Vanna.

"Often," Cara murmured, stroking his cheek again. "And if she does that for you, then I like her very much, Bene. I think that's what counts."

"Yeah, me too."

"Is she *that* kind of girl, then?"

"What kind?"

Cara winked. "The kind you could fall in love with—is she?"

Bene dragged in a quick breath, surprised at the answer that seemed ready at the tip of his tongue. His heart beat harder in his chest, moments of his time with Vanna flashing through his mind as other images—things that *could* happen, things he wanted to see happen—followed right behind. He wasn't expecting that, and his silence echoing after his mother asked the question only seemed to have her grinning as though she already knew his answer.

"Bene?"

He let out the air he'd been holding in as he told her, "Yeah, I think she's exactly that kind of girl for me, Ma."

Cara nodded. "Go and find her, then."

He didn't need to be told a second time, but he made sure to give his mother a hug, lingering with her for another moment, before he headed out of the kitchen. Only one thing, or rather, person, was on his mind, too.

Vanna.

Bene found Vanna easily enough in the grand entrance of the mansion, and he was glad to see she had stuck with his brothers. Not that any of the other guests at the dinner party would do anything to make a problem, but he didn't know them that well, either. However, if his mother cared enough to invite them for this thing to support the shelter, then they were probably decent.

Probably.

Didn't mean he cared to find out.

Instead of crossing the room to join Vanna and his brothers with the rest of the party guests, he stayed back near the mouth of the hallway leading further into the mansion to enjoy the view. It was almost as though she fit right in with the rest of them, laughing at whatever Marcus said to Christopher, and quick to bend down to speak to little Maria when the girl tugged on the side of her dress.

She looked happy.

Carefree, even.

And he wanted to appreciate it.

Bene was about to join her and his brothers when the sight of someone else standing across the entry had him grinning for a whole new reason.

Beni.

His twin stood near the front doors with his wife at his side, already passing off his jacket and August's to the woman handling that at the front. His parents didn't keep servants in the house often, but for parties and other events, they came to help. A team of maids came throughout the week to keep the large house spotless as well, although his mother was always quick to throw on old clothes and get down to business for that, too.

Knowing Vanna was okay for the moment, Bene left his hiding spot and crossed the room to greet his twin. As though he could feel his brother coming his way—he probably did what with their crazy, nonsensical intuition about each other—Beni lifted his head with a smile, his gaze already landing on Bene moving toward him.

"You didn't think to let me know you were coming?" he asked.

Beni shrugged, drawing his wife closer to his side. "Dad said he had a surprise for Ma this weekend, and asked if we could come to join in. I guess Corrado got called to Vegas last minute for something, and the baby has an ear infection, so Les and Ginevra didn't want to fly."

Ah.

That explained why they weren't there, too, then.

Although, he never thought to ask.

With his other brother living in New York with his two spouses and their baby girl, they didn't get to see him nearly as much as they liked. But if he was being fair, sometimes that was okay with Corrado … because the man had his moods.

He was joking.

Mostly.

"Didn't even see you come in until you were already inside," Bene said, clapping his brother on the shoulder. Then, he leaned in to give a smiling August a kiss on her cheek, too. "And good to see you—you're looking good. Keeping him in fucking line, right?"

A softness lit up August's gaze, as though she could just tell that Bene was doing better, and while she wouldn't say it out loud, she still recognized it for what it was. He appreciated that, and her. She was great for his brother, no doubt about it.

"Someone has to," she replied, "because God knows if we left it up to the two of you, well … nothing good comes from that, huh?"

Beni laughed. "Come on, now, we're not that—"

"You're terrible. Both of you."

"Worse together," Bene added.

"Don't take her side, man."

Bene shrugged.

Because where was the lie, though?

Beni sighed, giving his brother a cocked eyebrow before his gaze drifted across the room. "And hey, maybe you didn't notice us come in because you were distracted by staring at someone else, yeah?"

He didn't even need to look the same way Beni did to know who he was staring at. Vanna with their other brothers at the party.

"That her?"

"How do you know?" Bene asked. "She could just be some chick—"

"Dad said you were bringing her. You described her well

enough."

"And you *did* stare at her in a room full of a whole bunch of other people, Bene," August added.

"You told her?"

Beni smirked. "I tell my wife everything."

Of course, he did.

August winked.

"Okay, so yeah ... that's her," he murmured.

"Well done—she's hot."

He gave August a look.

She shrugged, saying, "Beni can't say it without losing his chance to get ass tonight, and all, so I figured I would do it for him."

Bene barked out a laugh.

Yep.

Perfect for his brother.

"That's enough of—"

Before his twin could finish his statement, applause lit up the room. Bene spun on his heels to watch his father, with help from the men from their *famiglia* who kept an eye on the house during parties like these, push a large *something* to the middle of the grand entry. Right under the tall chandelier hanging between the two staircases.

Covered with a beige sheet, rectangular in shape, and at least ten feet tall and wide, they had it sitting on a rolling platform dolly to move it while the men held it on both ends to keep it steady.

"Is that the surprise Dad has for Ma?" Bene asked.

"Think so," Beni responded.

"What is *this*?" his mother asked, moving closer.

"A surprise—or an updated edition, rather," his father replied.

Cara beamed.

His father grinned. "You ready?"

"I would love to know where you hid it."

"I have my ways."

"Show me, Gian."

That was all his father needed before he pulled the sheet away from the item, letting the fabric fall to a heap on the floor in front of a beautiful painting. A portrait that looked familiar in the way that the woman sitting on her throne in a forest surrounded by trees was the very same as the one as the one in the corridor that dominated the space compared to the others of their family. Only this one was different—now, all his brothers were older, young men or near to their current ages—but their mother stayed the same.

Still beautiful in her gown.

Still surrounded by life and love.

Forever the Guzzi queen.

"Oh, Gian," Cara whispered, "it's beautiful."

Despite her low tone, the room had grown so quiet that everyone heard her just fine. All over again the applause started from the guests. Bene, his twin, and August joined in. He looked around the room to find Vanna once more, ready to join her.

Problem was …

She was gone.

∽

"There you are."

"Here I am," she whispered.

He came to a stop in front of the chair she sat in, twisting her phone around repeatedly in her hands. Bene had no clue how Vanna found herself on the third floor of the mansion's largest wing, never mind why she sat outside his father's office, but at least he found her.

The guests had started to disperse before he finally was

able to pull way from his twin, and the rest of his family. It seemed like once his father showed off the portrait, everybody and their mother suddenly wanted a damn picture with everyone and it, too. And then each of the boys with the painting, and then all the boys that were there together with the painting.

It didn't end.

Vanna wasn't far from his mind, though.

Stuffing his hands in his pockets, he tried to ignore the fact that she wouldn't look up at him. Not that she needed to because he could still see that sadness in her pretty, downcast features. Something that killed him with its silence, yet its presence still felt oh, so heavy.

But why?

That was the better question.

What made her sad?

If she told him …

Well, he'd kill it.

Whatever it was.

She continued playing with that phone as he took a step back to lean against the wall opposite to her in the hallway. Right next to her chair was the opened doorway to his father's office—rarely did Gian leave it open, but sometimes, he did.

Had it been open?

"Where did you go?" he asked.

Vanna sighed, and let out a tired laugh. "Just … needed a few minutes."

"You looked like you were having a great time."

"I *was*—I did, Bene."

So, what was this, then?

He didn't think she wanted him to ask.

And really, he didn't want her sad.

Never with him.

All at once, Vanna glanced up, her stare meeting his. He swore a line of water wet her eyes, but when she blinked, he couldn't be sure because those long lashes of hers made it all disappear. She gave him another one of *those* smiles.

Soft, and *sweet*.

Still somehow sly and sexy, too.

"I came looking for you," she said.

"Sorry, I didn't mean to—"

"I heard you with your mom."

Bene stilled.

Vanna swallowed hard, her throat jumping when she added quickly, "Did you mean what you said to her—that you could love me?"

Well, damn.

"I did—*do*," he murmured.

She dropped her gaze back to her hand, and the phone. "Even if I'm a liar?"

"What are you talking about?"

Vanna didn't answer.

Bene just waited her out.

Eventually, she shook her head, and glanced up with another one of those smiles. "Maybe I just got stuck in my head … this place, all these people, your family, and *you*. It's a lot to take in, that's all."

Was that it?

Or was it something else?

"Why come up here?"

"I got lost," she said, laughing under her breath as she stood from the chair, picking up her clutch from the floor at the same time. "Sorry, did your parents think I was being rude? I didn't mean to—"

"No, not at all."

"Oh, good."

"And they said we should spend the night, if you'd like to."

"Did they?"

He nodded. "This time, we're not picking a room, though."

"Well, that's not nearly as fun."

His chuckles colored up the hall before he pushed away from the wall, snagged her hand in his, their fingers weaving tightly together as he pulled her down the hall. "Come on, it's down this way. The room I shared with my twin—*rooms*, really. It's two bedrooms connected in the middle with a large sitting area that we used to use to game, and shit."

Not that he intended on giving her a tour. Once they were at the end of the hall and slipped into the middle room that connected the two bedrooms, he slammed the door behind them. Vanna was already moving for him. He reached back and kissed her, the force of them meeting sending her flying back to the closed door with a hard *thud*.

She didn't look so sad anymore.

He liked that more.

CHAPTER
14

Sometimes, being weak was easier.

Vanna did her best to never be weak in situations—it didn't matter which kind, really. And yet, right now with Bene, she found it was easier for her to just be weak. To let him react from seeing her sad, wanting to make her smile, but doing it in the way he did best.

By fucking her *crazy*.

Vanna barely remembered moving from the door to the bedroom to the left side of the room. She didn't even get a chance to admire the set up of two private bedrooms connected by a main sitting room because Bene yanked her into what she assumed had once been his bedroom in the mansion. She heard the door kicked closed behind her, but she was already walking to the bed. Already yanking her dress high, and letting it fall to the floor. She came to stand in front of the leather bench resting at the foot of a four-poster bed covered in black and red sheets, and draped in a matching duvet.

That was really all she got to see of the room. But did it really matter right now?

By the time she turned around, Bene was *on her*. His dark words whispered along her skin as his hands fisted into her black lace thong, and yanked it down her thighs, dropping to his knees as he went.

She stepped out of the underwear when he murmured,

"Get these fucking things off and spread those legs so I can have my dessert, Vanna."

"God, yes."

The sight of him on his knees in front of her, his hands sliding up her thighs while his dark eyes drank her in, and he grinned in that wicked way of his … Jesus, it was more than enough to promise she was good and wet when he spread her thighs wide.

"*Sit*." He flashed her a wink. "And give me this pussy."

He didn't need to say it twice.

Vanna dropped her ass to the leather bench.

The coolness of the supple material soothed her over-heated body for a split second. Just that second, though, because in the next, Bene was between her thighs. He licked her from her slit to her clit, and back down again. He took his time enjoying her. Making her squirm with the way he'd flick his tongue along her slit, while his hands kept her thighs pried open even when her hips jerked forward against his mouth to get more.

"You wanna come?"

"So bad," she breathed, "please."

"Please, *what*?"

He teased her further, grinning salaciously as his mouth grazed over her inner thigh, moving higher along the edge of her pussy, but not quite giving her exactly what she wanted. And his hands moved inward, the sides of his thumbs stroking along the sides of her pussy just enough to make her tremble.

"Please, Bene, please eat me until I come."

"That's what I wanted."

Of course.

Her words.

Her sounds.

It all got him off.

And she loved that.

His gaze met hers for a brief second as his tongue finally found her clit with fast, hard strokes that hit her in just the right way. Her head fell back, and the sounds that came out of her didn't feel *real*.

Just like the way she felt.

How he ate her.

It all mixed together in a tornado of sensation and pleasure. Until she felt his teeth scrape along the sensitive bud of her clit before he sucked it into his mouth with enough force to send her flying over the edge.

Vanna was sure she scratched the leather bench to hell.

Ruined it.

Bene didn't seem to care.

"Holy fucking *shit*," she breathed. "Love the way you eat my pussy."

His deep chuckle rocked her to the core as he kissed a wet path up her still clenching stomach. Those kisses found her heaving breasts, his attention on her nipples enough to get her thighs shaking again as he shuffled down his pants and the boxer-briefs underneath. She was already reaching for his shirt—he'd discarded his jacket *somewhere*.

Once she had the fabric separating them gone, and his thick cock jutted out between them, Vanna leaned forward and took him into her mouth. There was something about the image of him losing control—he *always* did whenever she sucked him off, and it didn't take her any time at all to get him that way, either—that made her hotter than ever.

"You're gonna make me come doing that, Vanna."

Maybe that's what she wanted.

He must have saw that sly twinkle in her eyes when she dragged her teeth along the silky length of his erection. A burst of salt hit her tongue—his precum. And that was all he gave her before he pulled away, leaned in to wrap his arms around her waist, and pulled her to the bed.

Vanna's knees hit the bed, and Bene pushed in behind her, his feet still rooted to the floor. That first thrust of his cock ached in the best possible way. Spreading her open, and filling her full, getting his dick soaked with her slickness with fast, deep strokes that had his groin beating against her ass.

His hand smacked down, too.

Reddening her skin.

Making her hot.

Sending her higher.

"Fuck that dick, baby," he murmured.

God, she did.

Bouncing back on him.

Taking him deeper.

Moaning into the sheets.

"Look at this pussy." His hand grabbed her ass on the next slap. "So wet and greedy—*shit*, I wish you could see what I see right now. You look so good like this, huh?"

Vanna whined a response through clenched teeth.

Because soon, she was coming again.

High again.

Wishing she could change everything again.

Because soon the bliss would leave.

She knew it as he pulled out of her, rolled her over, spread her wide, and came right back to fuck her again. As she stared up at Bene while he held her thighs opened, and watched, enraptured, by the way his cock filled her full …

Soon, this would end.

She'd be good for a moment.

Then, she wouldn't.

Because she'd have to face what she'd done here.

That she fell in love with a man she was supposed to hate.

That her misdeeds would hurt a man she loved.

She'd done this.

It couldn't be fixed.

~

Vanna blinked awake in the bedroom, the vaulted, gray ceiling staring back at her from her position on the bed. On her back, with sheets tangled around her legs, and Bene's arm tight around her middle, the room still smelling like their sex, and her body warm from his close proximity … well, it was the *best* way to wake up.

And on another night, if everything was different, it would have been the perfect way for her to wake up. She would have rolled over, tucked her face into Bene's chest, pretended like morning was never going to come, and went back to sleep.

But she couldn't do that.

Not when her mind ran a million miles a minute, bouncing from one thing to the next, all her mistakes and misdeeds warring with one another while her guilt climbed on top of all of it to roar and make itself known, too.

Who knew what it was?

Maybe it was the fact that Vanna was weak. That she had a heart—emotions and real feelings. That she couldn't be cold, and see these people, their family, and the life they made for themselves behind their closed doors the same way her father had. She didn't see monsters. *Yes*, they were bad people who did bad things, and the past had been colored a bright, violent red by those same things … but this was now.

Or maybe it was the fact that Vanna wasn't made to fulfill a vendetta for a lot of the same reasons, and others, too.

None of it even mattered.

She couldn't do this.

She shouldn't *be here*.

What was she *doing*?

Tipping her head to the side on the pillow, Vanna found Bene still sleeping peacefully. Like this, the hard lines of his handsome face smoothed out, and he looked almost *boyish*. Still sexy, and everything bad for her heart.

Still *hers*.

Because that was the thing.

Somehow, this man felt like hers.

He became hers.

Sure, he hadn't said it. Never breathed those three little words that would inevitably change everything between them, but he didn't really have to, either. Love wasn't *words*, she knew. Love was a feeling—a promise, and a loyalty to another soul. Love was so much bigger than just words, and if she continued to let this go on … it was going to be so much worse than what it already was, and that was her fault, too.

Vanna did this.

She understood that.

A part of her still felt like she was betraying her father, his memory, and the promise she made to him. Vanna didn't know what to do about that, or how to deal with it. So, she did the next best thing—and it was still the fucking coward's way out of this situation.

She couldn't tell Bene she loved him.

She also couldn't hurt him or his family.

Instead, she slipped out from under his arm, doing her very best not to turn and look at him as she found her clothes scattered around the room. Pulling the items on as quickly as she could, with as little noise as possible, she let her heels dangle from her fingertips instead of slipping them on, too, knowing they would make too much noise as she left the room.

No doubt, she looked a mess.

Makeup ruined.

Hair all over the place.

Clothes crumpled.

The walk of shame.

Funnily enough, she felt every ounce of that shame, too, as she left the room without a look back over her shoulder. Not because of the man she'd fucked *three* times before they fell asleep, but the fact she was leaving him at all when her heart screamed for her to get back in that bed with him, and pretend like the rest of her life wasn't falling apart.

Her heart kept whispering lies.

Tell him.

Tell him the truth.

He can help.

He'll understand.

He'll forgive you.

Maybe, maybe … maybe …

None of it was true, and she didn't need to test the theory out to know it was fact. The one thing Bene loved the very most was his family—that much was clear. Just like the rest of them. Finding out she had been working to tear his family apart at the seams would only be the final nail in the coffin, and she doubted he would give a shit about what was happening to her in the clan after he knew what she did to him.

She didn't need that pain.

Neither did he.

It wasn't fair.

Vanna crossed the sitting room that connected the two bedrooms, noting the door on the other side had been closed. She couldn't remember if that was open when they first came in—the door to his twin's room—because everything happened so fast. They went from kissing against the door, to fucking like animals on the bed in a blink.

She couldn't waste time wondering, either.

Leaving the sitting room, and coming out into the hallway, Vanna nearly ran into a form turning to come through the doorway. She almost lost the shoes in her hand as her eyes widened, and she came face to face with Bene's twin.

For a second, she wished she was dead.

That would have been easier.

Beni blinked, a glass of water in his grip as he tried to make sense of what he was seeing in front of him. *Goddamn*, she understood that feeling far too well. "You're leaving?"

Vanna swallowed hard. "I—"

"Bene didn't say you were leaving at …" He checked the watch on his wrist, muttering, "Three in the morning —*what*?"

She struggled to come up with a lie, blurting, "Got a call, something came up, and I don't want to wake him up. You'll let him know in the morning that I said sorry, right?"

"Yeah, sure … can I help with anything?"

"No, I'm good. I just have to get out of here."

Beni nodded. "Sure, and uh, sorry we didn't have a lot of time to chat earlier. I was worried about my brother, but he's doing okay now, and it seems like that's partly because of you. He does better with you, huh?"

God.

Her heart split *more*.

"I have to go," Vanna muttered.

She didn't even wait for him to respond.

She just needed to leave.

It was another two hours before Vanna finally faced the front door of her penthouse. Her hands trembled as she slid the key into the lock, seconds away from a breakdown that she had been keeping at bay lest her cab driver watch her ugly cry in the backseat while he drove her back to the city.

She wasn't thinking about anything except getting inside, stripping off her clothes, and finding her bed for the next *several* hours. Maybe days, who fucking knew? As long as she could get away with it, then that's what she planned to do.

Vanna stumbled into her penthouse, expecting a darkened hallway and the safety of silence. Instead, she was met by every single light turned on, and the loud sigh of a guest that in no way was invited to be standing at the end of the hallway like he'd been waiting there for her all night.

Mario.

She sucked in a breath, the clutch dropping from her hand as he tipped his head to the side when their gazes met. There was no hiding the way his stare took her in—from the dress she wore, to the heels that were currently killing her feet. His scowl deepened when he took in her messy makeup, and ruined hair.

Shit.

It wasn't that she forgot about him.

Quite the opposite.

Vanna simply figured this would be like every other time that she blew Mario off in the past. It wasn't like this was the first time she was supposed to meet up with him, but instead, fucked off somewhere and came back later. He'd be pissed, sure, but he got over it.

Because he didn't own her.

Except now he does.

The ring in her clutch that she took off to attend the party with Bene said so.

"I will give you exactly twenty seconds to tell me where you were," Mario murmured.

"I—"

"No lies. I already know. Start speaking the truth."

What?

He couldn't possibly know.

"Out," she said.

Mario's jaw tightened. "Don't fuck with me tonight, Vanna. Do you know how long I've been here waiting for you to get back from being with that fucking *scum*—that goddamn *Guzzi?*"

Her eyes widened.

He sneered. "Oh, you didn't think I knew? The bitch downstairs at the front desk—she calls me whenever someone comes around here. Your fucktoy was just stupid enough to give her his name when he came around."

"Mario—"

"*The truth.*"

Jesus.

"What does it matter?" she asked.

That was the wrong thing to say, apparently, because the very second the words left her lips, Mario pushed away from the wall he was using as a leaning post, and came flying her way. She didn't even have time to react before he was at the end of the hallway, and Vanna found herself shoved against the door with a *bang.*

Unlike earlier, with another man who shoved her against a door to kiss her like his life depended on his need to have his mouth on hers, she didn't like this. *At all.* Mario's hand found her throat, partially covering her jaw as he forced her head back, crowded his body along hers, and made her stare up at him.

That fire in his eyes …

The hate …

Sure, she saw it before.

Never toward her.

Not like this.

She didn't give a single fuck that he was feeling some

kind of way about the things he knew she had been doing. She felt *zero* shame about the fact she'd been fucking someone else while she was intended for him because she never wanted him in the first goddamn place, and told him exactly that more than once.

However, the sight did startle her.

It made her pause.

His grip on her face tightened to a painful point, surely leaving bruises behind while his fingers dug into her jaw, He shook her face, and tears sprung to her eyes. A reaction from the pain, but she refused to let him see the fear he caused.

She wasn't *that* weak.

"See, I thought you were fucking someone else," he said, leaning down close enough that his lips nearly brushed hers. If he kissed her, he better be ready for her to spit, or bite him because she would not be playing this game with him. "But I figured it was like the other times you acted like a whore for a man—some prick was pretty enough to make you spread your legs for him, and you were just smart enough to keep him out of my sight this time, huh?"

"*I was never yours, Mario.*"

She felt the ache spreading in her jaw when he grabbed even harder a second before he pulled her head away from the wall, and then slammed it back against it. *God.* Did that crack her skull? With the stars in her eyes now, it was very possible.

Vanna shut the fuck up.

Before he *killed* her.

"And look what I found," he ground out through clenched teeth, the vein in his forehead starting to pop out from his rage, "you're not fucking just *anybody*. No, you're spreading your legs for a Guzzi. Jesus, you won't even fuck *me*, but you'll lay down with that piece of shit, Vanna? What kind of woman are you?"

"One you don't deserve."

For a second, his grip loosened.

Then, it came back harder than ever.

He kept their gazes locked on one another, not that she had any other choice given the way he was holding her head up. The silence stretched on between them, giving her ample time to watch the rage of violent emotions wash over his features, but unsurprisingly, he was the first to speak again. Not that she cared because she had nothing to say to him.

She never would.

"But who fucking *has you*, huh?"

Vanna swallowed hard. "Fuck you."

"Yeah," he added, chuckling sardonically, "because that's the truth, isn't it? Doesn't matter what you do now, girl, you're still going to end up with me for the rest of your life whether you like it or not. And I have waited far too long to give up now."

"I'll never be yours. *Ever.*"

He needed to know that.

She had to say it.

It should be *clear.*

"But you *are.* And you didn't get a say about it."

She shook her head, as much as she could manage in her current predicament with the tears streaming down her cheeks. It was getting harder to breathe now, too, but he didn't show any sign of letting her go.

"Not like that," she whispered painfully, "not like he has me."

Mario shoved her harder against the wall, starting to say, "I—"

"I'll never love you—I love him."

"Fucking *bitch.*"

His words were punctuated by him shoving her against the wall, then he let her go, and slammed his hands to either side of her head. Vanna sucked in a deep breath before he stepped back altogether, fists clenched down at his sides while he stared her down with enough contempt to burn her from the inside out.

If only she cared …

He pointed a finger at her. "You *will not* fuck up what I have worked for all these years—do not make me look like a fool to the clan, and my father, or I will be the one who chokes the fucking life out of you, and I will enjoy doing it, too. Go near the Guzzi bastard again, Vanna, and that's it. You're *done*—you hear me? I will kill him, *and* you."

He would.

She knew it.

"Do you hear me?"

She nodded. "I hear you."

"Things will be changing soon. Understand that. You've lost the right to have your life the way you wanted it, and you've got nobody to blame but yourself for it, too. Try to fight me from here on out, and *everyone* will know what you've been doing. I'll let you live just long enough for you to suffer for the whore you are before I kill you. Be ready—a truck will be here tomorrow to move your shit out. This is over."

He didn't give her time to respond before he was leaving. Vanna slid down the wall, her backside meeting the floor while her palms dug into her eyes to press the tears away, as the door slammed shut.

It felt appropriate.

An end.

The coffin closing.

This was her life.

Mario was right, though.

She did this.

~

Vanna's life in the week after coming home to find Mario waiting in her penthouse became a series of her doing only what she had to. Wake up, get dressed, go to school, and come back to a home that wasn't hers but where she now had to live. It felt like she had walked straight into a fog with no way out.

But at least like this, she didn't feel as much.

It didn't hurt as much.

She stayed in that hazy bubble, content to let it drag her under until it swallowed her whole and drowned out everything else. At this point, feeling and being nothing was better than the alternative option.

Maybe that was why she hadn't expected the detective to be waiting right outside the last class of the day at her college, if only because the fact that she completely ignored his calls should have been more than enough of a hint to him.

Or not.

"Miss Falco," he greeted.

Not *unkindly*.

Still, a tension lingered in his voice.

Vanna's eyes flew wide, and students blew past her in the hallway as she came face to face with the man. For a brief second, she swung back and forth, checking the hallway to make sure the man who regularly followed her now wasn't standing anywhere nearby. Jacob Keefs seemed to understand exactly what she was doing.

"He's currently standing on the front steps waiting for you to leave."

She gave him a pointed look. "Then, you should know how *dangerous* this is."

"What choice did you give me? You ignore my calls, my

messages, and my texts. You haven't sent anything for me to use on the Guzzis when I know you were inside the mansion again just last weekend. What am I to think?"

"That something *happened*."

"And here I am to find out what that is."

Vanna steeled her spine, needing this *thing* with the detective to be over now. She didn't have a choice because of Mario, but even if she did, she no longer wanted to play this game. She certainly hadn't given him enough information to really hurt the Guzzis, but it was probably enough to begin the damage.

And wasn't that enough?

That alone killed her.

"I have nothing else for you, and my connection to the Guzzi family is dead."

The man smiled tightly. "Is that so?"

"It is."

"Or … is it something else?"

Vanna frowned. "What?"

"You were getting very … close to the young Guzzi man, weren't you? Did you get in your feelings, start getting a conscience about it all, or what? Do you think you're going to become the next Guzzi queen of that family if the man takes enough of a liking to you?"

She blinked.

And just as quickly, recovered.

"No," she snapped, "and again, I have *nothing*. I will no longer be helping you, or whatever investigation you have started on the family."

That wasn't the answer he wanted.

Rage dotted his cheeks red.

Taking one step toward her, the detective narrowed his eyes as he said, "You think it's only the Guzzis who could be hurt here, Vanna? What about *you*, hmm? The Dettis—they took you in, didn't they? You think I don't know what they do for business? What are the chances that something in their dealings will tie to you, and you'll suffer for it, too? How do you think jail will suit you?"

Fuck him.

She tipped her chin up. "Is that a threat?"

"Does it need to be?"

No.

She wouldn't play this game.

Not with this man.

Or another.

Ever.

"You know," she murmured, "my father kept recordings … and he journaled. Every single little thing about this life, all of it. I don't know if it was because he never wanted to forget, or because he wanted me to have something to go back to, but I know all about you, Mr. Keefs. I know the dirty deals you used to do with my dad, and how you helped him out a time or two. Oh, and I know how he helped you, too. The loans—guess your wife blew through money like it was fucking candy. What was that, to make up for the fact you were too focused on a career that was going nowhere instead of being home to warm her bed like she wanted, or something else?"

He took another step.

Vanna held firm. "I know all that, and more. Threaten me again, and it'll be the last thing you ever fucking do, I promise you that, sir."

He sneered.

She smiled.

"You fell for their trap, it's all over your face," he muttered, looking as though she disgusted him just by being in her presence. "That's what the Guzzis *do*. They dazzle you with their wealth, promise it can be yours, too, and then when you're in their web ... they drain you dry. You're just another weak little girl who can't measure up to them, but sure you were going to do your best and try to make it work, huh? It doesn't matter if you won't continue to help my investigation—I have enough to move forward from here, anyway. Thanks for that, couldn't have done it without you."

What did that mean?

What did that fucking mean?

She didn't get the chance to ask before he spun on the heels of his cheap loafers that still squeaked when he walked, and left her standing in the hallway.

It was empty now.

A lot like her.

Completely empty.

CHAPTER
15

Two fucking weeks.

Two weeks with no calls, texts, or otherwise from Vanna. Bene woke up alone the morning after his mother's dinner party, and it pissed him off. Not because Vanna had left like that, but because it didn't make sense. Never mind the strange conversation his twin apparently had with the woman at three in the morning when Beni caught her sneaking out of the house like she was running from something.

What was she running from?

That was the better question.

Bene had no clue, but his pride was just enough for him to wait her out, or that's what he thought he was doing. He figured, whatever shit had happened that sent her running like that, she would work through it, and come back eventually.

Right?

Weren't they working on something together?

Doing something?

Being something?

God.

He thought so.

So yeah, he gave her two weeks. Fucked around with his anger and stupid pride about not going to her first when she kept refusing to answer his texts and calls. Then, he decided to suck it up and do what he had to do to see her. It was all about making the first step, or that's what other people told him. Besides, maybe she had a good reason for running off like she did. Not that he would know that unless he went and spoke to her.

Which was why he was currently parked in front of her downtown building, sitting in the front seat of his Lambo, while arguing with his oldest brother. He had a million other things he would rather be doing, including getting inside that building to see Vanna, but one thing at a time. Rome wasn't built in a day, and all that good shit.

"Where are you?" Marcus demanded.

"In the city."

"*Right now?*"

"Uh, yeah."

"Bene, there's a meeting at the mansion today. For *everyone.*"

Right, everyone that was made.

Bene hadn't known about that until thirty minutes ago, however, and he had already been on his way to Vanna's penthouse, and he wasn't turning around just because his father decided to make all his men run in circles for him.

Okay, now he was crossing lines.

He fixed his thoughts, and put his attention back on his brother on the other end of the call. "Listen, I am on my way, Marcus."

"You're already *late.*"

"Yeah, well—"

"Yeah, well, fucking *nothing*," Marcus snapped. "Get on the goddamn highway, pull thirty over the limit if you have to, and don't make the boss wait another second longer, Bene. Do you hear me?"

Of course, he did.

Didn't mean he would listen.

Bene straightened up, sure.

He could still bend the rules.

Just a little.

"You were doing good, you know?" Marcus sighed loudly. "What happened?"

That woman.

All of her.

Instead of saying that, Bene replied, "I'm on my way."

He hung up the phone before his brother had a chance to respond which was just fine with him. Marcus would keep repeating the same shit, and Bene had nothing new to say. What was done was done—he'd work on fixing it later.

Simple as that.

Knowing he didn't have much time to fuck around, Bene left the Lambo running on the side of the street— risking a ticket, no doubt—as he headed into Vanna's building. The same as the last time he visited, he headed to the front desk first, ready to charm the woman waiting there with a smile on her face to get upstairs through the private elevator.

A new woman, actually.

She wasn't the same as the one from before.

What happened to her?

"Vanna home?" he asked, grinning. "In the penthouse, I mean."

Instantly, the woman's smile drifted away. "Sorry, no."

"So, she's not home or she doesn't want anyone up there?"

"No, she no longer lives here, sir."

Bene blinked.

What?

"I'm sorry?"

"The remainder of Miss Falco's things were moved from her penthouse last week, and the building has been made aware that a realtor will take over the sale of the property. Excuse me, but are you a friend or—"

What did that matter?

She wasn't here.

Where the fuck are you, Vanna?

"I have to go," he said, turning away from the front desk to make a beeline for the door. He didn't have time to stand around and have a conversation with someone who either didn't have the information he needed, or simply wouldn't give it to him. Throwing a hand over his shoulder at the woman's call to him, he added, "But thanks."

For nothing.

Bene's mind was still running a million miles a minute as he headed out of the building. Jumping into the still-running Lambo, he was happy to find that he hadn't managed to get a ticket stuck under the car's wiper, but that was likely only because he hadn't been inside for very long. It was the one good thing about this day.

The rest of it was just *shit*.

Where was Vanna?

That's what he kept asking as he raced out of the city limits.

Where are you?

Bene expected to find Marcus waiting for him when he arrived at the mansion—best case scenario, really. He figured his oldest brother would be at the ready to rip him a new asshole for being *way* too late to a *famiglia* meeting with the boss. Worst case? He thought maybe the meeting would be over, and his father would be sitting in his spot behind his desk, giving Bene *that* look. The one that said he wasn't even mad, just disappointed.

He found none of those things.

Nah, because it was a *raid*.

Of cops.

Like an infestation.

He pulled his Lambo in past the gate, watching the scene unfold up the long, winding Guzzi driveway leading to the mansion. He couldn't park farther in because of all the vehicles—police cars, a couple of SUVs, not to mention, all the vehicles that belonged to men who would be at the meeting with his father.

Fuck.

This was not good.

What was happening?

Bene jumped out of the Lambo with every intention of finding out. He weaved in and out of cop cars, trying to get as close to the mansion as he could. He slipped under the line of yellow tape that cut across the driveway about halfway up, uncaring that he probably just made more trouble for himself by doing it.

"Marcus!"

His brother turned at his shout, seemingly unbothered by the cop who was readying a pair of cuffs. Were those for his brother? *Why?*

"Bene, get the fuck out of—"

It was pandemonium.

Chaos.

Men were shoved out of the mansion one after another, two cops per guy. Each had their hands tied at their backs, and the closer Bene came, the more he realized this was getting worse by the fucking second. They hadn't even used proper cuffs to hold the men of the Guzzi Cosa Nostra, but instead, goddamn zip ties.

What were they?

Animals?

"Where's the fucking respect, huh?" Bene shouted at a cop who was currently shoving his other brother, Chris, against the side of a car with a set of zip ties at the ready.

"Bene, *don't*," he heard Marcus warn.

Too late.

Bene was already heading right for the mansion the second another couple of cops dragged out a familiar man. *His father*. It was unusual for Gian to *ever* leave his house before he was entirely ready for the day. That meant his hair was combed back, his three-piece suit was on, and his shoes were shined. He looked his best because his image had to come first when it came to the public, no exceptions.

Now, though?

His father looked *rough*.

Thing was, he'd been in a meeting.

So, he would have been dressed, and good.

Why was he missing his jacket?

Why was his shirt a mess?

His hair skewed, missing a shoe, and—

"Gian!"

"Cara, it's okay, *bella*, it's fine."

"Let me talk to my husband!"

Bene came around the last cop car keeping him from getting to his parents when his mother came flying out of the house, too. She moved for her husband, her hands curling around the arms that were tied to his back as she *begged* the cops holding him to give her just one second.

Please, she cried, *please let me hug him. Please, just allow me a moment with him.*

Instead of being decent, and giving his mother what she begged for—something Cara never did—the one cop let go of his father, and literally ripped his mother away from Gian.

She stumbled on her way to the ground. His ma *fell* because a cop dared to put his hands on her when all she wanted to do was hug her husband goodbye, and Bene saw red. He wasn't sure what happened after that, really.

Bene went *all fucking in*.

Might have hit a cop.

Might have threatened a couple.

It was how he found himself bent over the hood of a cop car, blood in his mouth, and his hands cuffed at his back, too.

Fucking perfect.

His night could only go up from here.

Right?

"Where were you before you arrived at your mother and father's mansion earlier?" the detective asked.

Bene tipped his head sideways, eyeing his lawyer for a response on that. This interview, as the cops posed it, although really it was just a fucking interrogation, had been going on for an hour and a half, but he was already done with it. Entirely. Depending on how the lawyer replied would determine whether or not he answered that question. The lawyer gave him a slight nod, and shrug, saying, "Your discretion to answer, as long as you feel safe to do so."

Right, right.

"I was in the city," Bene said.

"Where?"

"Downtown."

"Where?"

"At a friend's place. Or, I tried to see her. She wasn't home."

"What friend?"

Bene sighed. "Why am I still sitting here? You've pressed no charges, and all you've done is piss me off, and try to insult me. Now, you want to play another round of twenty questions? I don't have the patience for this shit."

Keefs peered at Bene over the rim of his reading glasses. "First, you were arrested because—"

"A cop thought it was okay to rip my mother away from my father after they practically dragged him out of his home with his hands zip tied at his back. What, they don't give you fucks enough money for a set of cuffs or two per pig, or what?"

The lawyer to his left coughed. "Easy, Bene."

Yeah, easy his motherfucking ass. This cop could eat his whole fucking ass, too, if he thought he was going to get a single drop of respect from Bene.

Unquestioningly, his father handled the arrest with the same grace, respect, and dignity he faced everything else in his life. That was what Gian Guzzi *did*. It's what a Don had to do for his family, and organization. These things were inevitable, and it was how he would be portrayed to the public *after* the arrest because of how he acted during the arrest that made all the difference at times. It was the same thing he taught his sons, too, even if Bene sometimes preferred to handle things in a more ... *undignified* manner.

Gian would have been fine.

But then his ma got in on it.

Bene wasn't doing that shit.

At all.

"*What friend?*" the man asked.

Jesus Christ.

The man wasn't going to let it go.

Not that it made a difference. Bene wasn't concerned with letting Vanna's name slip in this interview. She wasn't connected to the mob, and certainly not to his family. Hell, the woman hadn't even really known about his connections, right? She asked a bit, *hinted* that maybe she knew what the rumors were, but that was it.

It wouldn't hurt.

"Vanna Falco."

The second her name came out of his lips, the detective's writing—whatever he was scratching to the pad of paper in front of him—stilled all at once. He continued staring at Bene, though, and while he caught the hesitation in his hand, he also saw *something* in his eyes.

Was that … recognition?

Bene held the man's stare.

Keefs swallowed hard. "Hmm."

"Do you know her?"

The man shook his head, but Bene didn't miss the way his gaze narrowed a bit before he looked down and said, "Can't say that I do."

"You sure about that?"

Tells.

Everybody had them.

Including this cop.

"Absolutely sure," the detective replied. "I just find it interesting you were there, that's all."

"Why?"

"You don't ask the questions here, young man."

Bene scowled. "I heard what the RCMP were saying at the mansion, you know? About the maple syrup farms, and how they believe it's being used to launder money for my father and his associates. See, the thing is … our name isn't even attached to those farms. Not on *paper* … you look, see if you can find something, it's all third party companies who own those yeah? My knowledge of these farms are not an admission of guilt, put that on the record, thanks, and you won't find shit in those farms, but here's the thing, *Keefs*."

The detective arched a brow. "What about it?"

"Only *family* knows anything about us and those farms."

Or famiglia.

Or anyone who might have gotten inside his father's office.

Things were falling together.

Bene didn't like it.

It started with the way the detective seemed to recognize Vanna's name. And then he had to think about other things, too. Like the fact she just *showed up* one day in his life, and while things like that were certainly possible, he didn't believe in coincidences when he started adding up other facts. Her place was empty. She left him high and dry.

That woman was not who he thought she was.

"Did you have a rat talk?" Bene asked.

The detective laughed. "Again, you don't ask the ques—"

"Then, we're done here."

He looked to his lawyer.

Keefs huffed. "I'm not done with this interview."

Bene still didn't grace the man with his attention. He simply kept his attention on his lawyer, and let the man do whatever talking for him that he needed to do to get him out of this goddamn room and interrogation. Nothing had been found on him when he was arrested, and the arrest was only because he threatened a cop that got handsy with his mother. He knew for a fact they searched his penthouse in the city because they showed him the warrant, and so far, nothing came out of that, or they surely would have let him know.

They couldn't keep holding him.

That much was true.

Every Guzzi knew how this game with law enforcement was played. It wasn't their first rodeo, and it wouldn't be the last, either.

And that game?

It was all about waiting.

~

"To appease the bastards," his lawyer said as they exited the building, "I set up another interview with them next week. Only this time, it'll happen in *my* offices, and they'll be required to send their questions to me three days before the interview, so we can go over it and make sure your answers are appropriate."

Bene nodded, listening to what the man said, but more interested in the person standing on the steps of the police station. Marcus looked ready to throw a goddamn fit in his crumpled suit—but hey, at least he was standing on the steps and not inside in a jail cell.

"Later, okay?" he told his lawyer.

The man nodded. "I'll call the others. Get everything together."

"*Grazie.*"

Once the lawyer left his side, Bene headed for his oldest brother. Marcus glared at the building with a scowl that could rival the devil's. Before he even said a word, Marcus muttered, "They're holding dad—it's all fucking sketchy, and I am pretty sure the charges they've got on him are bogus bullshit meant to keep him in a cell until they can work something out on the money laundering and whatever else."

"You're off, though."

"Because they couldn't hold me." Marcus's gaze swung his way. "A lot like you, it seems."

"Yeah, well …"

The two quieted.

Where was everyone else?

"Anyone called about Ma?"

"Corrado is flying in—the rest of them, too. She's staying in their penthouse in the city for now, but I imagine she'll head back to the mansion once more of us come home."

"Chris?"

Marcus sighed. "His lawyer is finishing up inside, and he'll be out soon, too. It was only dad, and a few other men from the family that they're holding. It's all about Gian, though, not them. They're hoping the longer they hold a few made men, the better the chance they'll start talking. Which is exactly why—"

"We're out here."

His brother shrugged. "They'll never turn a Guzzi son on their father. *Ever.*"

Wasn't that the fucking truth?

They'd die first.

Bene shifted on his feet, his next words playing at the tip of his tongue. He had to say them, spit it out because all his suspicions seemed more real by the second, and this was bad. For all of them, so his feelings—that shit he felt for the woman he thought Vanna was—couldn't factor into this at all.

That *hurt* in his heart?

The way his soul twisted?

It was love.

Fighting to live.

He choked it out when he said, "I need to find out who she really is."

Marcus turned to Bene, brow raised. "Who?"

"Vanna Falco. I'm not sure she's who I thought she was."

His brother just stared.

Bene explained everything.

CHAPTER 16

"I knew that dress would look good on you."

Mario's compliment bounced off Vanna as she continued working at the stove. Stirring the melting chocolate to ready it for a glaze on a cake she made earlier, her work was far more interesting than anything he had to say. Especially now that she could no longer attend classes at the college. Everything was different, now.

And this home didn't feel like hers.

Even if he said it was.

"Did you hear me?"

His footsteps approached from behind.

Vanna sighed, still refusing to turn away from the stove. She didn't want to listen to him at all, but she was. She had to, otherwise his moods could shift faster than she blinked, and if she wasn't ready for the next swing, it might not end well for her. Mario always had a bit of a temper, but it seemed his fuse became *far* shorter with her.

She walked a fine line living with him.

Every single day.

"I am—I also have to continuously stir this chocolate because stopping at all will make it burn at the bottom, and the glaze won't be nearly as good, Mario."

"You can't talk and stir at the same time?"

Vanna's gaze narrowed on the swirling chocolate under her whisk. Not that he ever cared about her cooking unless he was eating it, but it was clear the man just didn't appreciate or understand what went in to cooking a dish like this.

"Do you want cake later, or not?" she asked.

Mario sighed, coming to stand directly behind her. So fucking close, in fact, that she could feel his hot breath on the back of her neck. As if that wasn't uncomfortable enough, his fingers drifted over the column of her neck, and he leaned in *closer*. He always did that. Invaded her personal space whether he was wanted, or not.

Then, he pressed a kiss to the side of her throat.

Vanna would vomit.

Soon.

If he didn't stop …

"Easy," he murmured at her stiffness. "Imagine how good we could be together, if you would just let it happen."

His hand skimmed up the side of her body, tracing her curves with his fingertips, but not *appreciating* them. No, his touch didn't want to enjoy having her, but rather … to *own* her. That was why she felt nothing when he touched her. She would rather take a short dive off a high cliff than be living in this man's home, sleeping in the bed across the hall from his, and playing pretend house until their wedding.

Except this was her life, now.

Hell.

And it would be her life long after she married this bastard, too. That much became painfully clear over the couple of weeks she'd been forced to be here living with Mario. He controlled everything from the clothes that she could wear to how she spent her days, and far more with no end in sight.

He tried to be nice—*sometimes*. He tried to make her think he cared—when he wanted to make an effort. Then, he went back to the asshole. The same person he always was.

Vanna wasn't stupid.

He only did that shit when he was trying to get something out of her. And for the last several days, he kept wanting the same thing. For her to fuck him, or at the very least, give him *something* physical. He seemed to be convinced that if the two of them jumped into bed together, it would change the fact that she was only there with him because she had no other options.

If she left, he would chase her.

If he caught her, he would kill her.

If she tried to get help … that wouldn't end well, either.

And unfortunately, she didn't even have the money to run. What little money remained in the trust fund her father left for her after his death was practically gone. She'd used it to live on from the time she was eighteen and put her through college—bought her penthouse that was now on the market, and likely wouldn't sell until *after* she married Mario, who would then take the money from the sale.

She had nothing.

At his fucking mercy.

The bastard knew it, too.

"Come on, Vanna," he said lowly in her ear. "It could be *so good.*"

"No, it'll be you fucking a dry hole, and me wishing it was over before it even begins."

Okay.

So, maybe she should have kept those thoughts in her head. Thing was, she had been tired of this game a long time ago, and now that she had clearly lost here, she no longer cared what happened when she opened her mouth and told the truth.

Mario's hand connected with her hip, his fingers digging in painfully and taking her breath away. Her hand on the whisk stilled as she dragged in a quick breath. "*Why?*"

Vanna swallowed hard. "What?"

"Why will you fuck anything else with a dick, but you won't even *look* at me?"

She didn't fuck anything with a dick.

A whole total of three sexual partners.

Bene being one of three.

Mario's real problem was that he wasn't one of them.

"I—"

"Once we're married, I'll no longer give you the option of coming to me willingly. I hope you understand that, Vanna."

"So you keep saying."

His hand left her hip and found the back of her neck instead. He grabbed hard enough to leave bruises behind, she was sure.

"Knock off the fucking *attitude*," he snapped. "Because I don't mind showing you what that attitude gets you in this house, you rude little bi—"

His threat—the same one of many that he simply recycled with Vanna—was cut off by the sound of a door opening and slamming shut before footsteps echoed in the entry hallway leading to the moderate sized kitchen. All at once, with the chance someone might see him being physical with her in an abusive manner, he let her go and stepped back.

Vanna breathed a sigh of relief.

And also scowled.

She'd burned the bottom of the chocolate.

Perfect.

Well, he could eat his disgusting glazed cake.

She didn't give a fuck.

"Mario, man," came a familiar voice as the footsteps came closer.

Mario swung away from Vanna, and she removed the pot from the burner. Shutting the stove off, she turned with the hot pot to take it to the kitchen island and begin the process of straining the chocolate as Mario's sidekick—demeaning? Yes, but also true—Jase came into the kitchen with a grin that annoyed Vanna instantly.

His next words only made it worse.

"Got some news you're gonna like, man."

Mario rounded the kitchen island, picking up a pear from the fruit basket as he passed. "And what is that?"

"Got word a certain boss was arrested at his house today."

"You serious?"

Vanna glanced up from her work, knowing better and that she should mind her own damn business, but she had never been very good at those things. Thankfully, neither man seemed to notice her interest in their conversation.

"Yeah, Guzzi," Jase said, "guess a couple of his boys were taken in, too, and a lot of the family's men."

It took every ounce of willpower Vanna had not to react to that statement. She knew better, anyway, because if Mario saw it, she would pay for the mistake later. Hadn't she already pushed his buttons enough for the day?

She thought so.

Better not to play with fire.

"How long until they're out?"

"Hard to say—some of them are already released. Not the boss, though."

Mario whistled low, turning around slightly to eye Vanna, and give her a look that screamed for her to keep quiet, and say nothing. "Sounds like something that might be good for our business. When the Guzzis are away, other families can *play*."

"Want me to call the boss, and—"

"Nah," Mario said, turning around again and taking a bite from his pear, saying as he chewed, "I'll call my father and let him know. See what he wants to do—there's a racket the Guzzis have on the east side with a distribution company that he's been trying to find a way into for a while now, and with them in an uproar, the company might be willing to switch to our side of things to keep the cash flow coming in for it."

Yeah.

She bet he was enjoying this.

Snakes never missed an opportunity to creep in.

"And we should celebrate this turn of events in the city," Mario added after a moment, taking another bite of that pear, "because business should always be celebrated."

The only time Vanna could leave Mario's home now was when he wanted to show her off. It could be a dinner at his parents' home with the rest of the clan, or taking her to a party at someone else's house, but it all came down to the same thing.

Showing off his beautiful thing.

His thing he *won*.

Vanna didn't get a choice either way, but she had learned quickly enough that the better her behavior on these little trips out, the easier Mario was to deal with when they returned to his home. *His home* because it still wasn't hers. She didn't care—it would never be hers.

Tonight, he'd brought her to a restaurant opening. A business that he'd apparently decided to invest in, and because he wanted to show off his growing status to the people that would eventually determine his fate after his father stepped down as the boss of the Camorra clan, the majority of his people were there to celebrate, too.

Vanna hugged a drink at the bar, trying her best to stay civil as each new person who had yet to see her ring, although they all knew of the engagement, came around to get a peek, and congratulate her once again. Thing was, no one seemed surprised about the marriage, even if it had been announced a month ago, but more like ... this had been inevitable to them.

Perhaps, that bothered her the most.

She'd lived in delusions.

The other thing no one noticed?

How all her smiles were fake and forced. The way she angled her body away from Mario when he stood at her side. And that despite her efforts to join conversations because that was polite and expected of her, she had little interest in these people or their life.

She'd always thought of it as *her* clan, too.

Even if that came with pain.

She no longer thought of them as hers at all.

"What are you doing over here again?" Mario asked as he came to stand next to her at the bar.

Vanna tipped up her glass for him to see. "Getting another drink."

Bullshit.

She'd been nursing this glass for fifteen minutes.

He didn't call her out on the lie.

"Well, my mother wants you to show her the things the designer picked out for the wedding. Indulge her for me, would you? It'll keep her happy, and then Senior will get off my fucking ass, maybe."

Ah.

She often wondered if Mario dealt with the same shit from his father that he put her through on a regular basis. Senior expected his son to behave *exactly right*—no excuses. The next potential boss for the clan, he didn't dare step out of line now, or risk facing the wrath of his father which never pleasant for the man on the receiving end. It even stretched as far as Vanna because God knew if Senior found out the truth about her involvement with another man, he'd blame Mario before he came for her, too.

As for his mother …

Vanna fought not to roll her eyes.

That fucking sham again?

She didn't pick anything for the wedding—the designer did it all. She couldn't even be bothered to choose a goddamn color scheme, and now he wanted her to pretend like she was having the time of her life planning this wedding just to keep his mother happy?

Great.

"Sure," Vanna said, sighing.

"Thank—"

"Mario, we got a problem."

He swung around, and Vanna followed the same path, although slightly slower. A problem for Mario usually meant good things for her, if only because it got him away from her for a little while. Vanna wasn't about to complain should that be what this was, too.

"What do you mean, a prob—"

Mario's words cut off as a group of men flooded the entrance of the restaurant. Vanna's heart stopped for a split second as her gaze landed on the man fronting the group dressed in black, tailored three-piece suits, their aloof auras spilling throughout the room and bringing the restaurant opening to a fast, silent stop.

All at once.

With just their presence.

"Bene," she whispered.

Thankfully, neither man standing there heard her.

But *God* …

She felt Bene.

From all the way across the room.

Worse was the way she felt his gaze when it turned on her after scanning the large space. It was as though he just *knew* she was in the place, and he intended on finding her. The two of them stared at one another from across the floor, and she swore the room disappeared for a moment.

Everything else went away.

It was just him.

And that rage in his gaze.

It burned.

She deserved it.

Did he know now?

Had he figured it all out?

The hatred in his eyes said *yes*.

"What in the fuck are they doing here?"

Mario's sharp question brought the situation back into sharp focus for Vanna. She tore her stare away from Bene, though it was the very last thing she wanted to do. Quickly, she counted the six men who accompanied Bene, two of which were his brothers … and the third, well, apparently his older brother's—Christopher—twin came back into town because a third brother that looked identical to Chris stepped around from behind the other men to stand with his brothers.

"They know we've been trying to get in on their racket with the distribution company for the last couple of weeks while they've been trying to get a handle on their legal issues, and—"

"Shut up," Mario snapped.

The man did.

His gaze slid to Vanna, but she stayed neutral, her expression holding that same indifferent stare while his burned with fire and fury. She could see his silent questions and demands without him needing to vocalize it, too.

Did you get them here?

You better not have done this.

Keep your fucking mouth shut.

"What do we do?" the guy to Mario's left asked.

The silence in the restaurant stretched on.

"Get them the fuck *out*."

"And cause a scene? It's not just the clan in here. *Outsiders*, Mario, think about it."

"*Fuck*."

His snarl slithered across the quiet floor.

Vanna saw the way it made Bene smirk.

"Go assure my father I have this handled," Mario ordered, eyeing his father fuming at the table nearer to the middle of the dining section, "before he blows a fucking gasket."

The man didn't hesitate.

Then, Mario turned on her, his back to the room, and his viciousness coming back out to play when he grabbed her arm hard enough to make it ache.

"And *you*," he muttered.

Vanna gave him a look. "What about me?"

"You stay put—don't draw that prick's attention while he's here. If *anyone* finds out you were fucking him, I will put a bullet in your skull, Vanna. Do you hear me?"

Yeah.

She heard him.

"*Answer me*."

"Yes, Mario."

"Have another drink. Don't even look at him."

Involuntarily, her gaze drifted over his shoulder to find Bene again. Now, the group had come a little farther into the restaurant, and Bene currently snatched a drink up from a table. One that another member of the clan had just ordered, but never even got the chance to enjoy before Bene downed it in one go, and then set it back to the table.

Mario yanked on her arm, bringing her attention back to him. "What did I just say to you, huh?"

"They're just flexing," she told him, "they know the Camorra was fucking in their business while they were distracted, and now they're here to show you how big boys play. If you're going to make moves like you did in their world, you better be prepared for them to answer you. Move is on you—keep throwing your threats at me or focus on making sure they know you won't be pushed around. It's your choice, but *everyone* is watching, Mario."

That did it.

She knew it would.

He let her go and turned to face the room again.

The room watched on.

Now, Mario walked the thin line.

Vanna liked that better.

The restaurant separated into two distinct sections, with a row of tables directly in the middle with regular patrons who didn't seem to have the first clue about the danger they were currently in that Vanna had dubbed *no man's land*. On the left side of the business, the Guzzi men dominated three tables, passing drinks back and forth, laughing at the jokes told between them, and ordering more food every so often.

On the right …

Well, the Detti clan *fumed*.

Perhaps it was because they couldn't actually do anything here when the Guzzis had yet to cause a problem. And that was the thing, wasn't it?

They just *were*.

Their presence, solid and loud.

A power play if she ever saw one.

Mario hadn't been ready for that.

"All right, I think it's just about time you *cafones* take your leave here," came the thundering voice of one of Senior's closest men as he stood from his table. With a narrowed gaze locked on the Guzzi men across the way, it seemed *he* had at least reached his limit of dealing with the outliers. Silence stretched on in the business, and for the first time, Vanna figured some of the diners who were just regular people off the street were starting to understand this situation wasn't normal as they glanced between the two groups.

Perfect.

So much for not causing a scene.

Marcus Guzzi spoke first. "We'll leave when we're ready —sit down, don't make none and there won't be none."

"What the fuck does that even mean?"

"A problem," Bene said over his shoulder, but passing something that looked like a card to his brother across the table. "Don't make a fucking problem, and there won't be one."

"I—"

"If your boss wants to have a discussion about why he's been encroaching on our business on the east side, then we'll chat," Marcus said, "but otherwise, I'm going to continue enjoying my food, and then *maybe* I'll leave when I'm done. And unless you're going to make me do something different, I would love to see you try, I suggest you sit down, and shut the hole in your face before someone else does it for you."

The air sucked out of the room.

Silence reigned.

Marcus went back to cutting the piece of chicken in front of him as though he wasn't bothered at all by the turn of events, and he hadn't just threatened a man. "This is good, not dry at all," he told the man to his left at the table, "so someone give the chef my compliments."

It took another ten minutes.

The Dettis conversed in hushed tones.

And then chairs were moved.

Tables pushed together.

On one side, Marcus sat with his plate of food, now alone at his table as the rest of his men scattered to all the corners of the room. On the other side of the table, Senior and Mario sat in their own chairs to face him for the *chat* he wanted to have.

With no one watching her ... or so she thought, Vanna took the chance to slip into the back hallway leading to the bathroom. She needed a breather, a second to be alone, and deal with the emotions warring in her mind and heart.

She didn't get the moment.

Bene followed her.

And when she spun around to face him as he entered the bathroom behind her, she swore the only thing she saw in his stare was pure hatred. It only worsened when his gaze dropped to the large engagement ring glittering on her finger.

Yeah.

He definitely knew.

CHAPTER
17

"Were you engaged to him the whole time?"

Bene wasn't sure why *that* was the first thing he decided to ask Vanna when he got her alone—a dangerous thing to even attempt, considering their circumstances, and yet he couldn't control the urge to follow her when he saw her leave the dining room. No one was even watching them when everyone's eyes were trained on the men sitting at the table opposite to one another.

God knew he should have asked her a million other things. Who in the fuck did she think she was coming after his family, to start, and had he been her target from the very beginning because she saw him as the weakest link in his family … or was he just a chance encounter that she couldn't help but take?

No, instead he asked about *that man*.

The one he saw touch her.

Get close.

Who he had been told, just recently, she was engaged to.

Engaged.

Vanna shook her head. "No, that was—"

"No suffices," he bit out.

"It's not the whole story, though."

"You think I care about your story?"

She blinked. "If not for an explanation, then why follow me back here at all?"

"Maybe I wanted the chance to choke the fucking life out of you while I could."

He expected to see fear from the threat.

She showed none.

Because *of course* …

She had to know it was an empty threat.

A lie.

One of many he was sure to speak with her.

"My whole life," she tried to say, "I was told this was my purpose … to take from your family the way they took from mine. That I didn't *have* a family because of yours. And by the time I started to think a past I had never even experienced wasn't enough to justify what I was doing, it was too late for me to fix it. No one knew what I was doing with you, or about my plans until much later when I was already trying to figure out a way to make it better, and it went downhill fast."

Things made sense, then.

It clicked all at once with the shit he knew about Vanna —information he had been able to get pulled about her family history, and where she came from—with the stuff he knew about his parents' history. How their worlds had intertwined before either of them even knew one another all because of a manipulative woman his father married before he ever even met Bene's mother.

Pasts always came back to bite.

And it *hurt*.

"I don't need you to tell me anything, you know?" he said, shaking his head as he sneered a bit. "Once I finally decided to really look into you, it turns out you weren't very fucking hard to figure out. Where you came from? Why you did this to us? I don't need you to say it because I know."

"I—"

He didn't care to hear what she had to say.

At all.

"No, it's my turn now," he snapped, taking one risky step toward her, "because I think you've had more than enough time to lie and tell me stories, didn't you?"

She said nothing.

Bene nodded, expecting that. "Yeah, you know, our parents never hid shit from us. They didn't want us to be ashamed of their life—of this legacy they made for us. I bet you think I didn't know about my father's first wife, huh? Or is it *you* that doesn't know very much about her, Vanna?"

Her brow dipped. "I only know what my father told me."

"Another bastard made by Gabriel Canali—the only thing he ever gave my father's first wife was his last name, and she was so desperate to get rid of *that* small piece of him that she was willing to trick my father into a marriage with her to do it, too."

Vanna straightened a bit.

Bene didn't back off in the slightest. "Oh yeah … and then when she had what she wanted from my father—to get away from *hers*—she couldn't get away from him fast enough. But don't worry, she came back just long enough to almost get my mother and brother killed, before she swallowed a bottle of pills, making sure to kill my uncle's child she was carrying while she did it."

Her throat jumped as his words slashed through the still air between them, settling like a heavy weight. He could see the understanding dawning in her eyes, the fact that she knew he was telling the truth … or at least the truth as he knew it.

And it didn't match with what she had been told.

Clearly.

"I get why you hated us—you thought we took from you, I bet," he said, ignoring the thickness building in his throat the longer he spoke, "but it means nothing to me, and it won't save you when the time comes for you to answer for what you did."

"I'm sorry, Bene, I *am*."

She reached out for him, but he couldn't have that.

"Don't touch me—don't fucking even come near me," he snarled at her. That surprise in her eyes, the *hurt*, had him barking out a bitter laugh. "How dare you look at me like I just did something wrong to you after *everything*? After what you did, you think you get to be hurt?"

"I do care, I care so fucking much, no matter what you think or say. It won't make that less true. Nothing else you said was a lie, but nothing I just said was one, either."

Bene glared.

Vanna held firm. "And I can't touch you now?"

"No."

"Why?"

"Because then you'll be too goddamn close." He pulled in a burning lungful of air, wishing it wasn't so hard to breathe lately. "And when you're close, all I can think about is how much I want to love you, but because you made me hate you, too, I don't know how to do both."

"But—"

"Don't speak because when your lips move, you lie."

"I don't *lie*."

"You *do*."

"I don't! Not right now. I'm not, I swear."

Her staunch denial only served to have his control breaking altogether. Before he could think better of it, he crossed the three feet between them, the force of him coming forward for her making Vanna step backward until she hit the edge of the counter. Not that it stopped Bene from crowding her altogether, his hands resting on either side of the wall for the vanity to keep her locked in place.

Now, she wasn't going anywhere.

"Go ahead," he said, getting closer until their mouths were only a breath apart, "go on and lie to me *again*."

She let out a shaky breath against the bathroom counter. "I *am* sorry. I would do anything to go back and—"

Still leaning over her, Bene dragged a handful of her hair back behind her neck so that he could murmur in her ear, "Except you can't change what you did to my family—to my father, my *mother*. And I'll do whatever to make sure I ruin you ... like you could only *try to do to us*."

She let out a cry as he pulled away from her. He turned to leave the bathroom. To just get the fuck away from *her*. He heard the shuffle of her dress as she, too, pushed away from the counter to probably come after him.

"Bene, please just listen to—"

"Fuck you. This is *it*. This is over."

Vanna's choked gasp made his shoulders tense. "Don't say that."

Again.

Again with that fucking shocked disillusion of hers. As though he was hurting her. Like she really fucking *ever* cared. As if this thing they had been wasn't just manufactured by her lies and bullshit, and not from something that was real on her part.

He swung around on her before he could think better of it. But she was already there. Right at his back. And turning so fast had him chest to chest with her. Her petite height caused her to still need to look up at him, and he leaned down further, too. Until their noses touched, and their eyes were level.

She needed to see it.

What she did to him ...

She should *see it*.

"You don't get to be the victim here. Don't look at me and act like I'm doing something *bad to you*. Do you fucking hear me? You never gave a shit about me before, not when you only wanted to tear my world down, right? Well, *good*, you did it, Vanna. But just because the person I thought would be my world turned out to be a fucking liar doesn't mean it stops turning for everybody else. And you don't get to act like I'm hurting you right now when from the start, it was all just bullshit."

Water lined her eyes.

Her bottom lip trembled.

He could already hear what she was going to say before she did—*knew* it would be the truth simply because her pain was most obvious, even if he was trying to ignore it while hurting her with his words because fair was fair.

Right?

They couldn't *be*.

Even if her original intentions for him changed.

After everything?

No way.

"If you would only let me explain," she whispered. "Let me tell you that I lov—"

"*Don't*."

He was so hyper-fucking-aware of their close proximity again. Of that sugary perfume lingering on every edge of her. How her makeup stayed perfect—a feat, he was sure—despite the tears that she freely let fall down her cheeks.

That she was more beautiful when she cried.

Somehow.

That he still wanted to kiss her.

Those lips, though.

And that something inside him just craved her—every horrible and perfect part of her.

Because he loved her.

But she didn't get to tell him the same.

Not now.

He understood well this was exactly why he didn't want to get closer to her when he first entered the bathroom. His entire mind went crazy around this woman. Stupid, maybe, if he were being honest. He reacted from emotions with her; he found himself willing to debase his integrity and raising *for her.*

To have her.

And that spelled bad news all over.

Vanna blinked, tears slipping from the corners of her eyes as she swallowed hard. She spoke as though she knew exactly what was running through his mind when his gaze fell to her lips, and then darted back up to her eyes. "Just do it, Bene. Will it make you feel better to use me because that's what I wanted to do to you? Don't pussy out now—you put the knife in, I'm letting you twist it. That's what you want? *Then, just fucking do it.*"

He lurched forward—those pesky emotions again—to get his mouth on hers. Their lips crashed together as he slammed her back against the counter. Those fingernails of hers, always manicured to perfect points, scored against his throat as she took his kiss just as rough as he wanted to give it to her.

All teeth, and tongue clashing.

Ruining her lipstick, probably.

Her taste in his mouth.

God.

Her back hit the sink counter hard, but she barely reacted to it at all. He only kept her pinned against the counter just long enough to drag her skirt up over her thighs and bunched around her waist. He lifted her to the granite counter, and her legs widened while her ankles hooked at his hips. Her hands did the rest of the work to undo his pants before dragging them down around his hips with his boxer-briefs to let his cock spring free to her waiting palms.

Tight strokes of her hands made his already hard cock feel like pulsing steel. Her words a breathless plea when she mumbled against his kiss, "Fuck me … please, just fuck me one more time, Bene."

Not that he was in any position to deny her, but all he needed was to hear his name on her mouth to cement that decision. But unlike all the other times the two of them had fucked—all the moments he took to enjoy himself with her, to *feast* on her and take her so high again and again, he wouldn't do that this time. Wouldn't give her all of that again when it would only kill him that he couldn't allow himself to keep loving this woman.

But he could fuck her, sure.

Like he hated her, and the very ground she dared to walk on.

It would be a lie.

A *terrible*, fragile lie.

Still, he could do it.

"Show me that pussy," he demanded. "And I'll fuck you the way you want."

Vanna dragged in a lungful of air as he drifted away from her lips, and without question, she let go of his cock to get her hands between her thighs. She showed no hesitation about pulling her nude panties to the side, the slit of her pussy a soft, wet pink already.

"Your turn," she urged.

The thing Bene loved to do the most when he fucked this woman?

Kiss her while he filled her full.

All those sounds she made.

How she tasted.

It was electrifying.

He didn't do that this time. He kept his hands on her thighs, forcing them wide as she tipped her head back to the mirror and let him stuff her pussy full of his cock. She didn't try to take more than what he gave her while he pounded into her, their words gone as they chased one last high.

It was so familiar.

Everything he wanted and needed from this woman.

All the things that no longer felt like his.

She shattered in his hold, her orgasm drowning him under a current of anger and lust all at the same time. Another three pumps of his hips, and he followed right after her, emptying himself deep as he held her tight to his cock.

Vanna whispered an apology again.

And a soft, *I'd give anything to change this.*

Yeah, him, too.

He was still as empty as ever when he left her spread open and leaking his semen on the counter when he exited the bathroom a minute later wishing so many things himself.

Too many things.

Impossible things.

~

Bene was still trying to shove the image of Vanna's heart-broken face out of his mind as he reclaimed his spot in the dining room. No one seemed to notice him coming back, and the meeting at the table continued as though nothing was out of the ordinary.

They were only here to make a statement, anyway. They wouldn't cause a problem as long as the Dettis didn't react to their presence with violence. Seemed simple enough, didn't it? That's how Marcus intended it to be when he demanded they do this.

Bene went along with the plan because …

Well, Vanna.

That, and because when he heard she was engaged to the

Detti boss's son, he—and probably the rest of his brothers and the men in *la famiglia*—assumed this whole thing had been one big plan on the Camorra's part. Put a woman in front one of them, see how close she would get, and go from there to adjust their plans accordingly.

Except in that bathroom, Bene learned that was likely not the case at all. This had been something *Vanna* did alone. After all, her desire to hurt them came from her own broken history. The Detti Camorra hadn't fucked with the Guzzi family in decades; they didn't have a reason to. So, that simply meant whatever the Dettis planned for the Guzzis came after Vanna was already involved. He found himself wondering why, and what might have changed for that to be the case.

And *goddammit*.

That just pissed him off more.

That he wondered *at all*.

The only thing he needed to worry about now was ruining that woman, and everything about her. *Anyone fucking near her*.

But her sad face drifted through his mind.

Those tears.

It felt like a betrayal to his family that he felt anything at all for her now, even if it was something like sympathy. It meant he had a heart—that he *cared*. It said he was a decent guy, but *fuck* … he didn't want to be a decent guy right now.

She fucked him over.

Lied to me.

And she was engaged!

Bene didn't have so much pride that he couldn't admit her engagement was the thing that bothered him the very most. It wasn't what made him want to commit violence— no, that was reserved for the fact he watched his mother cry one too many times since his father had been arrested because Gian still hadn't been able to come home.

In his own heart, though?

The engagement hurt like a bitch.

While Bene had the chance, and he was sure the meeting would go off just fine without him standing in the corner, considering the number of men they brought along for their side of things, he slipped out of a side exit door. The alleyway beside the restaurant gave him a moment to breathe alone, and try to piece together the rest of the shit that still felt entirely unknown to him in this whole mess.

And what a mess it was.

All because of *her*.

Bene fully intended to go back inside and rejoin the rest of his people to finish out this fucking shitshow once he had gathered his thoughts, but he didn't get the chance before someone else exited the door, and joined him in the alley.

He eyed the man.

Sized him up.

The guy did the same to him.

They were pretty even in height—towering over six feet, but he had an inch on the other man. Not much, though. Mario, to his benefit, looked like he regularly played on a defense line for a football team, and while Bene had a boxer's form from all his training with his twin, the man across from him still had a bit of size to his benefit.

Not that it mattered.

The bigger they were, the harder they fell when he broke their face.

"Mario Detti, right?" Bene asked.

Mario didn't confirm.

He didn't really need to.

"Let me make one thing very fucking clear to you, Bene Guzzi."

Bene tipped his chin up, considering his choices here. He didn't like the man's attitude, or the way he looked at him as though he were scum under his shoe. He hated the fact that Vanna wore a ring on her finger that came from this man. Part of him wanted to make sure Mario knew those things, but also had the greatest urge to rip the man's pride and dignity from him as he did it.

Broken hearts were the *worst*.

"And what is that?" Bene asked.

"You stay the fuck away from my woman."

He took a second.

Absorbed that warning.

"If she's *yours*," Bene said, "then why was she fucking me?"

"I—"

"And why would you need to tell me that at all?"

The man's face reddened. "She might have fallen in love with you, but she's in my bed now. Remember that, Guzzi."

… *huh*.

That was a strange way to phrase something like that.

Bene wondered … "But is she actually doing anything worth while in your bed?"

Mario blanched.

That answered Bene's question even if the man did try to come back with, "But she isn't in yours, is she?"

Oh, so they were being really petty now, huh?

"Is that because she wants to be in your bed, or because you forced her there?"

"You heard what I fucking said. Stay away from her."

Right.

He'd remember it, too.

Not for the reasons Mario thought, however.

∾

"Corrado, is Ginevra—"

"She took the baby over to see Ma."

"Good," Marcus murmured, his voice drifting over the mostly quiet office space in his mid-city penthouse, "she loves Caroline. At least, the baby will make her smile."

"She's not doing any better, then?"

The question from Beni had Bene flinching, although the rest of his brothers couldn't see it what with his back turned to the window. Here, he could let his mind run wild, and not have to worry about one of his siblings seeing the emotion on his face. It was hard enough listening to them try to make plans to take care of their ma while also attempting to figure out something for their father.

A mafia boss in jail was a dangerous thing.

For *la famiglia*.

For their father.

For *them*.

A Don behind bars, even if it was on trumped up charges while the police tried to gather the information they needed to make a better case on the wire fraud and money laundering, put him in a vulnerable place. Open to attack, which meant they needed to make sure their father was protected in jail.

As for their organization, with a boss away … men tended to become emboldened in the worst goddamn way. Like they thought this was their way to the top, as long as they could make it there before someone else did. They needed to keep an eye out for any of that shit happening while they handled everything else, too.

And for them?

Well, they just had to survive.

"And we're sure Papa's protection is going to hold while he's in that jail, or …?"

Chris's question hung in the air.

Corrado passed his twin a look. "Les is making some calls —it all looks good, though."

"Yeah, okay."

"Bene," Marcus said.

He glanced over his shoulder. Behind the desk, his oldest brother looked far more like their father than he should have, except right then it also seemed like he had the weight of the world resting on his shoulders. Bene didn't want to add to the pile of crap Marcus was dealing with, so for now, he just did whatever his brother told him.

"Yeah?"

"Make a trip to see Ma, yeah?"

"Of course."

"Take Beni with you—how long are you going to stay, anyway?"

Next to him, his twin shrugged. "As long as I need to. Tommas gave me the okay to be away from Chicago for however long this might take."

"Good to know. Back to these fucking *Dettis*."

Right.

Bene went back to staring out the window. He had other shit on his mind. Going over every moment he ever shared with Vanna, their encounter at the restaurant, the shit she told him, and then after … with the Detti bastard.

Something just wasn't right.

He *felt* it.

In his bones.

Something was wrong.

Maybe it was still those tears that had been in her eyes when she stared at him, begging for him to listen and to let her apologize. Or maybe it had been Mario, and the way the man's face drained of color when Bene asked if Vanna was actually *fucking* him when he tried to say she was in his bed now.

"You okay?"

Bene met his twin's gaze. Behind them, the conversation between their other three brothers continued like they couldn't hear the two of them. Given how low Beni asked the question, the rest probably didn't hear their conversation.

He nodded. "Yeah, sure."

"I know when you're lying."

"You could leave it alone, too."

Beni lifted one shoulder. "I mean, I *could* … but that's not really what I do, and definitely not where you're concerned."

Not a lie.

The bigger problem for Bene was that the things running through his mind wouldn't spell out anything good to his brothers, or the rest of their family. The fact he felt anything at all for Vanna, or that a part of him wanted to keep digging until he figured out what was wrong here, would only cause a major issue with his brothers.

She fucked them over.

Messed with their life.

Hurt their parents.

That should have spelled the end.

Completely done.

And yet …

"I don't know if everything with this, and *her*, is as simple as it seems," Bene murmured, "but if I said that to Marcus, or—"

"Yeah, that won't go over well. He'd kill her first, and not even bother to ask questions later."

Exactly.

"It won't get out of my head, though."

"Or is it her?"

Bene let out a hard breath. "Both, maybe."

"Do you think she—"

"Wanted to hurt us, yes. Got in over her head. But it's something else, too ... something more, Beni, and I don't know how to let it go."

"Maybe," his brother drawled lowly, "you don't let it go."

The two of them stared at one another until Bene put his attention on his reflection in the window. "Then, Marcus would kill *me*."

"Only if he finds out you're looking into shit, though."

Good point.

CHAPTER
18

"The red lace set certainly has an extra—"

"White. It needs to be the white one."

The seamstress who had been called to Mario's home to do a fitting for Vanna's wedding dress and brought along a half a dozen sets of lingerie for her to pick through to wear under the gown, met her gaze in the mirror. It was as though she was waiting to hear *Vanna's* opinion on the items she wanted to wear for her wedding day, but it wouldn't work like that.

"Why not pick something a little different for under the dress? Like a … surprise," the seamstress suggested. "That's what most women do."

"Vanna isn't most women, and she will be *my* wife, and since I will be the only man who gets to see what she's wearing under her dress, shouldn't I get the choice of what I want to remove from her body the night of our wedding?"

"Mario," Vanna muttered.

Not that her warning would do any good.

It was clear the woman helping Vanna try on the items wasn't comfortable. And to be fair, this wasn't the first set of comments—lewd, or otherwise—that Mario made while she was having her fitting. Undoubtedly the most unprofessional fitting the seamstress ever had to do, and Vanna felt bad for her because of it, too.

"What?" he demanded.

"The dress is white, Mario."

"I know, I've seen it."

Of course.

Because she couldn't even pick her wedding dress alone. Mario had to be there to do that, as well. Lest she pick out something that might make him look bad in front of the parish, and priest because apparently she didn't know how to act.

All of it … entirely ridiculous.

Vanna knew better than to cause an issue over it, though.

"Although …" Mario said, tipping his head sideways, his reflection in the large mirror showing off the action from where he stood in the bedroom doorway. Even her fittings weren't private, and since he kept such a strong hold of control over her now, it had to be done in his home because he didn't trust her to do it outside of his view. "That red set does *very* nice things for your ass, Van."

The girl—Courtney, was her name—cleared her throat. Otherwise, she said nothing even as Vanna stared hard at Mario in the mirror, clearly unimpressed with his behavior, and not trying to hide it at all. Not that it mattered.

She hadn't been hiding anything, lately.

She was unhappy.

He would be, too.

Vanna made him a promise, after all.

"Pick the white," Mario demanded.

"Fine."

He chuckled, taking a few steps into the room to come and stand alongside the bed. Fingering the sexy lace items on the bed, Vanna felt her stomach start to twist and turn at the sight. The heavy realization that she would be wearing those things *for him* coming to rest on her chest like a weight that just refused to be moved.

God.

She could barely breathe.

In a *month*—just thirty days from today—she would be married to Mario, and his to do with what he wanted. Including ripping all this lace from her body to use it as he wanted, and she wouldn't get a say.

For a while, she had done well to ignore it, but now as the wedding drew closer with every passing day, she could no longer pretend like this wasn't happening. As if this wasn't her reality, and her new life wasn't waiting right around the corner.

Mario picked up another item from the bed, holding it high and grinning salaciously at her from the end of the bed when he said, "White for the wedding night, but we'll be taking the rest of these sets to enjoy, as well."

He hid nothing.

Not his intentions.

His disgustingness.

Or anything else.

Courtney gave Vanna a smile—awkward as it was—and picked up one of the garment bags from the bed. "I will let you try on the last one alone, so I can go grab the dress from the back of my car, and we'll get on with the fitting. Okay?"

Really, she could tell what the woman wanted because it was written clearly all over her face. She needed to get the hell out of that room, and away from Mario. The same exact thing that Vanna wanted, but was unable to achieve, now.

For the rest of my life.

She didn't fault the woman.

No.

Simply envied her freedom.

"No problem."

Courtney wasn't gone from the room for more than a few seconds before Mario took another step toward Vanna. Even if she couldn't see his goddamn figure in the mirror, she could still feel his presence. Oh, she was still able to sleep in the bed adjacent to his bedroom. He had yet to force her into anything, but it was coming. Every day, his control snapped a little more, and he crossed yet another line.

How would it be on the wedding night?

That terrified her.

Even if she wouldn't admit it.

Mario came to stand directly behind her, his thumb skimming across the back of her neck as he admired the sight of her in the red lace. "Look at you, huh?"

She shivered.

Not from lust, though.

The disgust was strong.

"Could you not?"

His hand landed to the side of her neck at that response, flexing tightly enough to take Vanna's breath away, but not quite hard enough to *hurt*. After all, he left that for places where his marks and bruises wouldn't be seen by others. They were getting married in a month and had dinner after dinner to attend leading up to it which meant dresses, and blouses that would show off the column of her neck.

Makeup could only do so much.

"That mouth of yours …"

"What about it?"

She was done playing games.

Done playing along.

If he was going to hurt her, force her into this life with him, and do whatever the fuck he wanted with her, then he was going to have to fight for every piece he took from her. She settled herself on that, and it wasn't changing. She would give him nothing willingly.

Not after everything.

His fingers tightened again, *almost* hurting, as he leaned in close enough to murmur in her ear, "Don't worry—your mouth will pay for every comment you make to me. You'll only act like an ungrateful bitch for so long before you'll either learn to like the pain, or straighten up. It's your choice, Vanna, so choose wisely."

Fuck him.

That time, she didn't even bother to give him the decency of a response. However, if he wanted one, she couldn't be sure because the ringing of his cell phone coming from his bedroom across the hall had him spinning away from her without hesitation. Vanna might have breathed a sigh in relief, but she knew it would only last so long.

He would be back.

They both lived here.

This was her hell now.

Not sure how long it would take Courtney to get back with the wedding dress, Vanna decided to step out of the bedroom she used to sleep in, and head down to the bathroom where she left her silk robe the night before. Then, at least if Mario came back before the seamstress, she would be slightly more covered from his view.

Coming back down the hallway, Vanna heard quiet murmurs coming from Mario's bedroom. Not unusual, if he was chatting on the phone. He'd even closed his door, or *tried*, but it looked as through it caught on the tip of a shoe. The man was a total mess in his private spaces, and she didn't have the first clue how he could stand to be around it. Like a hurricane constantly went through his room, everything was *everywhere.*

Shoes kicked off where they fell, clothes tossed anywhere they landed, and more. For someone who looked so put together on the outside, Mario was a mess otherwise. Or maybe it was that he was just a spoiled man who needed someone to follow him constantly and pick up his shit like his mother had done his entire life.

The woman *did* come over to clean.

Often.

Although, his mother was quick to let Vanna know that once the two of them were married, it would be *her* responsibility to keep the house, and the man, in appropriate condition.

Right.

She kept it in mind.

Not.

Vanna stopped directly outside of Mario's bedroom instead of turning right to enter her bedroom. Not because he was talking on the phone, he did that all the time, but because of the voice that spoke back to him.

He thought he closed his door.

And put his phone on speaker.

The idiot.

Constable Keefs—the detective Vanna had been feeding information on the Guzzis—spoke to Mario as if the two of them were familiar, and this wasn't the first time they had a conversation with one another. She wanted to be surprised as she neared the crack in the door, and listened to them share a few words, but she couldn't be.

As Vanna had come to learn, Mario knew *a lot.*

About her.

The shit she did behind his back.

Her life away from him.

The man watched her more than she thought, and it only landed her in hot water. She was more interested in *why* Mario would do something insane like risk being attached to a cop, even if said cop was a fucking dirty bastard.

His next comment to Keefs on the phone explained exactly why. "No, with the Guzzis distracted elsewhere, they can't cover *all* their points of business, which is giving our clan ample time to creep in where they can't be at the moment. And yes, you'll certainly be reimbursed for your help here. I never thought she would take the bait like that, but Vanna has a way of surprising me whenever I think I have her figured out."

Oh.

That was it, huh?

Her meeting with Keefs wasn't because he thought she would be the perfect informant for his purpose, but because *Mario* thought she would be the easy ploy to use to further his endgame? Just how long had he known what she was doing with Bene?

The whole time, she bet.

Asshole.

Vanna had a good mind to enter his bedroom, and let him know she heard everything, but the smarter part of her brain had a better idea. Spinning on her heel, she headed for her bedroom as fast as she could go without making noise. A sense of victory spread in her heart at the item the seamstress had left sitting on the table next to the bed.

Her *phone*.

Vanna no longer had one of her own. Mario took it from her, and refused to give it back, citing the fact she could use it to call *that Guzzi bastard* as a reason. Like he couldn't just check her history and go through everything if he wanted it. Really, she figured it was just another way for him to control her.

Nonetheless, someone else's phone would do the job, and she'd noticed that the seamstress didn't seem to keep her device locked with anything more than a swipe on the home screen. Knowing how dangerous it was, and if she was caught … well, she might not make it to her wedding, not that she cared, Vanna headed back across the hall with the phone in hand. She already had the text messages up, and a familiar phone number typed in to ready for sending. Putting the video on record, she stuck the phone into the crack of the door, letting it pick up any sounds of the conversation Mario was still having with the detective.

Had she missed the good bits?

The stuff that might help?

Vanna didn't know.

But she had to *try*.

A part of her heart had never given up hope that she could somehow fix this mess she made—that eventually, Bene would hear her apologies, and understand that she knew she had made a horrible mistake.

This wasn't the apology, but it might help *him*. It wouldn't get her out of the marriage, but it very well might help his family somehow. And if it meant sacrificing herself, if he only used what she sent him to help his family and not her … well, Vanna would understand.

She wouldn't blame him at all.

The phone sent through the first recording, stopping at the max time it could record before it started recording again.

"And you're still good with the ten thousand a week transferred into the account?" Mario asked.

Keefs was quick to respond with, "Well, if you're doing better because of my work, then I'm not opposed to you paying me for advancement."

"Is that a demand, or—"

"It's whatever you want it to mean, Mario. I'm not sure how your father would feel about the fact you worked with a cop to get your clan further ahead in controlling Toronto, but if you think he'd like to sit down with me and have a chat about it, I am willing to do that."

"No need," Mario muttered gruffly, "an extra ten percent on top of the pile, then?"

"That'll work."

"It'll be in the next payment."

The phone automatically sent the next text message.

Vanna couldn't afford to record more, however. Downstairs, she heard the front door to the house close, letting her know the seamstress was done with her break—it was never about going to get the dress, she knew—and was now coming back.

Not wanting to risk it, Vanna headed back to the bedroom, texting a simple, *I'm sorry, Bene, and I hope this helps. Don't respond, it's not my phone. –V.*

Bene would know who it was. He could do with it what he wanted. She had done what she could. It took all of ten seconds for Vanna to go back and delete the text message thread so that the seamstress wouldn't know someone used her phone.

And by the time the seamstress was back in the bedroom, Vanna was already pulling down the straps of the red lace bra, readying to slip into the wedding dress that would surely feel more like a prison than it would a fairy tale.

Not that she could focus on those thoughts—her heart couldn't afford it, and she was not going to become that blubbering, weak woman who just gave in. That wasn't her, and it wouldn't be her simply because everything felt hopeless right now. Besides, she was already heartsick, it simply wasn't over the man she would marry in a month.

No, it was over the one she couldn't have.

The one she hurt.

The one she'd been meant to hate.

Every single night … Vanna cried for him. When no one could see, and no one would know, she broke down. She allowed herself to think of him, their short time together, and what might have been. He filled her thoughts all the time—day in and day out—but it was only at night, when she was truly alone, that she let herself be weak over it.

In a way, it felt like a punishment.

One she deserved, after everything.

He probably hated her now.

She deserved it.

And no matter what, she would do *everything* to help Bene fix this mess she made. At the risk of her own life, she would do it.

Today wouldn't be the first time.

Vanna settled on that.

What else could she do?

"All right," Courtney said, tossing the wedding dress in its protective bag across the bed, "let's get this on, and do a quick fitting. I suspect this will be the only one we'll have to do, considering you're quite trim, and haven't changed in size since last month when you picked the dress."

She hadn't picked it.

Mario's mother did.

Vanna didn't correct the woman.

"Sure," she said, turning away from the mirror.

"And be quick about it," came Mario's order from the doorway. Vanna met his stare, and he raised an eyebrow right back at her. It didn't seem like he was aware she knew his secret, or that she had been spying on him. "Because we have dinner at my parents with the rest of the clan in two hours, and I don't want to be late."

If the clan would be there, then business was happening.

Or *talks* of it.

Vanna wondered … what else she might be able to collect about the Detti Camorra? No doubt, a lot if she cared to try. She had focused on gathering damaging information on the Guzzi family, but tides changed all the time.

Right?

Vanna smiled at Mario. "Can't wait."

CHAPTER 19

"Unless something happens to Constable Keefs," Marcus said, "seeing as he's acting as the verifying witness to the information that was provided by the … informant, and he's the only one that can prove those documents came from your office seeing as how your name wasn't actually on the contract for the farms well—"

"We can't *kill* him," Beni snapped. Still on his sabbatical from Chicago to help them out until their father was released, or otherwise, Bene's twin had to state the obvious. Which only earned him a glare from Marcus. "I'm just saying, we can't do that, but you posed the statement like it might be an option."

"I didn't pose anything," Marcus replied heatedly.

"Relax," Chris muttered, "both of you."

In the corner of the room, standing in the only portion of shadows, Corrado scrubbed a hand down his face, his sigh echoing. "Marcus and Beni are both right. I mean, if you want to get technical, and Chris has a point—stop snapping at one another. It doesn't help, and it gives me a fucking headache."

"*You*," their father said from behind the metal table where his hands rested on the top, wrists cuffed, and connected to a bitch link in the middle, so he couldn't even stand from his position, "need to go back home to Ginevra, Les, and the baby."

Corrado dead-stared their father, saying nothing. His lack of words said it all, anyway. He, like the rest of them, wasn't going anywhere until this was said and done. Until they either got their father *out* of jail, and off these bullshit charges of wire fraud and attempted money laundering, or they figured something else out. Which so far, was proving impossible.

"As I said," Corrado drawled slowly, turning his attention back to their brothers, "Marcus is right in that something has to be done about the detective. Constable Keefs is the star witness to all of this, it'll be his word that seals the deal on the authenticity of the photos of the documents taken from Papa's office. The only thing *saving* us right now is the fact that when they raided the house, all of those documents had already been destroyed. So, what they have is his word, and if they don't even have that ..."

Yes, because their father only kept something that showed illegal activity just long enough to look it over, do what he needed with it, and then he burned everything. Keefs was the only person, considering the informant—Vanna—was no longer cooperating with the investigation.

Apparently, for the protection of the anonymous witness, as the police had stated in their last media conference, they would not force her in to testifying when they had enough using the Constable on the stand for trail, should they make it that far.

"Except we can't kill him," Chris said to Corrado.

"No, and Beni was right on that, Marcus, so chill."

Marcus, the only one of the five brothers sitting at the metal table with their father, considering there had only been two uncomfortably hard chairs placed in the private conference room at the jail for them to visit with their dad, scowled but stayed quiet. Because he knew Corrado and Beni were right, no doubt, but it still pissed him off a great deal.

Bene didn't blame him.

"Killing him," Corrado continued, ignoring their oldest brother's attitude, "would instantly come back to us, no matter how we framed it. And when we get Papa off these charges, because we will somehow, we need as little attention on us as possible. Then, he can slip back under the radar, and we won't have someone up our asses every single time we do business. It's the smart thing to do, but killing that bastard? That'll ruin everything. We need to figure out another way to make the detective unreliable to his superiors and the judge."

Things were not simple.

It wouldn't be easy.

This was bad all around.

No one needed to say that out loud for the rest of them to know it was true. Whenever they were around their ma or dad, the boys kept an upbeat demeanor. They never made it seem like this was a hopeless situation, and Gian would be stuck right where he was until he was found guilty, and then moved to a prison. Never did they suggest to their ma that her husband wouldn't be coming home to her.

Still, there was a chance.

They were running out of time to figure it out.

"I hate that detective," Gian muttered. "Just like his fucking partner years ago. They're cut from the same cloth, and it isn't like *ours*."

Bene did well to keep his mouth shut at his father's comment. Not that Gian was wrong—he also wasn't entirely right. The phone burning a goddamn hole in his pocket constantly would confirm that, given the recorded phone call Vanna sent him a couple of weeks prior. The detective was just as bad as any of them when it came to dirty money and bribery, but he liked for everyone else to think he was the good guy cop at the same time.

Still, he kept his mouth shut.

Now wasn't the time.

And … well, if he were honest, it wouldn't end well for Bene if he outed to his brothers and father during their weekly jail visit that he was still—even if it was only through random text messages from phone numbers he didn't recognize—attached to Vanna Falco. No, he wasn't seeing her, and he sure as hell wasn't fucking her, even if she made regular appearances in his dreams, but he was in contact with her.

He was using her for all she gave.

She was willing.

He had to do something for his family because no one else was getting anything done on their side of things. Their father was still in jail, his first bond hearing denied because he was considered a high flight risk what with his available funds and ties all over the world. His brothers pulled every single string they had, called in every contact they might be able to use, and still nothing.

So yeah, they might hate him later.

They'd be pissed he used *her* info to help.

Bene would do what he had to—if it worked, and it got his father free, then wasn't that all that mattered at this point?

He thought so.

Now, it was just a matter of figuring out *how* to use the info he had been given from Vanna on the detective, and more recently, about the men of the Camorra. Mario, and the bastard's father … their people. All their recent, illegal business dealings were on his phone to be used whichever way he saw fit, but he just hadn't figured out how yet, or if it would even help.

"And you," his father said.

Bene looked at his dad, doing his best to ignore the fact Gian's usual three-piece suit had been replaced by a drab, gray jail uniform that didn't even fit him that well. "What about me?"

"Make sure you stay out of trouble, son."

Right.

What his father really wanted to say was *make sure you stay away from that woman, Bene.*

He could see it in Gian's eyes.

"Let's just worry about you right now, Papa."

That's why they were all there.

And Bene had never been a good liar.

Bene and Beni lingered midway on the steps of the police station where their father was still being housed in the jail as the rest of their brothers conversed a few steps down. Corrado was apparently hitting a flight to New York to spend a day or so with Ginevra while Alessio needed to head to Vegas for *something*. He'd be back soon enough, he promised. Chris was heading across the city—a politician to bribe, if he could make it work.

Marcus had to handle business.

The world didn't stop turning.

It only felt like it.

"Handle your shit, yeah?" Marcus called over his shoulder to the younger twins. Bene and Beni, still mirrors of one another even after everything, nodded in sync without prompting. "Good, and keep me updated on Ma, Beni."

With that said, the rest of their brothers dispersed. Bene and Beni, however, still remained on the steps of the jail until every single one of their siblings had disappeared, and it was safer for them to chat about the phone burning a hole in Bene's pocket.

Because *of course* ...

He trusted his twin more than anyone. There was no chance in hell he would do something like go behind his family's back without telling Beni. No judgement, his brother would do whatever he needed to help him, and that was that.

"Anything new?" Beni asked.

Bene nodded. "Where's your phone?"

Saying nothing more, Beni pulled his own smartphone from his pocket. Bene's came out, too, and he placed the phones back to back. Turning his home screen on, all he needed to do was touch the transfer data button on the settings app, and everything Vanna had sent him from random phone numbers in the last two weeks went straight to his brother's phone. After it was all done, Beni spent a minute or two going through some of it.

"You're not answering her back, huh?"

Bene swallowed hard. "What, you think I should? After what she did, you think—"

"I think you're in love with her, and sometimes, people we love do things that hurt us for reasons we can never understand. It teaches us about forgiveness and just how capable we are of forgiving someone else in a way nothing else can, Bene."

He sighed.

His twin waited him out.

"She's getting married in two weeks," he muttered.

Beni shrugged one shoulder, as though that little detail didn't matter to him a bit in the world. And who fucking knew, maybe it didn't. It mattered to Bene. *A lot.* "Yeah, still not sure that's because she wants to, or someone demanded it."

"Doesn't matter. It's still happening."

"And you still love her," his brother pointed out.

"What is your point?"

"Well …maybe I'm worried about you."

"I'm *fine*."

He couldn't tell a bigger lie.

He was far from fine.

Bene's thoughts warred with his heart. His loyalty to his family battled with the love he felt for a woman whose only intention had been to take away the things that meant the very most to him. And then he remembered her tears—the way she tried to apologize, even though he refused to let her even speak the words. He couldn't get the image of her pain and grief out of his head when he said horrible things to her, even if they were deserved.

Those images were burned into his mind, now. Impossible to remove, and because he couldn't get rid of them, he was forced to think about them all the time, and what they might mean. Like the fact that yes, he absolutely believed she loved him, too.

Yes, after her attempt to help him with whatever info she could gather and send, he believed she spoke the truth when she said she regretted the things that she had done, except it was too late. She couldn't fix it now.

They were doomed.

An impossible thing.

And he still wanted her.

Fuck him for wanting her.

"It's a complicated thing," Bene murmured, staring at the building across the street from their current position. It was far easier than staring at his brother who would see the truth in his eyes the moment he met Beni's gaze. "And not a thing I think is worth trying to fix, if it even can be now, you know?"

"Don't say that. Anything is possible."

Bene barked out a laugh. "And what do you think would happen if after everything was said and done, I brought her home again? *Oh, let's have a do-over, Ma, meet the girl I love that helped put your husband in jail.*"

"I'd be more worried about Marcus, actually."

"Fuck off."

He laughed, though, as weak as it was because his brother wasn't wrong. Marcus's protective nature really came out to play lately, but especially where their family was concerned. He wasn't fucking around anymore, and he wouldn't hesitate to end someone if their intentions for the Guzzi family was less than innocent.

Beni cleared his throat, glancing down at the phone in his hand. "Anyway, on this shit here ... I'll take it to Uncle Tommas and see what he can do."

"Don't let him—"

"He won't tell Papa it came from you, or that Vanna had anything to do with it. And besides, he's just going to pull his contacts, work some shit, and see what he can get done for the Camorra and the detective. *Maybe* it'll work for what Corrado was saying in there earlier about making the detective unreliable. And hell, if we can throw in removing that Camorra clan from the equation, too, then even better."

"Yeah, okay."

"You gotta give the process time to work, man."

He would.

It was still hard.

"What if she doesn't get married?" his brother asked after a moment.

Bene's chest ached. "They'll still hate her."

"But you don't."

Didn't he?

God knew it felt like it sometimes.

Love.

Hate.

Such a fine fucking line.

"I'm heading over to see Ma at her and Dad's penthouse," Beni said, "do you want to come, or—"

"Tell her I'll be by later."

His brother shot him a look. "What else do you have to do?"

More things he shouldn't.

What else?

Bene shrugged instead of answering.

Basically, his life in a nutshell now.

She didn't smile.

At all.

In fact, Vanna constantly looked as if she was ready to kill her fiancé whenever the man was in breathing distance. Sometimes, she did well to hide it, and other times … she didn't even try to hide her displeasure.

Now was one of those times.

Bene, from his position hidden in an alley across the street from a restaurant that Vanna and Mario frequented throughout the week, he watched as the two of them stood face to face in front of a running town car parked on the curb. The man driving in the car stood near the rear passenger door, ready to open it for the two when they wanted to leave, but they weren't paying him any attention.

Probably because they were too busy glaring.

And their voices?

Loud enough for him to hear.

That was not a couple in love.

Not in the least.

God knew he had no business spying on these two, especially because he wasn't doing it to help his family in their current situation. No, he followed the two because a part of him still wanted to know what was happening here—*why* was she marrying that man, and had everything between them been a lie?

Bene learned more than he wanted.

More than his heart could handle.

"What did I tell you, huh?" Mario demanded.

Vanna stared back, unbothered. "I'm not going to be pleasant just because you tell me to fix my face, put on a dress, and go out to look pretty on your arm, Mario."

"You will do whatever I tell you."

She let out a bitter laugh.

God.

It hurt in Bene's chest just to hear it, and it wasn't even directed at him. It sounded like a mixture of desperation, anger, and *more*.

"You really haven't figured it out yet, have you?" Vanna asked.

"That you're going to be my wife whether you like it or—"

"You can't *make* me want you, and you won't force me to be your fucking pet. You didn't like the way I acted in there tonight, then too fucking bad for *you*. I'm not a doll for you to play with whenever you feel the goddamn need."

"Listen, you'll either get in line, or you won't like what happens when you don't."

"I don't love you!"

"Watch your fucking *tone*," Mario snarled, "before I cut the tongue right out of your mouth. We'll see how much attitude you give me then, huh?"

Jesus.

He was still mad at Vanna.

Still had things to say to her.

Despite all that, it took every ounce of his will power to stay hidden in his spot when what he really wanted to do was cross the street and beat that man into the pavement for threatening Vanna like that. For some reason, he doubted it was the first time.

One of many, likely.

Even from his position in the alley across the street, Bene could still see her jaw clench. That fire in her eyes? Clear as day.

Her pain?

Echoing.

"I hate you," Vanna said loudly. "And that won't change … not now, not after you make me walk down the aisle, and not after you force me into your bed to act as the easy hole to stick your dick into. *It won't change.* I hate you."

Yeah, Bene learned all kinds of things.

And it only hurt more.

Mario's hand struck out, his fingers catching Vanna under her jaw in a tight grip as he forced her head back so that she had to stare up at him. Bene's hands clenched into tight balls at his sides as he willed himself not to move.

He shouldn't even be here.

Shouldn't see this happening.

He shouldn't *care.*

This only made a complicated situation even more complex. He had so much shit he needed to say to that woman—some of them would hurt her, and others were simply the truth that needed to be said. The phone in his pocket, with her text that said *I'm sorry* constantly mocked him because yeah, he knew she was. He still didn't know if it changed anything, though.

But this?

Knowing what he did?

Seeing her with him?

Well, that changed everything.

Bene still didn't know what it might mean. He did know that whatever it meant, he wouldn't try to figure it out over random texts that he couldn't even answer back. And he couldn't have that woman at all if he couldn't get back the things she'd helped to take from him.

So, where did that leave this?

And them?

A mess.

That's where.

"And yet," he heard the man tell Vanna while he squeezed his eyes shut, "even if you hate me, you'll still be mine to do with whatever I please. So, who's really winning here? You should make this easier on yourself, Vanna, and give me what I—"

"I'll never be yours."

No.

Because she was Bene's.

Fuck his whole life.

CHAPTER 20

There were several things Vanna didn't want to do.

She didn't want to be getting married today. Not to mention in a church that wasn't the one her father used to take her to every Sunday morning. She didn't want to wear a dress that looked more like something straight out of a princess movie instead of something more suited to her style. She didn't want to be promising her life to a man she could never love when she still hadn't even been able to properly apologize to the one who still owned her fucked up, broken heart.

And what she *really* didn't want to do?

Be bent over the toilet in her private suite, puking into the porcelain bowl while a pregnancy test on the counter told a truth she had refused to admit until now. Somehow, she managed to pull the *many* layers of her chiffon gown away from the toilet before her small breakfast came rising in her throat.

A feat of fate, she was sure.

Standing from the toilet, she quickly flushed the mess down, avoiding looking at the spinning, disgusting water as it went down. That wasn't the only thing she pointedly ignored, either. The blinking pregnancy test with it's flashing *Pregnant* on the small screen taunted her as she went about washing her hands and checked her reflection in the mirror.

Make up still perfect.

Dress unstained.

Certainly nothing to say her life as she knew it was ending today, and it was all because she had brought it on herself.

Oh, her stare was dead, for certain. In her gaze, she found *nothing*. No emotion, and no life. So far, she had managed to hold it together for this horrible day. How long that would last … Vanna didn't know.

Finally, she dropped her stare.

The test looked back at her.

Pregnant.

The word flashed as fast and clearly as it had when she took the test twenty minutes ago. The test was supposed to take thirty seconds to give the positive or negative result. Like everything else in her life that seemed to be one giant joke lately, the test took all of ten seconds before the word *Pregnant* started to blink.

That's when she puked.

When had she started to suspect?

Vanna couldn't put her finger on it. Maybe it was the fact that two months ago, when Mario forced her into his home, she'd lost her freedom which meant also losing access to her doctor who handled any medication she needed. A missed appointment left her without the birth control shot that she had done *religiously*.

Never failed.

Until now.

And then she had that moment with Bene in the restaurant bathroom. A split second of weakness where she didn't think to say—*I'm not safe.* It wasn't his fault, or hers, really. Bad decisions seemed to be par for the course with them, and this was just another one of those added onto a very high pile that was still growing every single day.

Her period never came a month or so after missing the

shot. It could take a while, the doctor had explained when she'd first starting getting it, and they were required to tell her every last detail of the birth control. She kept holding onto that—it *would* come.

It didn't.

Her mornings went from ignoring the passing days on the calendar to attempting to hide the fact she vomited *minutes* after waking.

Because God …

If Mario even suspected she was pregnant, he would know it couldn't possibly be his child. She'd not let him touch her once, despite his efforts. Apparently, even a monster like him could have limits because he kept his word on that.

For now.

Until tonight.

And damn … what happened then?

She stared at the pregnancy test again, remembering how quickly she had slipped into the gas station around the corner from the church to grab it while her chaperone stayed in the car, convinced she just needed some Tylenol for a headache.

She had to know.

Before she walked down the aisle.

Before it all ended for her.

She had to know.

And now she did.

She was pregnant with the child of a man she loved, but who hated her, and she learned the news on the day she would be forced to pledge her life, body and soul, to a man who wasn't worthy to lick the soles of her white leather heels.

Mario would kill her.

And her child.

Bene hated her.

And he didn't know about the baby.

How did she fix this?

She couldn't.

A knock on the bathroom door had Vanna glancing up and meeting her gaze in the reflection of the mirror. Gone was that passive, dead stare. Now, she found a line of water dampening her dark eyes, threatening to ruin her composure and the perfectly applied makeup that hid the bruises on her throat and her skin that didn't quite gleam the same way it used to.

"Yeah?" Vanna asked.

"Are you okay in there?"

She wished it was someone she cared about behind the door, waiting for her to finish helping her ready for her wedding. Her mother … *God*, her father, even. She still loved her father; she always would, and she wished he was here to help her get through this awful day if she couldn't, at least, have what she wanted.

Someone who loved her.

She wished this day was for her and someone else.

She wished *so many things*.

Things that could never be.

Sorry, Daddy, she thought, *sorry that I couldn't do what you wanted me to. Sorry that I wasn't who you wanted me to be. I'm sorry your vendetta couldn't be mine.*

Because that was the thing, right?

This vendetta had never really been hers.

And look where it led her.

Her gaze found the bouquet of white roses that she'd managed to toss on the side of the counter before throwing up her breakfast, and the string of rosary beads that twisted around the stems covered in white silk.

Her father's rosary.

One of the only things she had left.

She understood now that undoubtedly, her father's choices and beliefs about a man and a family he thought wronged him was likely the making of his own blood. *His father* did that with his mistreatment, and constant rejection of Adam. He'd believed that if only he could convince his father he was worthy, and not the bastard he'd been told he was his whole life, then he and Gabriel would be better.

Instead, his father died before it could happen.

And he just passed on that unhealthy love to her.

In a new way.

"Vanna, are you listening?"

No.

She spoke so they didn't break down the door.

"I'll be out in a minute," Vanna said.

A lie.

Another to add to the pile.

Maybe Bene was right.

Maybe she was just a fucking liar.

In her blood.

Fused to her DNA.

How else could she survive now?

How else would she protect this child?

Bene's child.

Even if he hated her, she would do whatever she had to … everything she needed to, even if it meant sacrificing her own happiness, to make sure his child was born alive, well, and *loved*. And maybe, *someday*, she could fix this.

But today was not that day.

And after today, her life was not her own.

"You have five minutes before you need to be downstairs," the woman behind the door called. "So, let's not waste time. Everyone is antsy to get the ceremony started."

Right.

"I'm coming."

Except she didn't move.

She couldn't.

Someone would drag her out of the bathroom.

That she could promise.

Run.

Run.

Fucking run.

Vanna's thoughts kept screaming at her even though she knew it was impossible to do what her heart wanted. All it took was a look down the corridor outside of the doors leading into the main floor of the church to find the man standing there, watching her. At her stare, he had the nerve to cock his eyebrow, like she needed a reminder what he was standing there for. No, she knew very well.

Not that he needed to, but if he raised his suit jacket, she knew a gun would be tucked into his waistband. At the ready, in case she decided to do anything stupid. Or, that's how Mario put it when he visited her earlier. The bastard was determined to see this day through, no matter what.

She didn't have anyone to walk her down the aisle—yet another sad thing about this whole farce—so she was stuck waiting behind the large, double doors alone until the organ changed to the traditional wedding march.

With a new chaperone.

Who wouldn't let her run.

Her fingers curled tighter around the bouquet as she glanced to the side, in the opposite direct of her current chaperone. That way only led to the private quarters of the church where she had gotten ready under the watchful eye of Mario's mother, and other women from the clan. The same women who practically pulled her from the room, and dragged her down the hall when she didn't want to go willingly.

A beautiful day for a wedding.

Smile, it's your wedding day.

This is a privilege for you, Vanna.

Their words still rung in her mind.

Still taunted her.

Vanna heard the music change beyond the closed doors —the church organ muted through the thick, darkly stained wood. The song that meant it was her turn to walk through the doors after the only person who went before her, a young girl from the clan who acted as a flower girl. Her gaze went back to the door, her veil shrouding her features just enough to hide the fact that she couldn't smile, and she barely held back tears.

God.

She wanted to cry.

More than anything.

A part of her knew, though, Mario would like that too much. And besides, she had never been that woman. The one who cried her way through shit that was out of her control. No, she always fought her way through it, instead.

This wasn't one of those times.

There was no escape.

The doors were pushed open from the inside, making them swing toward her and giving her a good view of all the people standing inside the church. Instead of focusing on their faces, she stared at the white satin aisle runner dotted with red and white rose petals.

She breathed deep.

Willed away the pain.

Prayed for the nausea to subside.

The music played on—it was her turn to walk. All she needed to do was take one step, and then another. Keep going until she reached the end. To where Mario currently waited with a burning gaze zoned in on her like he could read her mind and knew exactly what was running through it. How she was still trying to figure a way out of this.

Something.

Anything.

She could force herself to do this. She could.

What choice did she have?

But *God* …

She didn't want to.

That made it harder.

Holding the bouquet tighter, letting her father's rosary bite into her fingertips, she held the roses closer to her stomach. Her fingers brushed against the beaded bodice of her gown covering her still-flat abdomen, but just having that moment was enough to settle her nerves for the moment. She didn't dare outright *touch* it.

Not with all these eyes—

"It's a *raid!* It's a raid!"

Vanna swung around fast at the shouting coming from behind her, the bouquet falling from her hands to the floor. Her father's rosary spilling to the carpeted entrance of the old church as the man rushed past her, one of the soldiers the Detti boss had demanded watch the outside of the church throughout the ceremony.

He blew by her.

Still shouting.

Raid!

It's a raid!

She didn't care about him.

It was the others coming in through the front of the church. And the ones she heard shouting from *within* the church, too.

"Police! RCMP, everyone put your hands up!"

"*Police! RCMP! Les mains en l'air!*"

Vanna's hands flew up high. She was one of the first to be arrested, RCMP officers spilling into the church through all entrances and exits. Hell, they brought everyone, it seemed. She hadn't seen that many cops in one place in … a long time.

She didn't get the chance to ask questions. Not anything beyond, "What am I being arrested for?"

The cop's answer?

"Precautionary."

What the fuck did that mean?

She also didn't get to appreciate they ruined the wedding in the nick of fucking time. And after the cop who slapped the cuffs on her had dragged her out of the church and put her in the back of a cop car, Vanna was sure she saw a familiar figure watching from across the street. He looked the same as he always did—black leather, a face made to sin, and a dark gaze she could feel on her long after it was gone.

Bene.

He'd been there.

Waiting.

～

"Miss Falco, is it?"

Vanna glanced up from the sleeves of her hoodie where she had been pulling at the fabric to keep her hands busy. The plain-clothed cop that slipped into the room she had been housed in after arriving at the station gave her a smile.

A tight one.

It wasn't warm at all.

"That's me," she said, "but I can't say I know who you are."

He arched a brow. "Constable Andrews, but you can call me Detective, if you'd like. I work with the division for—"

"Am I under arrest?"

"No."

"Then, why I am I still sitting here?"

At least, someone had the decency to grab the bag of her clothes from the private dressing room in the church. A female cop accompanied her to a bathroom to change, and pack away the wedding dress and veil she hoped to *never* see again.

No one answered her questions.

She asked a lot.

"We'll get to that in a moment," the detective said, closing the door behind him. "Before I ask a few questions, is there anything I can get for you?"

Vanna scowled. "A lawyer?"

"Do you think you'll need one being you're not under arrest, and I'm only here to ask a few cursory questions relating to your connection to your fiancé's family, their business, and your previous status as an informant for a ... Constable Keefs?"

She straightened in the chair.

No one should have known about that, but especially not another cop. Her informant business with Keefs had been strictly between him and her, and when she refused to keep feeding him information, well it was over.

That was it.

"If I had any say," Vanna muttered, "Mario Detti wouldn't *be* my fiancé, for one."

The detective narrowed his gaze, rounding the table to pull out the metal chair on the other side so he could take a seat. "And their business?"

"I don't know anything about that."

Mostly true.

"So, you wouldn't know anything about the shipment of heroin we just picked up at the Niagara Falls border crossing that was coming to an address of a warehouse owned by your future father-in-law?"

Vanna's jaw ticked. "Can't say I do, no."

All lies.

She stumbled upon that information during one of the clan's many family dinners, which she then snatched someone's phone, took a bunch of pictures, and sent it off to Bene to do with it what he could, if he even wanted to. That had been two weeks ago, or a little more.

"Are you also unaware of Mario Detti's connection to Constable Keefs, who he was paying a large sum of money to monthly in order to keep the detective from passing over the information he had on the illegal dealings of the Detti family to his superiors and the team of investigators he was working with for the Guzzi investigation?"

Her face stayed passive.

Still like stone.

"No, I don't," Vanna said quietly, "sorry."

The man nodded. He flipped through a paper in the folder on the table, and then another. The silence stretched on, causing her nerves to grow tight with every passing second. Was that his point? She hated to tell him, but this wasn't even her worst experience of the day.

"And you're going to deny that you were the informant for Constable Keefs investigation into the Guzzi Cosa Nostra, as well?"

"What would it matter, if I even was?"

"It wouldn't," the man replied, "except with Constable Keefs being caught up in this bribery scandal with the Detti organization ... well, his word is unreliable, and any prosecutor worth his weight wouldn't dare to put him on the stand. And without a cooperating informant to confirm the information pulled from Gian Guzzi's home, as we only have digital photographs and recordings that could have been faked, with the right programs, well—"

"His charges will be dropped."

"Most," the man agreed, "yes. Unless, Miss Falco, you have something you would like to tell me."

Did she?

Absolutely not.

"I can't say that I do," she replied.

As though that was the answer he expected, Constable Andrews dropped the folder to the table, and sat back in his chair, folding his arms over his chest. "Well, then I'm very sorry for wasting your time today. You'll be allowed to gather your belongings, and an officer will escort you out of the station whenever you're ready to go. Unfortunately, your fiancé and many others in his family won't get the same treatment … seems we have quite enough on them currently to keep them right where they are."

Oh?

Vanna *almost* smiled.

"Shame, that," she whispered.

Yeah, a real fucking shame.

Under the table, her hands stayed flat to her stomach. Protecting the growing life there. Hiding the proof of her baby away from the rest of the world.

What would happen now?

She had no clue.

CHAPTER 21

"At least, they let you get out of that monster of a dress."

Vanna's head snapped up, the revolving doors she'd just stepped out of still spinning behind her. Gone was the large, poufy dress he'd watch her be arrested in only to be replaced with gray sweatpants, a similarly colored hoodie, and running shoes. It wasn't her typical look, but he wasn't at all shocked that she still managed to pull it off.

Everything looked good on her.

Fuck him for noticing, too.

He might have enjoyed the sight of her surprise on another day, but today, he wasn't entirely sure what to feel. Except for maybe the fact he shouldn't be here at all. Not standing on these steps. Not waiting for her release from the police interviews.

None of it.

And yet, there he stood.

"Bene?"

Her hesitant call of his name had him standing a little straighter on the steps of the police station. Shoving his hands into the pockets of his leather jacket, he stared at the woman who had changed his entire life in far more ways than she could possibly know. He wished that so much of this between them had been different, but as this was what they were given, then he would try to do something with it.

Try being the keyword.

"Did you come to tell me you hate me again?" she asked. "To call me a liar, and leave before you let me explain? Do you want to taunt me because you have what you want, and now I have nothing?"

He didn't miss how she kept a good distance between them. She took a few steps away from the door, likely wanting to get far away from the cops in that building, but she didn't begin to climb down the stairs to come closer to him.

"Don't you think I would be owed that?" he asked back.

Vanna swallowed hard. "That doesn't mean I want to hear it."

"That's the thing about love and forgiveness, isn't it?"

Her brow dipped. "Pardon?"

Bene took one step higher, asking, "How about I ask you a question?"

"Well—"

"It's a good one, I promise."

"Okay," she whispered.

"Why *me*?"

"Honestly?"

Bene nodded, taking one more step on the stairs.

Vanna blew out a hard breath, her arms full with a large brown paper bag. Likely the items she had gone into the station with, or what they gathered of hers from the church when the raid happened. "You were the logical choice—all your other brothers weren't single, or *around*."

"Marcus—"

"Not my type."

For some reason, that made him grin.

And chuckle.

A little.

"And why did you change your mind?" he asked. "About coming after my family, I mean. What made you—"

"Because a part of me knew I was chasing someone else's wrongs—a part of me thought it was the only way to keep my dad alive when I worried, I was forgetting him. Because I blamed your father for the way my life went. Because I love you."

Each time she said *because*, he took another step. There were only three left between him and her, now, but Bene wasn't quite ready to close them. He thought there was still a lot left unsaid between the two of them, and if they didn't get it out now, then he doubted there would be another chance for them to do that.

And he needed to make a choice, didn't he?

To love this woman, and *fight* for her.

Or to let it go.

Give me a reason not to let it go, Vanna.

"What did you mean—about love and forgiveness?"

Bene arched a brow, tipping his head to the side a bit as he regarded her. "It only really works if you *want* to be forgiven, Vanna."

She just stared.

He looked back.

"When you hurt somebody," he added, shrugging and taking one more step higher, "then you don't get to decide anything about their forgiveness, but especially when it's someone you say you love. You hurt them, and so you should be prepared to deal with the consequences of their forgiveness, even if it hurts you. It's your willingness to accept their forgiveness in whatever form it takes that proves you understand what you did."

"You hurt me, too, but I don't think the same thing applies."

He had hurt her.

Said things in anger.

Behaved rashly.

Couldn't *deal*.

She'd taken the brunt of it.

"But I understood," she added softer. "So, I'm not sure if it's that there's nothing to forgive, or I already did. What about you?"

"I wish you could understand the weight of what you did."

"I do."

"Really, you think?"

Vanna dragged in a shaky breath, blinking before tears slipped out of the corners of her eyes and made glistening tracks down her cheeks. He expected her to quickly wipe away the tears, but she didn't even bother.

"I'm sorry I hurt you, Bene, and I'm sorry that I made it worse because you fell in love with me."

"But are you sorry for that?"

It took Vanna a second.

And then, two.

Bene waited her out.

"I'm not sorry that you love me, no, and I'm not sorry that I love you, either."

"This is a messy thing, Vanna."

She lifted one shoulder, holding that brown bag tighter to her midsection. "I wanted to fix it. It was too late, I knew it, but I still wanted to fix it. I tried everything I could to make it better and—"

"Stop."

She did.

Instantly.

She tipped her head down, and because of that, didn't see him climb those last steps, and cross the remaining distance between them. He didn't even think about it before wrapping Vanna in a tight hug at the top of those stairs. The second she was in his embrace, he found life became far more bearable. All the noise of the city faded into the background. Her sugared scent soaked into his lungs, the soft strands of her hair on the top of her head pressed against his lips, and for the moment, everything was good again.

Just fine.

Or they could pretend.

Vanna dropped the paper bag between them and hugged him back. He'd done well—did all he could to keep a respectable distance until they said as much as they could before his control snapped. Hanging on by a thread, watching her do what she needed to survive from a distance, all the while she still risked herself to help *him*, and his family …

Yeah, he didn't need to be told.

He knew she loved him.

It was just so fucking messy.

"I meant what I said that day," he muttered against the top of her head, "that I love you and I hated you, but I didn't know how to do both things at the same time."

"And now?"

"Seems you can't hate things you love."

He heard her heavy sigh.

Their embrace tightened.

"That doesn't mean everything is good, Vanna."

She nodded. "I know."

"But it does mean I want it to be."

Her head tipped back, and her wet gaze met his. He swiped the pad of his thumbs under her eyes, wiping away what remained of her tears because he couldn't stand that. She should never cry, but especially not with him. Sure, he understood *why* she cried now, but that didn't mean he wanted her to.

Hadn't this been bad enough?

"What bothered me the most," he told her, "was that for

a time, I wasn't sure you ever loved me, or this had just been a scheme."

"It was at first, but then there you were, Bene ... and you were not who I expected. You were nothing like who I thought you would be."

God, yeah.

"I know all about that."

She smiled.

All he wanted to do then was kiss her, so he did exactly that. Oh, they had a huge mess to clean. Apologies to make. More things to say between them. Of that, he was most sure. There were more obstacles in their way to face, yet, the number one problem being his family.

And yet, when he kissed her ... it didn't matter.

Just the press of her lips, and how her mouth parted for him without question, letting him find the taste of her on his tongue. Whatever remained of the world around them disappeared, and he had never been happier for it.

With a kiss, she had him again.

Took his heart back.

Held it so tight.

Bene was good with that.

His lips grazed down her chin, and then she pressed a soft kiss to his forehead. Bene stayed like that for a second, lost in a space where it could be just the two of them, and nothing else. Where they didn't have to deal with everything else quite yet.

"Everything else is just details after this," he murmured, "and we can figure them out as we go, if that's what you want to do."

"I thought the point of this was that it's what *you* want."

Bene straightened up, meeting her gaze with a smirk. "*Well ...*"

Vanna smiled back. "I'll go wherever you take me as long as you're there, too."

"That's all I need to know, then."

Something flashed in her eyes.

A whole change in her demeanor, really. She went from happy and sweet, if not still a touch sad, to nervous in a blink.

He didn't miss it.

Nor did he like it.

"What's all that about now?"

Vanna's gaze darted away from his, but just as quickly, their stares met as her lips moved to form words he hadn't been expecting to hear. "I'm pregnant."

"What?"

That seemed like the only appropriate response.

And the only one his brain formed.

"*What?*"

Vanna swallowed audibly. "It wasn't intentional, please don't think I did it on purpose."

God, that's what she assumed?

That he'd be pissed?

Bene blinked, asking, "The restaurant?"

It took Vanna a second.

"Yeah, I think so. You're not going to ask about ... him, or if he's the ... well, the father?"

Bene felt the way his face changed at that question—how his expression morphed into something *very* unkind. That's what the mention of Mario Detti did for him. He wasn't even jealous of the man, and the asshole wasn't *free* now, anyway. Wouldn't be for a long time, if everything went well, and it would.

Still, he hated that bastard.

"No," Bene said thickly, "because I know he isn't."

Vanna's gaze held strong to his. "I wouldn't let him

touch me."

"He didn't deserve to. So, like a couple months or so?"

"About nine weeks, I think."

Huh.

He was mad that he'd missed nine weeks.

Pissed this couldn't be different.

So fucking happy, too.

Then, he had another thought. "Why didn't you tell me that right away? Why wait until after we talked?"

"Because you had things to say, and you deserved to be able to say them whether they would be things that hurt me, or not. I'd done enough already ... it's your turn."

"Not a tit for tat, Vanna."

And then his hands slid down between them, palms covering the expanse of her flat stomach just because he could, and it felt so fucking *good*.

"Hmm," he said, tone thick with pride. "Love you."

"Love you, too, Bene."

"The pregnancy thing might make this a little messier."

Vanna grinned.

He loved that.

"But does it matter?"

No.

Not at all.

Bene dropped another quick kiss to her lips, adding, "It's my family we have to worry about."

Just in case she forgot.

Because he hadn't.

∿

"*What is she doing here?*"

Jesus Christ.

Bene hadn't even helped Vanna out of the car yet, and

already, it had begun. Marcus came rushing out of the Guzzi mansion like a man on a mission, his gaze laser-focused on Vanna who was currently letting Bene take her bag before she stepped out of the passenger side of his Lambo. Following behind his oldest brother was the rest of his brothers. The mansion had become a hub of sorts for them while their father remained in lock up, and their mother refused to return home until Gian came with her.

"Marcus—"

"What the fuck are you doing with her, huh? Why is she *here*, Bene? You know we got Chris's wife in the house, right? The *kids*. Ginevra is here, too, and the baby. And you bring that fucking thing here tonight?"

"Marcus!"

His oldest brother was all of two feet away from them, looking as though if he didn't rip Bene apart piece by piece with his bare hands, then he might go for Vanna next. Bene couldn't have that, so he quickly moved in front of Vanna, dropping her bag to the ground as his hand slipped behind him to lay flat against her stomach.

He pointed one finger at his brother. "Don't you *dare* touch her."

Marcus fumed.

Blazing eyes.

Clenching fists.

Pure fucking rage.

"Bene," Vanna whispered, her hands fisting into his jacket, "it's okay."

No, it really wasn't.

Except, he planned for this.

Figured it would happen.

Marcus was who he was—raised by their father differently than the rest of them, really. Sure, all the Guzzi brothers held a strong loyalty to their family and bonds. They protected each other first, and foremost.

Thing was ... Marcus couldn't be the same.

The *firstborn*.

The only singleton.

He didn't have a twin to level him out like the rest did. He never had someone else always watching *only* his back like Bene had with Beni, or even the way Corrado pushed Christopher to be more out going and take risks.

Instead, Marcus had the responsibility of all of them. He took it on himself—did what he had to because he was the oldest brother, and it was his burden to bear, not that he ever complained. He was more protective, and in a way, the same lessons they had learned came in another way for him because his rules had always been different from theirs.

"Marcus, relax," Corrado snapped, finally catching up with his brother.

The others soon followed.

Chris stayed with his twin.

Beni came to stand beside Bene.

Just like that, the family almost seemed divided in the driveway with two on one side, two brothers on the other, and Marcus right in the middle. It was everything their parents would *hate*. Even if the cause was justifiable.

It didn't matter.

"It's not who we are," Beni said like he could read his brother's mind. "This isn't what we *do*, Marcus, and you know that."

Marcus's stinging gaze flew to Bene, despite his twin being the one who spoke, when he replied, "You know what else we don't do? Bring home women who got our father put in *jail!*"

Bene gritted his teeth. "I—"

"Is that what you've been doing for the last month?

Chasing her ass around when you were supposed to be helping us figure out something for Ma and Papa? Every fucking time I called, and you didn't pick up, right?"

Every sentence brought Marcus closer to Bene until the two of them were chest to chest and eye to eye. On another day, it might concern him how physical his brother became because that wasn't like Marcus at all.

Today wasn't the same.

He *got it.*

Completely.

Didn't mean his stance changed.

"Hey, hey," Chris murmured, quick to leave his twin's side to slip in between Marcus and Bene, putting at least the space of his body in the middle. "Let's take a second and—"

"I don't need a second! I need her gone!"

"She's the only reason Papa will be getting out of jail, Marcus," Bene threw at his brother just as viciously as Marcus spoke to him. "Because of *her*, yeah? Because she was willing to risk herself to help *me*."

Marcus straightened, his stare narrowing dangerously. "You went behind our backs and worked with the same bitch that fucked us over the first time?"

Okay.

That pissed Bene off.

"Watch your fucking mouth before I make it bleed, Marcus."

Beni cleared his throat, giving Marcus a look. "Go easy with the names, huh? And it wasn't *just* Bene. I helped him, too, and knew what was going on. Uncle Tommas pulled some contacts for us as well. *You* couldn't get it done, man, and there was no way you would use anything we got from Vanna, so just relax."

"I want her the fuck out of here. *Now.*"

"Absolutely not," Bene replied.

Marcus tipped his head up, staring down at his brother over Chris's shoulder. "Or *what*?"

"Or nothing, Marcus. She's with me, and that's the end of it."

"She's a fucking rat—an *informant*. You brought her into our family, and she used everything she found to *hurt us*. If you think for one second that she'll be welcomed here, you're highly fucking misinformed, Bene. I will give you one minute to get in the car and take her away before I put her off this property myself."

Bene inched back a bit, closer to Vanna than before. Her hand came to cover his over her stomach—would he even get to explain that this was bigger than Marcus understood? Would he care that Vanna did everything she could to right the wrongs she made?

"*Shit.*"

Bene's head flew sideways only to find his twin's soft proclamation was punctuated by the fact he could see the protective nature of Vanna's hand overtop his. Right on her midsection. There was only one reason why someone held their stomach that way.

Beni glanced away, the dawning in his expression as clear as day, but it was already too late. Chris noticed, too, who only shook his head with a dry chuckle as he stared up at the sky with a muttered, "Are you fucking *serious*, Bene?"

"What?" Marcus demanded.

Well …

Now or never, he supposed.

"Vanna's pregnant," Bene said.

Marcus blanked.

Just like that.

His face became white paper.

Nothing to see.

"What did you just say?"

Vanna's hand tightened around Bene's, but still, she stayed quiet. Smart, really, all things considered. Better for her to just stay out of this right now, and let the rest of them handle it.

"Bene," Marcus snapped, "what did you just say?"

"You heard me."

His brother's gaze darted between him, and the woman behind him.

Corrado was the only one who thought to say, "Congrats, man."

"Thanks."

"But bad timing," came a new, but familiar, voice.

Corrado made a grunt under his breath, lifting his hand to show the face on the screen of his phone that he was currently video chatting on. Or rather, the call he must have been on before they call came running out of the house. *Alessio*, his other spouse.

"Like Corrado told you," Alessio said on the screen, clearly amused, "congrats, and all."

Yeah.

Really bad timing.

Didn't he know it?

"I'll call you back, or just call Ginny, Les," Corrado said.

"I was having fun, though."

"Let's not and say you did, okay?"

"Don't hang up the phone on me, Cor—"

He did just that.

However, the few seconds Alessio had used to make a joke clearly calmed them down a bit. The man certainly wasn't a Guzzi by blood, but he belonged with them just the same. He proved it time and time again, like now. The way he just knew when the right time was to step in, and make a bad situation better.

"Okay," Chris said, putting his hands up to pat Marcus

on the chest, forcing their brother to take a step back with every smack, "let's take a minute to breathe—*all of us*. We wait for Ma to get home with Papa, whenever they finally get around to seeing a judge about the possibility of another bond hearing, at least until the charges are properly dropped, and then we'll sit back down and revisit all of this, yeah? Let them figure all of that out first, she's still at the penthouse in the city, but said she would call as soon as she got the okay to go down and get Papa. *Then*, we will revisit this."

"There's nothing to revisit," Bene said, "she's mine—I love her. She stays with *me*."

Marcus still glared.

Except now, Bene knew, things had changed.

A baby changed *everything*. It made this written in blood. And his baby was still a Guzzi no matter who birthed the child.

Marcus was always going to be Marcus. He was who he was. The man their father *made*. He'd protect a Guzzi no matter what.

Until the day he died.

"Caroline, yeah," Ginevra said, "kind of a play on Corrado's and his mother's name, but with a little twist Les liked, too."

"I love that name." Vanna beamed at the eleven-month-old baby currently toddling from chair to chair at the small dining table his parents used in their large kitchen when they wanted a more intimate place to eat with their sons. She never let go of one before moving to the other, not quite trusting her legs yet. "And she's so beautiful."

"Like her mother," Valeria added. "Maria, don't you take another cookie from that pan. I saw what you were doing, *princessa*."

Even with all their Italian flowing constantly, or usually, Valeria still held tight to her Spanish roots. He figured it was good for their kid, though, because the girl got Italian from Chris, a bit of French from their dad and Marcus, Spanish from her mom, and English from everyone else.

"But I was only taking one for Daddy."

Valeria pursed her lips. "But were you really, though?"

"*Well ...*"

"Maria," her mother admonished.

"He would have let me have it anyway!"

Laughter from the ladies lit up the kitchen.

From his position in the doorway leading into the kitchen, Bene smiled at the scene but didn't move further inside where he could be noticed. He didn't mean to spy, really, but after Christopher forced him to take a walk around the property to chat while Corrado took Marcus up to their father's office for his own conversation, Vanna promised she would be fine to sit by herself.

He didn't think so.

His brother didn't give him a choice.

He found she was, in fact, just fine, and apparently made friends with Chris and Corrado's spouses. Valeria, who always had to be cooking something to keep her hands busy, and Ginevra who was never far behind in that respect, had a whole table full of sweets baked, it seemed.

For who, he didn't know.

By the looks of Vanna's flour-dusted hands, she'd joined in.

And probably loved it, too.

He'd thought after his walk that Vanna might want him to save her from whatever awkward conversation she found in that time, but it seemed she was doing just fine. Plus, wouldn't she need some friends in this family?

Before he could convince himself otherwise—because

God knew he wanted her all to himself—Bene turned on his heels and headed deeper into the mansion. Before long, he found himself standing in the sitting room that connected his old bedroom with his twin's. Unsurprisingly, Beni stood near the windows while he chatted on the phone to his wife waiting for him in Chicago.

"Yeah, soon, Aug," Beni said, "once we get everything settled out here ... nah, I think you'll like her, and she's exactly what I thought she would be considering him."

Bene smirked a bit.

His twin ... always the first to have his back.

Even when he was a shit.

Bene cleared his throat, gaining his brother's attention for the moment. Beni gave him a look over his shoulder, but quickly went back to his call with a, "Okay, love you, too, babe."

"I'm surprised she's not here, too."

His brother shrugged as he pocketed his cell and turned to face him. "She's working on an article and has a bunch of interviews to do for it ... some of them could be done over the phone, but others were better in person. I didn't want her sacrificing that for something we were handling, you know? Besides, she calls Ma every day just to talk to her about whatever book they're currently reading."

Huh.

"They read the same book?"

"Yeah, Aug picks one and then Ma picks the next."

Bene nodded. "Didn't know that."

"It's their thing, you know."

"Vanna might like that—huge fan of Ma's reviews, and all."

Beni chuckled, saying, "I will let August know. Where is Vanna, anyway?"

"In the kitchen with Val and Ginny and the kids."

"Oh?"

"They seem to like her."

It was just … *everyone else*.

Yeah.

Beni, seeing the nerves in Bene's jittery hands, said, "Give Marcus some time, huh? He'll relax and fall in line with the rest of us. He just needs to get shit figured out in his own head before he'll come around, that's all. It's been a rough couple of months for him."

"Doesn't matter if he does or not. She's mine anyway."

"No, right," Beni agreed, "I'm sure you're more worried about Ma and Papa."

Bene shifted on his feet, clearing the lump in his throat. "A little, maybe."

"Don't be."

Easier said than done.

CHAPTER

22

"Marcus headed into the city for the night and will stay at his penthouse, I guess."

Vanna didn't miss the way Bene's jaw clenched at Chris's statement.

"Because he has things to handle there, or he's pissed—"

"Oh, no, he's still pissed."

Bene grunted under his breath. "All right, thanks."

"Mmhmm. Have a good sleep. Hopefully, Dad will be out tomorrow."

"Right, right."

Over Bene's shoulder, Chris called, "Night, Vanna."

She managed a smile from where she sat at the foot of the bed in Bene's bedroom. "Thanks, you too."

Bene closed the door behind his brother, but he clearly hadn't missed the change in Vanna's tone when he turned around to ask, "You okay?"

She shrugged, focusing on her hands folded in her lap. After pulling on clothes to sleep in from his walk-in closet— an over-sized tee, and a pair of boxers—she just wanted to climb into bed and forget this entire day had happened.

"Tonight was supposed to be *very* different for me."

A new husband.

A bed she didn't want.

A life that wouldn't be her own.

And now, here she was.

"It's a lot to take in," she admitted.

Bene crossed the space between them, rounding the bed to come and stand in front of her. His hands came to land on her thighs, and instantly, she opened her legs for him to fit in between. Tipping her head up, the two of them took a moment to stare in silence before he was the first to break it.

"It's all on you now. You know that, right?"

"For now, maybe, until your parents—"

"*Vanna.*"

She dragged in a sharp breath at the strength in his stare. "As long as you want to be here with me, then that's where you're going to be. No matter what. Regardless of what anyone says. That's how it's going to be."

He made it sound simple.

She wondered if it would be.

"You shouldn't fight with your family over me, Bene. I'm not sure I'm worth that."

And she wasn't.

Truly.

Not after everything.

"Except you're worth the world and more to me."

"But not for them. To them, I'm just—"

"Mine," he said thickly, squeezing her thighs at the same time to make his point clear. "To them, you are *mine*. And that's what matters, Vanna. I promise, and it might not be easy at first, but we'll get there. Just trust me."

"I want to believe you. I do."

But everything that had ever been hers was taken away in one way or another. A mother she'd never known. A father she wasn't sure she ever really understood. A life that could have been so different. And almost a future, too.

She wanted him, though.

Bene.

More than anything.

She chose to *want* something, and she was willing to give anything to have him.

Vanna didn't pretend to be the victim, not anymore. She did terrible things for a cause that wasn't even hers, and she was just selfish enough to want to keep a man she knew she had hurt. She wasn't the *good guy* here ... she was a villain who wanted their happy ending. And still, she wanted to believe him that maybe there was something worthy enough in her to be given a second chance, to start over as someone better.

To be his.

Bene leaned down close enough to her that his body flattened against hers while her hands balled into the chest of his dress shirt. His lips found hers, words whispering along the seam of her mouth in the most wicked, but *promising*, way. "Then just trust me, Vanna."

That whisper turned into a kiss lighting up every nerve in her body all at once. It took nothing at all, just their lips dancing a smooth rhythm before his tongue found its way to hers, slashing with hard strokes that already had her wet between her thighs. Because she knew how good his mouth was going to feel once it was on her pussy again.

God.

It had been way too long.

"You want that—*me*?" he asked when his mouth skimmed her jawline. "You want me to fuck you now, Vanna?"

"Jesus, yes, *please*."

That was all Bene needed to hear. Her clothes were pulled from her body by his rough, fast hands, and she only wanted more. A shiver raced through her body when she fell back to the bed, and he took his damn time dragging her panties down her thighs, leaving her spread wide and bare to him when he stood back up.

She hadn't forgotten what it felt like to be under the weight of this man and his passion but she still loved how it managed to sneak up on her every single time. She heard the tug of his zipper when he leaned into her reaching hands. She found his kiss again, just as hot and heavy as it had been only moments ago before he was pulling away.

Vanna only took in one sharp breath of air before Bene was between her thighs. Her hands, fisted into the bedsheets, quickly left to find purchase in his dark head of hair while his tongue stroked her from slit to her clit, and then his tongue found a fast rhythm beating against the already-throbbing nub.

He knew how to make her fly.

So damn fast.

"Fuck, fuck, *fuck … Bene.*"

Her words came out just like that.

High.

Broken.

Unintelligible curses of his name. Because damn him for being the only thing in the world capable of taking away everything she thought she was and making her better if only for him. Damn him for making it feel so fucking good, too.

It was the sudden graze of his teeth along her clit that sent Vanna falling over the edge. The orgasm came rushing in fast, a cry catching in her throat when her back arched from the bed. She was still shaking and whispering his name when he slid up her body, already shoving his pants down to step out of them. Oh, he stopped just long enough to kiss the spot below her navel, a soft and *brilliant* smile tugging at those lips of his, before he was on her again.

Vanna took his violent kiss, and found his cock pressed between their bodies with her palms, stroking his hard cock fast while he grinded against her.

"*Vanna*, damn …"

She swore her name was a prayer on his mouth.

He worshipped her always.

That, more than anything, got her off like nothing else ever would. There was something about knowing she took away all his control like this that made her sky-high.

Bene's arms hooked around her thighs, pulling her legs high and wide as she dragged his cock against her slit, letting him feel just a bit of her slick heat before his hips jutted forward. He filled her full and stretched her wide with one thrust, making her let him go so that her palm could rest against the hard ridges of his toned stomach while he fucked her hard and deep.

Fast strokes that had their bodies trembling.

Her heart racing.

And her pussy aching.

She needed to come again, and he knew it. Bene let go of one of her legs to use his thumb to stroke along the seam of her sex where his cock continued to fill her pussy. And then he was circling fast with that same thumb against her clit, using her own wetness as a lubrication to have her feeling and sounding wetter than ever.

"Fuck yeah, I want that pussy to come, Vanna."

All his dirty words.

Those dark promises.

Of course, she came again.

Harder than ever.

Bene's arm tightened around Vanna's waist where they stood on the right, curving staircase in the grand entrance of the mansion. Three steps higher, Beni and his wife waited with them. Down in front of the main doors, Marcus and Corrado stood in tense silence. Apparently, whatever argument the two had been having just moments ago in hushed tones was now over, and they were comfortable with pretending as if the other didn't currently exist.

Siblings, Bene had said, *it's normal.*

She didn't know if that was true.

Or if it was—once again—the brothers arguing about her, or her presence in the mansion. She hadn't left the home once Bene brought her, although Christopher's wife had brought her some clothes to use, but she made sure to stay with him whenever she could. And not because she thought someone might hurt her, but rather, she didn't want any of them to be uncomfortable with her.

Hadn't she done enough?

It was already awkward.

Why make it worse?

Besides, it was about to get worse, anyway.

All eyes went to the front doors of the mansion when they were pushed open, and Chris stepped inside first. Right behind him came his mother, and father. Vanna was sure that they expected to come home to a celebration, of sorts. Or at the very least, *happiness.* After all they had gone through with the man being in jail, his future uncertain, this should have been a wonderful day.

Instead, the first thing that happened when the couple walked through the front doors of their mansion, returning to their grown children and grandchildren playing in a connecting room, was look *their* way. Directly at her and Bene.

Gian tipped his chin up, the hard line of his jaw flexing as he bit back words. She didn't need him to speak those words for her to know they were on the tip of his tongue. The heat blazing in his gaze, practically nailing her to the floor, said it all.

Bene's arm tightened on her side.

"So, what Chris explained on the way here is true, then?" Gian asked.

"Depends on what he said," Bene replied.

Chris dropped a handful of bags to the marble floor. "Everything."

"Oh, and Tommas called, Bene."

Right.

The man—the Guzzi brothers' uncle—who helped Beni and Bene put the information Vanna sent him about the Camorra and the dirty cop to use.

Basically, all of it, then.

He knew it all.

"While I understand that you might consider yourself in love with—"

"Gian," Cara said quietly.

Vanna's stomach flipflopped, threatening to spill what remained of her breakfast after her first round of throwing up that morning. At least, Bene had been there to hold her hair back, and make her feel better after. She willed the vomit away, begging her body to not betray her.

It was just nerves.

She could handle that.

His gaze flew to his wife instantly. "He brought her *here.*"

"See," Marcus muttered to Corrado beside him.

"Shut your face," Corrado replied.

"Well—"

"That's enough," Cara told the two, and then to Gian, "don't make rash decisions; because he clearly didn't."

"You don't think some of things he did were *rash*?"

"Stop it. *Think about it*, Gian. All he did, he would have known what it meant to bring her here, so consider that it means something, and we should discuss it before you say something you cannot take back. Is our son not worth that?

And the other thing Chris told us—we have to consider that, too, now."

What *other thing*?

Vanna knew better than to ask.

Still not the time.

"That's not fair, *bella*."

"*Gian*."

"Cara—"

"We'll talk, and then you can talk as much as you want," the woman said, offering no room for argument. "Please, Gian."

"It won't change what I think or feel."

Cara smiled softly. "Oh, is that what you think?"

"I know what I know, and that's more than enough."

"Exactly, what *you* know … but you don't know them."

Gian visibly stiffened. "I—"

"We'll talk, and then you can talk," she repeated, "please."

He sighed, gaze skipping to Bene and Vanna again in just enough time to see him press a quick kiss to her temple. "Fine, we'll talk first."

"Good. I miss my library. Let's go."

"Right *now*?"

"No better time, Gian."

That was that.

~

"You always had to do everything different, didn't you, son?"

Bene's chuckles echoed out to reach Vanna's spot in the hallway. She hadn't been invited into his father's office yet, but they knew she was there. It wasn't like she was spying, or anything.

"You couldn't make things *easy* … not once," Gian

added. "From the day you learned to walk, it felt like I was constantly chasing after you. Well, both of you."

"Where's the fun in anything *easy*?" Beni asked.

"Gives me less gray hair."

"Yeah, well …"

"So it's known," Gian continued, "and so Marcus doesn't chew my head off later, no one is impressed by how this came about. But because there are special circumstances here, and your mother locked me in a room to make me listen to everything she had to say about all of this, we have to make other decisions. We have a lot of things to discuss, but we're also going to do so *respectfully*."

"Or try," Marcus returned.

"No, we will."

A sigh answered that.

The conversation continued. For the most part, Vanna followed along, listening to a father act as the referee between his sons when things became heated like they had when she first arrived at the mansion with Bene. Except, it seemed with their father there, all the Guzzi boys were far more likely to calm down when told.

"I often try not to step in when they have these kinds of moments. Gian always managed the boys better alone than with me trying to step on his toes and remind him to be a father first, and their boss second."

Vanna spun around, stunned at how quietly Bene's mother managed to come down the hall without her even realizing she was there. Or maybe it was because she had been far more focused on the conversation happening within the office.

Cara, wearing a periwinkle dress that reached the floor, with her red hair let down in soft waves, didn't look like a woman who had spent months worried her husband would never see the outside of a jail cell again. She hadn't spoken a word to Vanna after returning to her home that day, but she didn't take it personally.

Sometimes, one needed a moment.

Just a single moment to *breathe*.

She was sure that's what Cara had done.

"Do they do this often?" she asked.

Cara shrugged as she came to stand next to Vanna, just a couple of feet away from the open office doors. She busied her attention on straightening a few of the items on the decorative table and rearranged the roses that had been placed in a vase near the back corner. "Whenever it's needed, I think. This is … a special circumstance."

It was habit for her to apologize, now. She felt like the more she said it, the more they might believe her. Besides, apologizing was really the only thing she could consistently do for them after everything. This time was no exception.

"Sorry," Vanna muttered.

Cara smiled her way. "Do you love him—my son?"

She dragged in a burning breath. "More than I can explain."

"You know," Cara said, raising a brow as she folded her arms over her chest, "I thought it was your face that reminded me of someone the first time I met you, but it wasn't that at all."

"Oh?"

"No, it was what you were doing. Getting close, lying to do it, and hoping to use it against us. It was the same thing your aunt did to my husband, and even though I wasn't around when that happened, I knew enough from him to sense it."

"I—"

Cara didn't even give her the chance to speak before she added, "Except there was something different about you, and it confused me. Because I felt that part of you that could do us harm, and I also saw something else in you … something changed when you looked at him. And I couldn't ignore that, so it made me overlook the rest."

"I don't want to be like my aunt at all."

She really didn't.

Not anymore.

"You can't be like her," Cara replied simply, "because she couldn't *love*, Vanna, and she never once tried to help when she only wanted to hurt."

"Thank you."

Before Cara could respond, she heard Gian say inside the office, "Have her come in, son."

Cara nodded toward the door with one of those knowing smiles. Bene came out into the hallway, his gaze darting between his mother, and Vanna. He offered her his hand, and she didn't hesitate to take it. Vanna took in the people in the office—only his father, and brothers. Downstairs, she knew the women and kids were keeping busy. A part of her wanted to be down there. If only because it was easier to be a coward.

"Sit," Cara said, joining them before she went to stand behind her husband where he currently sat at the large desk dominating the room. "And then we can all go downstairs and find out what that delicious smell is."

"Sit," Bene urged.

She let him lead her to the chairs opposite to the desk. He took one, and she took the other. She kept her hands folded at her middle, but Bene reached over to grab onto her jittery leg, the press of his palm against her jean-clad thigh more than enough to settle her nerves before he removed his touch.

Yes, she wanted it back.

Still, she kept quiet.

Now was not the time.

It was only once everyone had settled into their spots that Gian decided to speak, and Vanna was a bit grateful for that because she certainly didn't have the first clue how to begin. A part of her still wondered what she was even doing here.

Why did they let her be in their home?

After everything?

"Let's start from the beginning," Gian said, "and Vanna, I suspect that starts with you. Don't leave anything out, hmm?"

She took in a deep breath. "Sure."

"Whenever you're ready, then."

Gracious.

Kind.

Respectful.

All things the Guzzi family seemed to encompass, and even in the face of someone who had only intended to hurt them, they still offered her those things first. It wasn't lost on Vanna, and if anything, their silence as she talked, explaining how this had all come to be, made her feel more guilt than she thought was possible.

It was okay, though.

She deserved it.

She took it.

"There are a lot of ways I would like to spend my first day home with my wife after everything," Gian said, his expression neutral as Vanna finished, "but this certainly wasn't one of them, no offense."

She nodded. "None taken."

"It seems we have a lot to clear up, *oui*?"

God.

If Vanna could shrink into the office chair, and never be seen again, it might be the better option than the way she felt right then with Gian Guzzi sitting across the room from her. Not because he made her feel uncomfortable, but after an hour of admitting every single one of her secrets to the man, and all the shit she had done to him and his family … well, Vanna had never felt more ashamed.

It took a couple of days before the man was finally released. Apparently, a few missing papers could keep him behind bars longer than anyone thought. Then, he arrived home with his wife at his side, the first time she came home and stayed since her husband's arrest, if Vanna was to believe what others told her.

Standing behind her husband, Bene's mother kept her hands clasped to his shoulders during the entire conversation. A pillar of the family, it seemed.

Vanna wasn't surprised.

Women tended to be the powerhouses.

They turned the world.

Men simply went along with it.

"You know," Gian said, clearing his throat as his gaze flicked to Marcus who stood near the office windows, clearly unhappy, "there was a time when I thought I loved Elena."

Vanna flinched.

She couldn't help it.

"All of her making, of course," Gian added quickly, waving a hand as if to dismiss the notion he could have truly *loved* her dead aunt, "because she orchestrated it all. From *bumping* into me at a restaurant, to the lies she told about who she was and what she wanted from me. Instead, she used those things I trusted her with to get away from a man she hated, and then she left me high and dry for years while I felt like I would never have the chance to be with someone I loved entirely. I couldn't be with someone else when I was already married to her, after all. Until Cara came along, that is."

Cara smiled briefly, bending down to kiss the man on the

top of his head before straightening back up like she hadn't moved at all.

"Nonetheless, with Elena, nothing was ever true, and even after the things she had done to me and to my family … I would have forgiven her for it all, if only she loved me back the way I thought I loved her. That's the thing about love, when it's real, then nothing else really matters. You figure out a way to make it work—it doesn't give you another choice."

Beside her, Bene reached over to unfurl her fingers around the arm of the chair. His palm pressed against hers, the warm heat soaking into her hand and straight up her arm almost instantly. Their fingers wove together, and just like that, she felt settled again.

Better.

He made her better.

"Nothing was ever real with Elena," Gian said, still staring at Vanna as he spoke despite all the others in the room, "and so there was nothing to make *work*. I think that's where the two of you differ, isn't it?"

"How are we supposed to trust her when—"

"Hush, Marcus."

The man at the windows quieted instantly.

"I'm sorry," Vanna whispered.

Behind his large desk, Gian nodded. "I understand that even to the detriment of yourself, you did what you could to help fix your errors, and while I could be quick to punish you for the rest first … I'm inclined to learn from the past, and the mistakes I left behind there."

He glanced up at his wife, asking, "What is it you say this family does, *cara mia bella*?"

Cara smiled. "We forgive—we love."

"We do because that is how you teach it to others." Gian looked Marcus's way again, the other man stiff in his position in front of the windows. "Something you still have to learn, although your reasoning for wanting to do neither is justifiable. Still, we remain together, or we fight and tear each other apart on our way down, yes?"

It took Marcus a second.

And then, two.

Finally, with a hard exhale, he muttered, "Yes, Papa."

Gian's gaze turned on Bene as he said, "Also, I hear we have other news to share. Something … happier, even if you do know better. And Bene, you *do* know better."

What?

Bene's cheeks reddened.

Vanna almost laughed.

"That was not intentional," he started to say.

"And yet, here we are."

"Well—"

"We already know," Cara said behind Gian, her attention drifting to Vanna, and then down to her stomach where one of her hands stayed flat against her body, "because Christopher told us."

"Oh."

"I don't keep secrets," Christopher said from the back of the room.

"Yes, we know." Corrado's reply came out dry, and tired. "Which is why no one tells you anything, man."

No one turned to look at the two.

"Could have kept that secret for a bit," Bene returned.

"No, probably not."

"Bene," Gian urged, "less them, more me, please."

"I'm not a child."

"No, apparently, you're going to have one."

Yep.

There it was.

Bene laughed under his breath. "Yeah, so there's also *that*. And I know that probably pisses you off the most, but—"

"You'll be married before the child is born."

Vanna's head snapped up.

So did Bene's.

Gian raised his brow at the two of them. "It's non-negotiable. It's our way, and I won't have more reasons for the made men in this family to instigate issues with my sons, either, and this would absolutely do that being who she is."

The man shrugged, adding, "And I think it should be made clear that the child is the only reason why we're sitting here right now doing this instead of something else that would be a far more appropriate answer to your actions against me and mine, young woman. It was my *wife* ... and her reminder to me that we have all made choices in our life that hurt those we try to protect the most, who made me willing to sit down with you. In any other situation, I would not offer my forgiveness or a second chance. And you can absolutely expect that no one else in our family will want to do the same. You don't have our trust, Vanna, and neither do you, son, because of who stands beside you. Those are things you have to earn back now. I can't give it to you, Bene."

"I know, Papa."

"Good, and as for the rest ..."

Her lungs ached with every breath.

Gian was owed his moment, though.

"A marriage settles it," he continued, "and the child cements it. It's a Guzzi child regardless, and when you give the mother the last name, too, our line becomes clear. And unless there's a reason why the two of you would rather not be married, then—"

"No, *yes*," Bene said, stumbling over his words as Vanna still tried to find hers, "yes, I want to marry her, of course, I do."

"Good," Gian replied.

"Vanna?" Cara spoke up, then. "Because no one thought to ask you, I guess."

She smiled.

Cara smiled back.

"I just want to be with Bene."

Forever.

Truer words had never been spoken.

At least, not from her.

Bene's hand tightened around hers, and with a firm tug, he had her leaning closer so that he could press a kiss to her temple. "You got me."

We'll deal with the rest later.

Because there would be a later, now.

They should have sent her running.

Killed her.

After all she did to them, the Guzzis should have buried her in a shallow grave where no one knew she rotted, and her name became dust in the wind. Instead, because a girl fell in love with a boy ... *one of theirs*, they let her stay. They promised to forgive.

If you do the same, Gian told her. *Because you must do the same.*

He was right.

Those thoughts chased Vanna through the Guzzi mansion with every step she took, her laughter flying over her shoulder as Bene *almost* caught up to her when she rounded the corner at the end of the long second-floor hallway.

The nostalgia of it wasn't lost on her. The familiarity of it all comforted her like nothing else could because everything was different now. Oh, they had a way to go, she was sure. It didn't take a day for her to damage them, and she didn't think it would be fixed that quickly, either.

Vanna wasn't stupid.

Or selfish, either.

"Are you going to make this easy on me, or what?" Bene called behind her.

She winked over her shoulder. "Never."

He wouldn't want easy, anyway. He chased her like this once. She let him catch her, then. Only, that had been for entirely different reasons.

Some things didn't change, though.

Like when he caught her.

Kissed her.

Those things stayed the same.

Entirely perfect.

Like them.

Even if everything else still needed work.

That was okay, too.

She didn't mind putting in the effort.

BETHANY-KRIS

Bethany-Kris is a Canadian author, lover of much, and mother to four young sons, two cats, and three dogs. A small town in Eastern Canada where she was born and raised is where she has always called home. With her boys under her feet, a snuggling cat, barking dogs, and a spouse calling over his shoulder, she is nearly always writing something ... when she can find the time.

Find Bethany-Kris at her:
www.bethanykris.com

BOOKS BY BETHANY-KRIS

Always

Revere

Unruly

The Companion

Naz & Roz

Guzzi Duet

Unraveled, Book One

Entangled, Book Two

DeLuca Duet

Waste of Worth: Part One

Worth of Waste: Part Two

Donati Bloodlines

Thin Lies

Thin Lines

Thin Lives

Behind the Bloodlines

The Complete Trilogy

Filthy Marcellos

Antony

Lucian

Giovanni

Dante

Legacy

A Very Marcello Christmas

The Complete Collection

Effortless

Inflict

Cozen

Captivated

Dishonored

Find more on Bethany-Kris's website at www.bethanykris.com